What People Are Say
T*he Phantom of the F(*

MW01014462

This book pulls you in with pe. ... . was in the book myself.

Joshua Potter

This book was a page-turning thriller from start to finish! Alex, Gabe, Thunder, and Lightning jump into the middle of another exciting mystery, this time in beautiful Salzburg, Austria. Guaranteed to delight young and old alike, this book will keep you reading and guessing until the very end. Well done!

Dr. Kelly Snyder

This book is realistic, intriguing, and wonderful. The characters are smart, but can make mistakes. The villain is a perfect mix of misunderstood, crazy, evil, and genius. Readers of all ages can enjoy the thrill of *The Phantom of the Fortress*.

Rachel McIntosh

The Phantom of the Fortress is a thrilling ride from start to finish. I enjoyed following Gabe, Alex, and their friends as they pursued the increasingly elusive Phantom, all while learning who they can really trust. Complications mount as stakes are raised, calling our heroes to rise above their own fears and rely on their strength, intelligence, faith, and each other to save the day. I look forward to seeing what the next installment has in store for them.

Allison Maruska,
Author of the *Project Renovatio* series

I thoroughly enjoyed the book. It kept me intrigued all the way to the end. The story line was well written. I look forward to what's in the next one in the series.

Toby Zielinski

The Thunder and Lightning Series

Book 1 – *The Secret of the Castle*

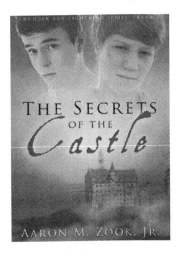

Book 2 – *The Salt Mines Mystery*

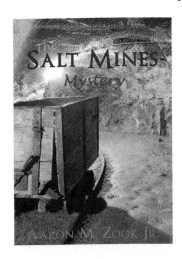

The Phantom

of the

Fortress

The Phantom

of the

Fortress

Aaron M. Zook, Jr.

Bold Vision Books
PO Box 2011
Friendswood, Texas 77549

Dedication

I dedicate this book to CLASSeminars, an organization that develops Christian writers through conferences.

The Thunder and Lightning series sprang into being through the encouragement of CLASS staff leaders, especially Gerry Wakeland, Linda Gilden, Karen Porter, and Larry Leech. Each CLASS staff member and volunteer sculpted my writing skills, the motivation to persevere, and the desire to strive for excellence.

CLASS inspires me daily to share the message that an individual's story or stories, fiction or non-fiction, are important to capture in writing. May we all strive to infuse our world with God's presence and love, influencing societal norms to achieve a mighty reflection of His majesty.

Table of Contents

Chapter One

The Troubling Trail

August 29 didn't impress me as the day I'd find a dying man. And I wouldn't have if not for Lightning and Mozart.

My brother, a friend, our dogs, and I stepped into Herr Gerlach's Print Shop in Salzburg, Austria, the hometown of musical boy-genius Mozart. Cool air washed over me, scented by musty books and the tang of inks and solvents.

Lightning bolted. Tail wagging like a storm flag in a hurricane, my canine buddy darted into a doorway. His tiny body slunk under a chain with a sign that read: "Employees only."

"Get back here," I said. My dog's reddish-orange form disappeared around a corner. I dodged a customer and ducked under the chain.

A yip drew me down a narrow passageway. I found Lightning, ears back, crouched with forelegs down. He barked. He'd found something important, at least to him.

"Can't you listen?" I bent down and slid a finger through his collar. I began dragging him back to the main store area and glimpsed red on the floor. I stopped.

"What did you find, buddy?" I knelt, double-checking to make sure I wasn't mistaken. My pulse pounded in my temples. "Stay." I raced back to my brother Alex and our friend Willie. I spotted them by the front window display. "Come here. Quick."

Willie, a nineteen-year-old Aussie, six years older than me, worked as a Polizei undercover cop. Months ago, he helped Alex, my fifteen-year-old brother, and me shut down a terrorist human-trafficking ring called Machete.

Thunder, Alex's huge black dog, bounded into my arms.

"Hold it, big fellah." I wrestled him to a halt, arms around his neck. Keeping his ninety-pounds under control, I snagged his collar. "Alex, control him."

"Heel." My brother took the collar from me and jerked it once. Thunder lurched to his master's side while Alex unclipped the green plastic chain into the private area.

"Did you find a filly, mate?" Willie cracked a big smile as he sauntered up. "You look a bit flushed."

"It's not a girl," I said. "Lightning's found…," I realized a few customers were within earshot, "something weird." I widened my eyes and tilted my head towards the back room.

Clipping the chain back in place, we hurried down the hall. I pointed at the floor in front of Lightning's nose.

"I think somebody's been stabbed." Alex dropped to a knee.

"Thunder, don't." Willie snatched at the dog's tail. Missed. The black canine shot off, followed by his wingman. Flying past a couple of long, built-in counters, they darted right.

Willie shoved us forward. "Mates, get those dogs under control. Now. We've got a crime scene here."

"Lightning. Thunder. Don't move another muscle." I dashed after them, squeezing past Alex. Around the corner, a leg poked out of the mudroom at the back entrance. Scattered papers and broken drawers covered the prone man. The air reeked of spilled ink. In two giant leaps, I captured Thunder and forced him to lie down.

Alex whisked Lightning away from the still form jammed against the wall. In his signature move, my furball struggled to lick the man's face.

Beyond the body, the exit door hung open, revealing stairs leading down into the alleyway. A man spun on the last step. Our eyes locked for a second. A horrible birthmark covered the right side of his face, interrupted by twisted scars. His lips curled in a sneer. Then, he vanished.

"Halt." I released Thunder and jumped over the victim to catch him.

"Gabe, get back in here," Alex said. "Help me. This guy's unconscious."

I killed my speed, catching the door-frame at the top of the stairs. "We'll lose the attacker." I slapped the wood hard and reversed direction.

"The victim doesn't seem to have lost much blood." Willie, restraining Thunder, sat beside Alex.

"That's fresh." I pointed at the red dots speckling the man's shirt. "Is he breathing?"

"Like a whisper." Alex crouched near the man's head, hand hovering above his mouth. "He's fading."

"I'm calling the Polizei and the Krankenwagen." Willie sprang to the phone.

"That ambulance better be quick." I surveyed the wreckage. Something caught my eye. "A note." I tapped Alex. "On his vest." As I reached out to snatch it, Alex caught my wrist. "Let go." I wrestled out of his grip. "The writing's covered by a shadow."

"Don't pull it off." Alex waved toward a reading lamp on a shelf opposite the slumped figure. "Use that light to see it better. Don't touch anything else."

"Party crasher." I seized the lamp, angled the shade at the man's chest, and flicked it on. I snagged one of the scattered pens and a crumpled sheet of paper from the floor to make notes.

"What does it say?" Alex set down the squirming Lightning and made him sit.

"29 August 1990. Most of the words are German." I held my scribbled copy next to the original. "We'll have to get it translated. And the last words are in English. He signed it, 'The Phantom of...' The rest is smudged."

"Mates, I reckon we've got a real dog's breakfast here." Willie hung up the receiver and examined the other counters for clues.

"Yep." I jabbed Alex. "A total mess." I decoded Willie's Australian phrases faster than my brother could blink.

"I got it." Alex whacked me.

"The Polizei are on the way." Willie searched the room, yanking drawers open. "The Krankenwagen will be here in two shakes to take this fellah to the hospital."

"Hey, look at this." I stepped over the victim's legs and touched a piece of brown cloth stuck on a nail head, poking out from the wall behind the man. "I bet that's part of the guy's jacket."

Alex and Willie came closer. Willie smiled. "He didn't hang around to say goodbye."

"Thunder. Lightning." Alex motioned them over to the cloth. "Track."

Thunder stuck his nose close to penetrate the store's inky odors. I lifted Lightning and shoved his muzzle into the cloth.

Sirens sounded outside the store. Willie dashed to the front.

I tapped Alex's arm. "Remember the package we got from "G" warning us of a trap?" G, a mysterious person, had sent packages to us before two dangerous adventures within the past year. "Feeling lucky again?"

"Maybe," Alex said. "Doesn't he usually send more details and clues about the real problems? It's not even a couple of months since our last adventure. After our first mystery in '89, we had at least six months to get ready."

"This store is closed," said a Polizei officer in the main store. In English and German, he told customers to leave the store. Four other cops poured into the back room. The senior policeman and Willie appeared in a heated discussion by the door, yelling. The Aussie shook his head and thrust a hand toward us.

The other policemen scoured the room, collecting the scattered documents. One cop watched as ambulance medics strapped their patient into a stretcher.

Willie trudged across the room, "Mates, we'll have to go to the Polizei station for questioning and statements."

"We have to meet Mom at the library in ten minutes." Alex darted a glance at the cop and back to Willie. "Didn't you tell him?"

"Sure, mate." Willie patted his shoulder. "Field cops don't always listen to undercover guys." Willie shrugged. "And my mission here isn't for every policeman's ears. Your Mom will have to wait until we can phone her from the station. We can leave her a message or have her paged."

"She's not gonna like this," I said. "I can see her—"

"She'll understand, mate. You're under my supervision for this homeschool project to find Mozart's missing scores and manuscripts." He shook his head at the Polizei. "Let's snoop around like actual investigators and find clues to solve the case."

I whipped out my notes. Willie ignored me, walking toward the medics who raised the guy to load him into the ambulance.

"Tochter. Meine Tochter." The words cut through the confusion of noise.

The medics halted. Everyone stared and waited, but no more words came out.

"Did he call for a doctor?" Alex said. "He's going to the hospital."

"You need to pay more attention in German class," I said. "He's calling for his daughter. He said, 'Daughter, my daughter.'"

Chapter Two

Change of Assignment

At the station, the policemen bustled us through the back entrance. After negotiating a maze of cubicles, we entered a worn-down office that contained a desk with a table lamp, a chair, and a trashcan. A uniformed officer sat behind the desk. He kept us standing and asked the usual questions: name, address, and the reason for being in the store. While the officer scratched notes before he talked to Willie, I cleared my throat.

"We're late." I tapped my watch, looking at Willie.

"Excuse me, officer." Willie smiled. "The Zanadu boys missed an appointment with their mother in the town's library. Could we—"

The officer silenced him with a gesture.

"Look, mate. I'm actually part of the force. I—"

The policeman got up, glaring at Willie, and said, "When I am done with these questions, then you talk. Not before."

Willie raised an eyebrow. After confirming he was the adult responsible for supervising Alex, me, and the dogs, ten minutes of questioning followed. Finally, the officer left the room.

"Now?" I glanced at Willie. "It's been close to an hour."

"Mom will skin us alive if we don't talk to her soon." Alex ruffled Thunder's fur. "She's gonna hate the fact that we're witnesses to an assault."

Another policeman walked into the room and sat. "Do you need to make a call?" He spoke English like an American.

"Yes." I explained the problem. He picked up the phone, punched a few numbers, and waited. After a brief conversation, he hung up. "The librarian has paged your mother. She will let her know your whereabouts. Before we discuss what happened at the print shop, I need your individual statements."

Standing, the officer led our group to a small classroom and handed all three of us a clipboard containing statement paper and a pen.

"You are being monitored. There will be no talking." He motioned to the chairs, left the room, and closed the door.

We're wasting more time. Shutting out the smell of cigarette smoke and burnt coffee, I repositioning the clipboard and wrote what happened. I was the last to finish.

A sergeant came and collected the paperwork. Another policeman escorted us to a nicer office with glass windows looking into and out of the station. Four chairs with cushions faced a mahogany desk. The seated officer was on the phone, looking out his window in the opposite direction. Our escort told us to sit and motioned for quiet.

"Why did you take that long?" Alex whispered, slouched in his chair. "Writing a novel?"

"I noticed a lot of details you probably skipped over." I picked up Lightning and stroked his hair. "I'm a better detective than you."

"Hold on, gents." Willie tapped my knee. "I reckon we all had our own viewpoint."

"And where are they?" Mom. Her voice's air of authority would make these cops move faster.

I dumped Lightning, jumped out of my chair, and stuck my head into the hall. "Over here. We're being held hostage."

"That's a bit dramatic." Call finished, the officer touched me on my shoulder and guided me back into his office.

"Are my children being held against their will?" Mom strode in after I sat, Lightning curled at my feet. "I've been waiting at the library for more than an hour. Why couldn't you let them call me?"

"Madam, I assure you—" The officer offered his hand.

"Let me *assure* you." Mom ignored him. "My husband's a U.S. military officer. He…we won't stand for this treatment. We are—"

Willie stepped between them, faced Mom, and held both hands up.

"What are you doing here? Why are my boys in a Polizei station?"

"Mrs. Zanadu, I can explain." Willie gave a quick summary. "We do have to finish discussing the case with the Captain here." He pointed at the policeman behind the desk. "Captain Hans Bergmann, may I introduce Mrs. Rachael Zanadu."

"This won't take long," the officer said. "It's half-past-two o'clock. We'll be done at three. A highly sensitive case. I'll have to ask you to wait outside in our visitor's lounge."

Mom nodded.

The officer walked her out and returned. He sat and didn't waste any time. "Why were you in the print shop?"

"Mom gave us a homeschool assignment," Alex said.

"The goal was to research some missing Mozart manuscripts, learn some music, and listen to other composers from the same period." I scooped Lightning into my lap.

"That's a little bit short of a full pint." Willie sat a little straighter in his chair. "These mates are under my watch. I'm like a kangaroo watching her joeys bounce around the outback." He eyed the policeman.

Captain Bergmann rubbed his chin and gazed at the ceiling as though wrestling with an intriguing thought.

"I'm sure the good Cap'n understands there are security measures?" Willie said.

The policeman nodded, rose to his feet, and closed the door. He settled back into his chair. "Out with it. Do these two *joeys* know what's going on?"

The dogs' ears came up on alert.

"It's all a bit hush-hush, you know." Willie motioned us in closer. "The missing documents are stolen compositions from several composers. The most notable is one of Mozart's famous pieces, *Fantasia for Piano in D minor*, K397. The second is from Josef Haydn, *Piano Sonata 9 in F Major*. And there are a few others. The working theory is the pieces are being fenced in Salzburg for resale on the black market. It's a ripper of a problem."

"How does that involve these boys?"

"They're part of my front cover to do some respectable research and bag some clues to the criminals. It's all legit." Willie winked at me.

"Does their mother know?"

"Yes." Willie shifted in his chair. "I mean, she knows about the missing manuscripts and the research. She doesn't know about the other part."

"Wait." I edged to the front of my chair. "We can do more. Our Dad trained us in detective work. And a few months ago, we broke up a huge human-trafficking ring."

"Let us be part of the police team doing the investigation." Alex grinned.

"Not so fast," the Captain said. "Solving a crime is dangerous work and your mother isn't aware of the problems involved."

"Mom will let us do junior detective work if it's under Willie," I said. "She'll talk with Dad. He'll agree. We've been training for over a year."

"I'd rather hear that from her." The officer rose from his seat and made a move toward the door. Willie held out a hand.

"Before you call her in, Cap'n, is today's victim part of the stolen manuscripts?"

"The man you found today, Mr. Gerlach, is the print shop owner." The policeman leaned against the door. "He recently discovered a complete 1773 manuscript of an original Mozart composition. A priceless national treasure. Amadeus Mozart sealed it and for some unknown reason, maybe spite or timing, buried it in the alleyway behind his apartment, the same building that the print shop occupies today. Mr. Gerlach was about to make a public announcement at the close of the tourist season. That's 31 August."

"If he kept it secret, how would the attacker know about it?" I said.

"He needed to get the composition validated." Bergmann sighed. "I guess one of his contacts sold him out."

"And now the work is in the hands of a black-market dealer." Alex patted Thunder.

"Now that's the funny thing." The officer rubbed his jaw. "We don't know that. Part of the original manuscript was left behind along with other papers. And the attacker pinned a note on the owner and signed it 'The Phantom of the Fortress.'"

"Well Cap'n, this is a bloody good mystery now." Willie opened the door, calling out in a casual way, "Mrs. Zanadu, may we speak with you for a moment?"

Chapter Three

The Search Begins

The police minivan dumped us off in the alleyway behind the Makartstrasse print shop. I raced Lightning to the exit where the man fled the scene. Though police tape marked the area, Willie convinced the Polizei sergeant to let us next to the door.

"All right, mate." Willie looked left and right. "Which way did the man run?"

"The door opened to the right into the alley." I mentally retraced my position inside and turned to my left. "From my position, he would have run to the left. That way." I pointed.

"Okay. That's Dreifaltig. The next alley."

"Let's see if the dogs can pick up the scent." Alex patted Thunder.

"Remember, Lightning." I tapped him on the nose. "You sniffed that torn piece of cloth. Track him down." I lifted him to the doorknob and set him on the concrete stairs descending to the street.

The dogs sniffed. Snorted. After a few false starts, Lightning, nose inches from the ground, trotted toward Dreifaltig. Thunder, not to be outdone, loped ahead.

The streets reminded me of the Altstadt or "old city" section of Salzburg. The alleys were a bit narrower than regular streets— usually one-way traffic for cars. And most of them were labeled as Fussgängers, pedestrian-only alleys during the daytime.

At the corner, the dogs searched for a minute, picked up the trail, and trotted into the Fussgänger on the right.

The street was thick with people. Tourists in bright colors and summer clothes jostled against each other, pushing around knots of sightseers. College students with bikes rammed them through the street, ringing bells to clear the way. A couple of kids played tag, ignoring the stern looks of the adults crammed into the narrow walkway.

"I can't believe Mom agreed to let us do this." I broke into a jog to stay with the dogs.

"I think she still wasn't happy." Alex pulled alongside me. "Dad must have lots of confidence in Willie."

"He did help us catch a crime ring boss." I dodged a lady with a red dress.

The street became clogged with tourists. The dogs weaved in and out without any trouble. Europeans relaxed attitudes about dogs made it easy for them to squeeze through, but the people slowed us down a bit.

"Don't let them get too far ahead," Willie said.

The dogs dashed to the right into another alley—Theatergasse.

I darted around a threesome to follow. The dogs galloped toward the main street ahead. I whistled loud and long, but they disappeared to the right.

"Hurry." I glanced at Willie and Alex and raced ahead.

I reached the Makartplatz Square, scanning for the dogs along the main road, Schwarzstrasse, which paralleled the Salzach River's south side. Horns blared when a taxi cut off a gray sports car. I almost danced at the crosswalk, waiting for the traffic light to change.

"There they are." Alex pointed.

Thunder's tail wagged as he bounded through the crowds on another smaller street that angled off Schwarzstrasse. The light changed. I sprinted.

"To the left." I raced across another crosswalk and waited for the pedestrian light to change. Willie and Alex squeezed in next to me, breathing hard.

"He led the dogs on three sides of a square. We're going in a circle." Willie pointed back to the print shop behind us.

The white man flashed on the crosswalk signal. We shot ahead, worming our way through the crowd. At the sidewalk, we nearly bowled over a young couple. After an apology, we dashed forward.

Thunder and Lightning were across the road, flashing past a restaurant and down the hill to a bike path that crossed under the Makartsteg Bridge.

A red man glowed from the final pedestrian light before the river. "Come on." I balled my hands into fists. "We don't have all day."

The figure flashed white. I sprinted ahead of the others onto the bike path. I ran in the path's center in spite of the furious ringing of bicycle bells from behind. One bicyclist whipped past on my left. I shifted right. A girl slammed into me, handlebars digging into my chest when I twisted and sprawled onto the ground. The bike tossed the rider and slid onto the down-slope toward the river. The girl rolled twice, then came storming back.

"What were you thinking?" She knelt over me. Long brown curls brushed my cheek. I squinted, checking out her blue tinted bangs. The initial hard lines of her anger faded into concern. "I could have killed you."

I massaged my chest and sat up. "I'm sorry. I—"

"Gabe, get up." Alex's hand appeared. "Quit trying to meet girls by having an accident."

The girl looked up at Alex and smiled. Alex affected girls that way. She took the extended hand, and he helped her stand.

"Don't pay any attention to these lads." Willie brought over her bike. "They're chasing dogs that have gotten loose." He pointed at Thunder and Lightning in the distance.

"Are you sure you're okay?" The girl's eyes sparkled a little, which cheered me up, even though I felt handlebar marks on my chest.

"Absolutely." I stood, straightening my back. "How's the bike?"

"It's right as rain, mate."

The girl smiled at Alex, let her gaze linger on Willie, then waved at me.

I waved back as she caught up with her friend.

"You need to quit chasing these young ladies." Willie slapped me on the shoulder.

"Or what?" I said.

"The next time you could get yourself killed." Willie nodded at the dogs. "Let's see what's got their attention."

When we arrived, the dogs wandered back and forth, sniffing the edge of the Salzach River.

I plopped on the ground.

"All that for nothing." Alex sat next to Thunder on the grassy bank.

"I think you're a bit hasty, mate." Willie gestured at a man on the other side of the Salzach. The river, wider than a football field, supported large and small boats. The guy was upriver lashing a small motorboat to a short pier. He wore a light brown jacket. His long brown hair, knotted into a ponytail, swung free while he finished securing the boat. He smiled and waved, showing the right side of his face. The hideous side.

"That's him." I jumped to my feet. "Let's get him." As I rushed up the slope toward the bike path, a hand on my shoulder stopped me.

"He's too far away." Willie held tight. "Relax, mate. We can't catch him now. Let's investigate the boat he used. Put a leash on the dogs."

We headed toward the pier, crossing over the bridge and past its famous collection of "love locks" fastened to the chain link fence.

"I wonder how G's riddle fits in this time," Alex said. "I bet we're on another adventure."

"What's that?" Willie said.

"G." I tugged on Lightning's leash to keep him on the sidewalk. "He sends Alex and me packages before something bad happens to us. The last time he warned us about dangers in the Salt Mines, where we met you. And he sent us clues for even more mysteries, to include seven keys and a riddle about all of the next seven adventures. We're kind of on a treasure hunt."

"I dunno if I got this straight." Willie guided us around a group of Russian sightseers, all wearing Mozart buttons and following a guide carrying a tall flag picturing a bear in the middle. "There's this guy, whom you don't know, and he tells you what's going to happen in your future?" He raised his eyebrows.

"The man hasn't been wrong yet," Alex said.

"All right, mate." Willie paused as the pedestrian light went red. "What'd he say about your next mystery? Where is it?"

"Our next adventure is here." I pulled a slip of paper out of my back pocket. Here's his last poem."

In the town of music, Mozart and charm,
A tortured soul plans chaos and harm.
Pursue him and all his accomplices
For terrible are his purposes.

Chase them aloft to the highest peak.
In fortress chambers, the phantom you'll seek.
Like a ghost of pain, he appears at will
And captures his prey with intent to kill.

His organ will bellow like a rampaging bull.
The town will shudder with the weight of this fool.
Forget not the key
Nor the path you've begun
And your fortunes in this town will not be undone.

"The Phantom? Isn't that how the attacker signed his name?" Willie tilted his head at me.

"Yep." I lifted my hands and shrugged. "Don't ask me how G knows this stuff. At first, I thought the G meant our Grandpa, but how could he know these kinds of details in advance?"

"And what's this key he's talking about?" Willie said.

Alex slipped it out of his pocket.

"Let's have a look, here." Willie examined the key, turned it over a couple of times, and handed it back. "Looks like an old castle gate key. Solid iron. Like the locks for the cages in the Bavarian Salt Mines."

I nodded.

Lightning sniffed, growling louder as we walked onto the ramp to the boat dock.

"Excuse me," Alex said to a dock-worker taking money from a customer. "Did you rent this motorboat to a man today? He dropped the boat off twenty minutes ago."

"Nein." The worker said. "No one has rented this boat from me today."

"Not true." Willie edged nearer to the guy. "We saw him leave this boat here."

"I'm a dock attendant. I'm not a babysitter." He began coiling ropes.

"We're working with the Polizei," I said.

The man stiffened. "You are not the Polizei. You are a boy. Leave me alone."

Willie cut off the conversation. "Perhaps we will talk with you later."

"Nice move, Gabe." Alex poked me after we left. "You've blown our cover."

"He didn't believe me." I punched Alex in return.

"He may not believe you, mate, but he'll report what you said." Willie's stride grew longer.

"Hey. I'm sorry," I said. "Where are we going so fast?"

"Back to the Polizei station. Now that we've blown our cover, they'll have to track the assailant right away."

Chapter Four

Hellbrunn Castle

We strode into the front of the Polizei Station. After an explanation to the desk sergeant from Willie, we weaved our way into the offices.

"Agent Gretzke?" A thundering roar made several heads snap up. "Get your tail in front of my desk now." A tall, muscular man sat near the back of the office area.

"Agent Wilcox." Willie stretched out his hand. "Seems like years."

"That it has." The big man motioned at the seat, ignoring Willie's friendly gesture. "Who are your companions?"

"Current assignment." Willie sat. "We're—"

"I know what you're up to. That's why I bellowed out your name." The man lifted a steaming coffee cup and slurped a bit. "Get this straight. Stay out of my territory, and I'll stay out of yours." He slammed the cup onto the desk, rattling some pens in another glass holder. Coffee splashed onto the wooden surface. "Got it?"

"Sure, mate." Willie pushed out of the chair. "Don't get your knickers all twisted in front of these boys." After a brief locking of eyes, he left Wilcox's area.

"Gretzke." A finger beckoned from the Captain's office.

When we entered, Bergmann shut the door.

"What was that all about?" I said.

Willie shrugged. "The man wanted credit for wrapping up a sting operation in Canberra, Australia, even though he didn't do a bloody thing to help. Instead, he left me stranded to fight two gunmen alone. I nixed his credit, which meant he didn't get promoted." Willie winked. "He'll be all right."

"Listen up." Bergmann sat down. "The print shop owner, Mr. Gerlach, nearly died today. His wife, Gertrude, is with him now. They almost lost him once. And he's still in critical condition, in a coma. He requires constant care around the clock. He could pass on at any moment."

The Captain toyed with a pen. "Our analysis of the scene tells us the following information. After a struggle, he was knifed and injected with potassium chloride, a killing agent. We studied the note on his chest. The Phantom wants a million Austrian Schillings or about $90,000 in ransom money for the man's girl, Heidi."

"Wait." I dumped Lightning off my chair when I slid forward. "What girl?"

"He didn't have a girl with him during the escape." Alex glanced at Willie and the Captain.

"Didn't you hear the man cry out for his daughter?" The officer set his pen on the desk.

"Yes." Willie sat forward, elbows on knees and chin resting on clasped hands. "But no trace of the girl with the Phantom. He might not be a loner."

"Or he abducted her earlier, stashed her away, and returned for the manuscript." Bergmann resumed twirling the pen. "Plus, he wants ten million Austrian Schillings or a little over $900,000 for the missing Mozart composition."

"I think he wants to be found," I said.

"Why do you say that?" Bergmann stared at me.

"He waited for us to catch him running away after we'd given our stories here at the station earlier."

Willie explained the tracking by the dogs.

"Unusual. The note he left said there would be a roar this week. I wonder if he meant uproar? There was a blurred word before that." The Captain tilted his chair back to think.

"I know," I said. "The roar—"

The door burst open. A police sergeant stormed through the doorway. "Sir, I have a new breakthrough on the Gerlach affair."

"Thanks."

The sergeant handed the note to Bergmann and left. After a quick read, he handed the note to Willie, who passed it around. "Now he's writing in English."

Alex read the note aloud. "It's 3:30 P.M. Meet me at Hellbrunn Castle in an hour. The tricks of the water works are nothing compared to the tricks I will play on you."

"The time on the note was ten minutes ago." Willie got to his feet. "We'll go find the man. Gabe can spot him on sight. And we'll need free entrance into the Hellbrunn Castle."

"All right. I'll send a few Polizei with you."

"The Phantom will spot the cops and run." Willie tapped a finger on his lips. "I've got another solution."

"Spit it out."

"Send a couple of plainclothes detectives that can make an arrest. They'll be hidden in the crowd. We'll point out the target."

"You've got it." Bergmann punched a button on his intercom. "Get Wilcox and Gardener in here immediately." He clicked off without waiting for an answer. "I want this man off the streets. If we can't get him under control and get that girl back in twenty-four hours, I'll have to bring in the Kobra Special Forces. And I don't want that. This is my city. Let's keep it clean without outside help. Do you understand?"

"Give me someone else besides Wilcox." Willie stepped closer to the Captain. He was with me in Canberra and …" His lips set in a firm line.

"Negative, Willie. They're the only two detectives we have on duty."

"Boss—"

"That's the end of it." Bergmann got on his phone and made a call.

Willie propped himself against a wall.

"We'll get him." Alex patted Thunder's neck.

Wilcox and Gardener pushed into the office.

"These plainclothes officers will assist you by making necessary arrests at Hellbrunn Castle." The Captain drilled me with his eyes. "Take a good look—you must recognize them out of uniform."

Gardener was a short, dumpy man. He wore a yellow sweater vest. Wilcox, Willie's enemy, was in a pale green shirt with a brown sports jacket.

We said our goodbyes and made a quick exit.

"The best way to the castle is by the Autobahn's fast lane—my favorite." Willie led us to his car. "Fifteen minutes, max."

The Hellbrunn Castle parking lot was about two to five minutes from the main entrance. The Phantom would arrive in twenty minutes.

"Been here before?" Willie picked up a few castle grounds maps and handed them to us.

Alex and I nodded.

"When we were kids." I glanced at the decorative pool containing three-foot-long fish. They looked like spotted catfish to me, with big whiskers brushing the bottom of the pool.

"When you were ankle-biters?" Willie shook his head. "You won't remember anything worthwhile. We need to race through the special fountain areas and come back in time to spot the Phantom."

Willie explained each water trick in detail. We ran from one location to the next until we'd completed one circuit of the gardens.

"That's it—back to the beginning for the five o'clock tour." Willie accelerated the pace.

"Why wouldn't he be in the main castle?" Alex said.

"He talked about the trick fountains." Willie stopped in the park's entrance area. "I think that means he'll use the fountains to hurt someone."

"He knows what we look like." I knelt and picked up Lightning. "How can we hide?"

"Let's split up around the first trick fountain, the stone table," Alex said. "I'm sneaking behind the bushes on the right."

"Are those plainclothes policemen going to work with us?" I checked out a hiding place behind a statue on the left.

"Gardener will—he's a team player." Willie cocked his head slightly. "Wilcox, I dunno. He can get real cheeky."

The last group of the day gathered around the tour guide, a blonde woman, as we hid. They started at the first water trick area, a table with four stone seats on each side and one at its head. Beyond the seating area was a mini-stone amphitheater, open end facing the table. The tourists sat on sculptured steps to listen and watch the action.

"Archbishop Markus Sittikus," the woman said, "designed the palace and water gardens in the 1600s for play. He would sit in the head chair and have his guests sit at the sides."

I glanced around the crowd. No suspect. Alex shook his head when I saw him. The plainclothesmen stationed themselves on either side of the table.

The guide enlisted several volunteers to take seats. She dragged Agent Wilcox to the table. She continued talking, and at the right moment, water spurted up from the seats, except at the head of the table. The seated tourists all jumped backward. Wilcox got soaked in the pants. And behind him and the seated guests, other water fountains sprayed them from the sides.

The people laughed, and the guide moved them past the two reflecting ponds to the next trick fountain.

Wilcox forced himself to fit in, smiling and laughing until he saw me. His eyes threw daggers of dislike at me with his lips curled in a snarl. A second later, the laughing tourist mask covered his resentment as he slid back into his role.

I chuckled at our incognito detectives and trailed along, moving further down the paths.

We passed trick deer heads mounted on the building that sprayed cool water for such a hot day. That mood didn't last. The next feature changed the party atmosphere.

"All the water in the palace is spring fed and excellent for your well-being." The guide strolled, talking over her shoulder. "Gather around this small reflecting pool to—"

"How disgusting." A mother picked up her little girl and hustled the child across the path. A few dead goldfish floated belly-up in the water. "This is no trick."

A fountain nearby on a slight rise, guarded by stone lions, fed the reflecting pool where we paused. Patches of a thick, ugly yellow-green spread through the crystal-clear fluid, transforming the gorgeous attraction into a sickly, rotten-egg-colored feature with an accompanying smell that almost made me choke.

"Ladies and gentlemen, please excuse this minor interruption to our fun-filled exploration of Hellbrunn's trick fountains. Onward to the next attraction." She waved us forward, stepping to the side to speak into a walkie-talkie.

"Lightning, he's here." I swiveled around, searching for the damaged face. "Can you smell him?"

My buddy wiggled, until I set him down, leash in place. He sniffed around the gravel trail, trotting up the concrete steps to the source of the water flow. Small walls to either side of the building got his attention. He jumped at one wall. I lifted him to the higher ground behind the wall and climbed.

Willie leaped the wall on the other side. He swept his hand forward. We met at a trail of trampled grass behind the building.

"Pretty recent." Willie plucked a blade of grass. "I'd say within the last half hour."

"I found an empty glass jar of colored fluid by the spring's outlet." Alex rounded the corner of the water feature with Thunder. "What made that print in the dirt?"

"A wheelbarrow?" I pointed back up the trail into the trees. A gardener's wheelbarrow lay on its side. "He must have wheeled it here as a disguise and wired a timer to the jar."

"We were close to catching him," Willie said. "Let's get back to the tour." Gardener looked at him for direction and he waved him ahead. We split up, following the tourists.

The guide settled the crowd, although the upset woman stalked toward the exit. We toured Neptune's grotto area, the water-driven musical theater, and the golden hat that was raised by a spray of water.

As the crowd went into another grotto, I stayed outside to check the woods behind the walking path.

A woman shrieked.

I raced back to the grotto.

Coughing and yelling, the crowd spilled into the clearing. A misty vapor crept from the grotto's mouth.

Alex and Thunder stumbled out. Alex rubbed his eyes, finding a fountain to wash them out while Thunder stuck his head in a decorative trench of water flowing by the sidewalk.

I scanned the greenery of the forest and the maintenance trail. The Phantom ran along the path.

"Go." I unhooked Lightning's leash. I rushed past the undercover cops on their knees, hands splashing water in their eyes along with the sightseers. Wilcox was ranting about babysitting young boys.

Willie, eyes red, stumbled and waved me to make the chase.

Sprinting to catch up with my canine buddy, I glimpsed the Phantom veer to the right. Lightning gained ground. The man raced off, however, my dog could outpace any short distance runner.

I'm going to capture the Phantom myself. I knew it. Alex would be jealous.

Brush crackled as the trickster hit the tree line about thirty yards in front of me. The sound lessened as he worked his way further from the path. In moments, though, the silence was broken by a lonely noise.

Lightning's barking changed from a steady roar to a series of weak yips.

"Lightning, are you hurt?" I redoubled my efforts to get through the bushes, breaking through onto another maintenance path.

I found Lightning pawing his face to get something off. He spun around a small space.

"Yew," I said. "That stinks like a skunk." I stepped on a mound of mulch toward a spigot with an attached hose. "Hang on, buddy. I'll rinse you off in a second."

A hidden noose snaked around my ankle and jerked me upside down, several feet off the ground. I swung my arms and stretched at the rope. My hands couldn't reach it.

The Phantom jumped from the bushes on the opposite side of the trail, laughing with gusto. He opened his brown jacket, revealing an assortment of knifes in leather sheaths.

"Alex. Willie." I yelled, trying again to bend at the waist. My struggles made me spin. Glimpses flashed by of the man pulling out different blades, shaking his head and stuffing them back in their holders. Like he was deciding to skewer me, skin me, or slash me.

Blood rushed to my head. My heart felt like it would break my chest.

Finally, he flicked out some paper, jabbed it with a pin and stuck the note into my forearm.

I yelled as the pin pierced my skin.

"Willie, hurry." I waved, pretending I saw him coming in the brush.

The man glanced behind himself and dashed into a thick set of trees and bushes, laughing as he disappeared from sight.

I tore the pin out of my arm.

"Gabe, you hurt?" Alex got there first, Thunder roaring past until called back. "What's wrong with the arm." He stopped me from spinning.

"Oh, nothing." I grabbed onto Alex, dropping the note and pin. "I'm a bulletin board for a criminal."

Willie arrived and climbed the tree to cut me down. "Have you down in a jiffy."

A minute later, my brother and I crashed into the mulch together.

"How about a little warning?" Alex bounced back to his feet first, brushing off his pants. "Like 'He's all yours' or 'Letting go now.'"

"Always be prepared." Willie tossed the rope onto Alex.

"That dirty, rotten—" I began to vent as I worked the rope off my ankle. The spot was raw from supporting my full weight.

"Watch that tongue." Willie dropped from the tree.

"I hope he uses sterilized pins." I glanced at the puncture where blood welled up. "At least it wasn't an artery. And I don't want any more tetanus shots."

"We'll get you bandaged up at the Polizei headquarters." Willie heard Lightning's whining. He bent down to check him out. "When were your last shots?"

"Before my Dad got stationed in Germany," I said.

"He left another note." Alex snatched the paper from the ground. "In German." He read it to us. "Altstadt. Bis Morgen."

I rolled to my feet and ran to my dog. I bathed his face with the hose. Afterward, he snorted for minutes, still pawing at his muzzle.

"Buddy." I kept his paws from moving. "You'll tear off your nose if you keep it up."

"I'd say we've botched this one, mates." Willie wiped water off his chin. "That suspect's not a total loon."

"The undercover cops got trapped too?" I sighed.

"Yeah. One good thing is that I don't have to wrestle with Wilcox for who caught the man."

"At least the guy used tear gas and not mustard gas." Alex scratched Thunder's back. "Guess we ought to get back to the vacation apartment."

"Right." Willie nodded. "The note said he'd see us tomorrow in the old town, the Altstadt. However, before we go, Gabe needs to describe this guy to the Polizei. He got up close and personal with him."

Alex and I nodded at the plainclothes cops on our way to the car. Back at the station, I wrote a description of the suspect and handed it to the desk sergeant. We left, walking past several stores. I spotted a box of Mozart Kugeln. I loved those chocolate balls. The candy wrapper pictured Mozart's right profile. Next to them was a Mozart chocolate bar showing the opposite side.

"Willie." I stopped. "See that picture of Mozart's face, the one of the left side? That's an exact match for the Phantom's face. His right side's messed up with some kind of purplish-red mark, maybe a birthmark, from his upper lip to the eye."

"Are you certain?"

"I have to go back and fix the description." I reversed direction. Fifteen minutes later we left for the apartment a few kilometers across the German border in the rustic village of Türk.

Chapter Five

Türk

"Are you guys for real?" I slapped my best friend, Peter Schultz, on the back. Pete was a couple months younger than me. "I can't believe we're together on vacation again."

"How did you track us down?" Alex hugged Jenna Schultz, his girlfriend. They spent all their free time together. She was about five months older than Alex.

"Your mom called our Mom, who talked to our Dad, who called your dad, and since your Dad left on a mission at the last minute… you know the rest of the story." Jenna pulled Alex into our apartment's combined living/dining/kitchenette room. The Germans believed in efficient living and packed everything in one small space like a tiny two-room cabin in the woods.

"Hi, Mom." I waved. Jenna and Peter's parents sat on the sofa. The four of us moved to the dining table and sat. "Is there anything here for dinner?"

"Where's Willie?" She glanced out the window. "He's not driving away already, is he? I worry about that boy."

"He's 19 years old," I said. "He's a man."

"Not where I come from," she said. "I wanted to hear about your day. He fills in the details I need to know. And he owes me a report about what you do. That's why I'm letting you work with him."

"It's pretty simple." Alex tipped his chair onto the back two legs. "We saved a guy's life. The dogs helped us track a man who ran away from the scene and we failed to catch him. Willie drove us to Hellbrunn Castle to point out the fugitive to undercover cops. The man escaped anyway and ruined the park tour for a group of tourists. He was a trickster."

"I'm sure it isn't as simple as all that." Mom went to the microwave in the kitchenette and heated some bratwurst and sauerkraut.

"I hate sauerkraut." I wrinkled my nose.

"Really? I could never have guessed that." Mom smiled. "Don't worry. I'm making some Käsespaetzle with bratwurst in a bun. Just for you." Mom pulled out another package and opened it up.

"I love German noodles and cheese." I grinned, glancing at Pete and Jenna. "Tell us what you two have been doing lately."

For twenty minutes we talked about chess, sports, dancing, school, and a ton of other subjects. Pete shoveled his food, talking with his mouth full. I devoured my bratwurst and Käsespaetzle while Jenna and Alex picked at their dinner. After we washed and dried the dishes, Jenna and Pete invited us over to see their apartment. The dogs tagged along.

"Okay, tell us the real story." Jenna opened the 'fridge, and we each grabbed a soda. "I know there's more."

Alex and I took turns sharing about the Phantom of the Fortress.

"Crazy." Pete gave me a playful shove. "You're always diving into trouble."

"Am not." I shoved him back. "Besides, now that you two are here, we can look around ourselves. Willie's a nice guy, but he likes to tell us what to do."

Lightning began to play-fight with Thunder by making little growls and pawing Thunder's ears and face. Thunder, who was lying on the floor, snapped back like an annoyed crocodile.

"The local policemen know you now. You don't need him, do you?" Jenna took her bottle to the kitchen sink and rinsed it out. "Isn't there something else he could do?"

"Mom wants him to supervise us." I sucked in a deep breath and let it out. "I think it was the condition for working on this case."

"Okay." Pete lay back on a pillow, feet working me off the couch. "What about the music research? Find anything interesting?"

"Maybe." Alex nodded. "Mozart showed his father a piano concerto when he was four. In spite of the smeary notes, his dad realized it was a real piece of music and not just a kid playing around on paper. We're looking for a score that's missing from when Mozart was a kid."

"Show off." I threw a pillow at Alex. "Pete didn't ask for a history lesson."

"Better to know than to be clueless like you." He threw the pillow back, knocking over my empty soda bottle. Lightning chased it under the table.

"Careful." Jenna snatched the pillow from me. "Break anything, and we'll all pay for it."

"The Polizei have a crack team on the music research." Alex bounced to his feet and gazed out the window. "We'll get a report tomorrow morning. I'd like to see that first. We don't have much time before they send in some kind of commando unit to track him down."

"We've got to do something." I wrestled Pete off the couch, taking his place while shoving him into the table and chairs. He hit the ground with a thump. "Nothing is happening. We're not getting anywhere. And who knows where he's taken that girl."

"When are you going in tomorrow?" Pete lifted his head.

"Willie's picking us up at seven-thirty." Alex sat on the windowsill. "Why don't both of you come with us? We'd have a lot more fun."

Thunder tracked Lightning, slinking up behind him as he went to nuzzle Pete's face. The black giant pounced, rocking the table. Chips flew into the air and chairs clattered to the ground. A bowl and chair crashed on top of Pete. His body lay twisted, legs askew like he'd taken a terrible fall.

The door flew open. Herr and Frau Schultz paused, observing the trashed room.

"Peter," his dad said. "Why are you lying on the floor?"

"Gabe wrestled me off the couch." He grunted, trying to untangle himself from the furniture. "And I'm comfortable here."

"Dad." Jenna beamed a smile at him and touched Alex's shoulder. "The boys invited us to Salzburg with them tomorrow. Can we—?"

"Before we discuss anything, you will clean this mess up immediately." Frau Schultz's directive allowed no room for argument.

"Yes, mother." Pete scrambled from under the chair. We all scattered, picking up the debris. The dogs lounged on the couch.

"Is this the same situation that Salzburg newscasters are reporting about a Herr Gerlach, who was almost killed?" Her dad righted one of the fallen chairs and sat.

"Maybe a little." Pete's head tilted at me.

"Herr Schultz." I snagged the soda bottle off the floor. "We've given our information to the Polizei. Willie, our Agent in charge, will work with them. The man who assaulted Herr Gerlach wants money for a music manuscript. The police will give a report on that tomorrow. After that, I'm sure we'll be released to wander the town and check out Mozart's life as part of our Home School project."

"I don't want my children involved in dangerous activity." Frau Schultz sidestepped the broken chips, secured her knitting, and sat across from us.

"Dad," Pete said. "We want to be with our friends. They need some company."

"I think after the last scare where we almost lost you in the Salt Mines, we must be cautious." He tapped his fingers on the table. "Hmm. Salzburg is a big city and many tourists are still around. You'll be above ground… No, this is not a problem. We should let them go."

Frau Schultz put down her knitting. She clasped one of Pete and Jenna's hands. "Stay together. Don't separate." With that warning, she nodded at Herr Schultz and resumed clicking her knitting needles.

"Great." I whistled for Lightning. "We'll tell Mom and she can tell Dad."

Alex and I left the room with our dogs before Pete and Jenna's parents could change their minds.

Chapter Six

Split Missions

The Polizei station buzzed with activity when we arrived for our third visit. Secretaries called out urgent messages. Uniformed Polizei rushed through the hallways. We ducked into the waiting lounge for something to drink. I grabbed a cold soda and followed Willie and the gang into the Captain's office.

"Your parents have flimflammed me." Willie slid into the Captain's chair as we waited for his arrival. "I've gone from watching two joeys to four. I'll be crackers by noon."

"We'll try to keep you out of trouble." I elbowed Pete's side and snickered.

"Don't you get any ideas—"

"I'm glad you're here." The Captain strode into his office. "Gretzke, what are you doing in my chair?" He motioned Willie out of his chair and caught sight of Pete and Jenna. "Give me a quick introduction."

After shaking hands with our buddies, Captain Bergmann dove right into work.

"New information came in last night." He went to a whiteboard on his wall and drew four red arrows. "We've faxed the Phantom's description to the town's Federal police and the Gendarme in the outlying districts. Police radioed in four separate sightings matching the description in the last half hour. Each reporting agent lost the trail in these tourist crowds. And Kobra can't get involved until we have a location for the kidnapped girl."

"Sounds like he's using accomplices that are look-alikes, Cap'n." Willie sipped on his coffee. "We can find him."

"My plainclothesmen will cover the most likely clue. That's Hellbrunn Castle again. We can't close down the attraction."

"Where do you want us?" I stepped forward. "We're great at detective work."

"Really?" The corners of the Captain's mouth turned up a bit. "Does that include yesterday's hunting trap you found? The one where you were upside down?"

"I…uh." I inched back, cheeks feeling a little hot.

"You were brave, but I need to keep you close at hand." The officer pointed at the board. "Two reports located possible Phantom suspects or look-alikes at the Hauptbahnhof—that's the main train station to you Americans—and another near Mozart's Birth House." He eyed the four of us. "We'll dispatch two teams to those locations. Can you manage those two areas between the four of you?"

"On foot?" Alex said. "Or by bus?"

"Too slow." The officer pointed at Willie. "I'd like Agent Gretzke to accompany you to both locations on his way out of town."

"What?" Willie almost choked on his coffee, spilling a little on the floor. "Cap'n, you can't be serious. These joeys are my charges. They're supposed to stay with me. Their parents—"

"You need to drive to Innsbruck. No delays."

"Sir—"

"That's all. I don't have the people or the time. Follow our minivan in the Peugeot we'll provide. When the minivan drops these young detectives at their locations, you start a high-speed chase. A fence for stolen manuscripts turned up in Innsbruck and the fourth Phantom suspect drove in that direction using the back roads through the Alps."

Agent Wilcox appeared in the door.

"Take over responsibility for these junior detectives in town." The Captain's deadly stare pinned the agent to his spot. "Gardener will assist. Stay with them at all costs."

"My pleasure." Wilcox folded his arms and smirked at Willie.

Willie's back stiffened.

"Well?" The Captain sat back in his chair. "What are you waiting for?"

We filed into the hallway.

"We'll take the main train station." Alex pointed at Jenna. "I like the Bahnhof."

"Suits me." I gathered Lightning in my arms. "While we're searching, I'll get one of those huge pretzels."

"Mates." Willie gathered us together. "I'll be back by 4:00 P.M. Meet me at the Polizei station for a debriefing on the day's activities. Don't take chances." His eyes darted over to Wilcox, then back. He whispered. "You can't trust the locals for any real help. You two…" He tapped Pete and me. "Ride with me."

In ten minutes we were at the main train station. Alex, Jenna, and Thunder jumped from the minivan with Agent Gardener who tucked a newspaper under his arm. After a visual once-over of my brother and Jenna, he shook his head. Something bothered him.

Willie stepped out of the car and spoke to Alex. Finished, he slid behind the steering wheel and blended into traffic. He didn't speak, like he was in another space.

Five minutes later, Agent Wilcox dismounted from the minivan. Pete, Lightning and me climbed from the Peugeot and joined

45

him in front of Mozart's Birth House on Getreidegasse, house number 9.

Willie waved our whole group over as though he wanted to talk.

I glanced at the old town and sucked in a deep breath. *At last. Now we'll see some action.* I felt strong, ready for anything.

"Come on, Gabe," Pete said. "Willie's in a rush."

Hurrying to the car, my thoughts flashed to Alex and Jenna at the Bahnhof. Gardener's disappointment in them was a bad sign. *Strange.* Goosebumps prickled my skin. I sensed a tragedy approaching.

Chapter Seven

Bahnhof

"Alex," Jenna said. "What did Willie say to you before he left?"

"Keep my head clear because the Phantom will play some nasty tricks."

"Brilliant. Takes a genius to figure that out."

"We've got this. The Phantom won't fool us." I bent in a mock bow. "After you, Madam."

Agent Gardener tried to blend into the crowd, looking at shop windows outside the train station. He made an occasional change in direction to keep tabs on Jenna and me. I tracked his reflections in store windows. He wasn't invisible to me.

I steered Jenna with an arm around her shoulder into the Hauptbahnhof entrance. Thunder padded next to my side. Salzburg's main train station looked like an indoor American mall. Shops and cafes with floor-to-ceiling glass windows lined the interior walkway, which was wider than four or five cars parked end to end. The tiled floor stayed level for the first four or five shop entrances, gradually sloping at least one floor underground to a flat central section, and rising back to street level on the other side. The ceiling was a mix of shiny white tiles and sections accented by stainless steel. We strolled past the information center on our right.

"Looks brand new." I took Jenna's hand and led her in the direction of the electronic train station schedule underground.

"Like a major airport." Jenna squeezed my hand and let go.

"How do you write Vienna in German?"

"Wien. It's pronounced 'Veen.' Why do you ask?"

"I'm a Mozart fan. I've read up on his life for a homeschool project."

"I'm listening." She window-shopped as we strolled.

"Mozart moved to Vienna the last ten years of his life because it was the music center for his world at the time. Salzburg wasn't good enough."

"Didn't Mozart travel everywhere with his father? I think he even went to Paris."

"True," I said. "That was to perform. And he didn't like Paris because his mother died there. He wanted to be the center of attention, to enjoy top dollar for his work. Like our suspect."

We stopped in front of the electronic board displaying departure and arrival times. Dark blue signs with white numbers hung from the ceiling at regular intervals to show the train track numbers. International signs for restrooms, ground transportation, rentals, and information were at the end of the sign. Orange arrows directed the way to each service.

"Gleiss number three goes to Wien." Jenna pointed. "The Phantom's destination?"

"Yeah. That's the track." I checked out another sign. "Two types of trains go to Vienna—slow, which makes a ton of local stops, and fast, a bullet train that stops a few times. I bet that's the one he'll take."

"Yes. The WESTbahn—Züge." Jenna read the board like a tour guide. "These trains have a bunch of different services. You can buy tickets on the train, store large bags, bring your bike, and lots of other things. Trains arrive one minute before departure. We'll have to be quick." Jenna slipped her hand into mine to walk away.

"Here's the schedule." I tugged her in another direction. "The bullet train leaves at fifty minutes past the hour and arrives about two-and-a-half hours later."

"9:45 A.M." She glanced at a clock hanging from the ceiling. "We have five minutes. Hurry."

The mall area ran under the tracks. To the right and left were escalators and stairs to different track locations. Track three was right after the glass windows of a SPAR store.

I spotted Gardener talking to a man in a blue coverall with the words Information and QBB printed on the back. Gardener's slight nod signaled that he saw us.

We weaved past metal barriers and ran up the escalator. Halfway to the top two men with large suitcases blocked our path. We waited. Three minutes. My fingers beat a rhythm on Thunder, who sat by my side.

"I hope Gabe and Pete are staying out of trouble." Jenna folded her arms.

"Gabe's reckless sometimes." I ruffled my dog's neck. "He doesn't think. He acts."

"That can be good." She shifted closer.

"Once or twice. And he doesn't seem to make the best choice in friends."

"You mean Jonathan?" Jenna leaned into my shoulder. "He doesn't care about anyone except himself. You could see that when we were trapped in the Berchtesgaden Salt Mines a few months ago."

"He blames his mean streak on a bad upbringing," I said.

"That's ridiculous. He's got a screw loose somewhere. I don't trust him. He's trying to pull Gabe away from your family. And Gabe's a sucker for the 'poor me' story."

"That will get him hurt some—"

Thunder rumbled. The men above us on the escalator turned their heads toward us.

"What's up, boy?" I rubbed his head. "Smell something?"

The men went back to their business and stepped off the escalator.

Track three's passengers crowded together on one side of the platform. Thunder trotted toward them, nose near the ground.

"He's got the Phantom's scent." I followed, pulse quickening. Jenna trailed me.

"Two minutes," she said.

Thunder weaved through the crowd. The adults made way, eyebrows raised or lips tightening to show their annoyance at the intrusion of an uncontrolled, unleashed dog.

"A doggy." A girl about two-years-old clapped her hands and rushed to Thunder's side. She patted him with exaggerated swats. Thunder nuzzled her with patience as she rubbed his side. He looked at me and made a thin, high-pitched whine like a question.

The WESTbahn train arrived. People streamed off.

"I don't see him." Jenna craned her neck to see around the packed bodies.

"Excuse me." I smiled at the little girl and her parents. "We have to go." I latched on to Thunder's collar, nudging him toward a boarding door.

Thunder lurched to the side and barked at the end of the train.

"Stop." I held him back.

At the end of the train, a man with a brown coat pushed a young girl inside. He seemed nervous, looking back and forth. I glimpsed his face's left side under the brim of a felt hat.

"That's him," I said.

"Go." Her quick shove forced us on the train. The door slid shut.

The train surged ahead. On the platform, Agent Gardener and the QBB guy quarreled with a cornered man holding a girl's hand. Until a woman joined them.

I rapped on the window. Gardener didn't notice. I sighed and started down the aisle.

"Hey." Jenna grabbed my arm. "Going someplace?"

"We've got to stop the Phantom."

"We need to think about this." She dragged me to a pair of vacant seats. Thunder followed. "We can't arrest the guy."

"Tickets." A conductor entered our car, punching papers handed to him.

Her blue eyes locked on mine. "Got any money?"

Chapter Eight

Mozart's Birth House

"Wilcox, if anything happens to these joeys, I'll tear your heart out." Willie's narrowed eyes drilled the agent behind Pete, Lightning and me. We waited near his car.

"Nothing to worry about, *mate*." Wilcox's emphasis on the last word showed his contempt for Willie.

"No worries." I patted the open window. "We'll keep our noses clean."

"I'll count on it." Willie motioned me around to the driver's side with his finger and whispered a few words in my ear. "That idiot looks out for himself and nobody else. Canberra wasn't the first time he left me hangin'. He's interested in promotion at any cost. Don't count on him for help."

I nodded.

"Remember. Four o'clock tonight. Full report."

"Roger."

I stepped back, and Willie's Peugeot pulled away.

"I'm headed for Mozart's Birth House." Wilcox pointed at a bright yellow building. "Care to join me?"

Getreidegasse is one of the main alleyways in the Altstadt, set at an angle to the main street, which follows the Salzach River. Rectangular gray pavers made up the road that doubled as a pedestrian walkway. With the outdoor cafe tables on half the street, the road seemed narrow, with room for one car. Grey and brown buildings rose several stories on either side. Mozart's Birth House, six stories high, was painted a bright yellow you couldn't miss. Gold letters nestled above the third story windows proclaimed this building was Mozart's Geburtshaus, visible to any sightseer arriving from the main street.

"Let's take the tour and see if the suspect is inside." Wilcox prodded us into the clustered tourists on the first floor. He positioned himself behind us at the ticket counter. "Two tickets."

"Two?" I stared and raised an eyebrow. "We need three, don't we?"

"How old are you kids?" Wilcox ignored my question.

"I'm twelve for another five days." Peter held up his fingers. "Can't wait to be a teenager."

"I'm thirteen," I said. "What difference does it make?"

"I'm not paying out extra department money unless it's necessary. You're both above the children's age limit." He made a face. "Barely."

"Why aren't you coming?" I pocketed the ticket from the cashier. "Afraid to be around some top-notch detectives?"

"That's a good one." His deep laugh attracted attention. "I'll have to tell the Captain."

"You still didn't tell us." Pete faced him. "Why?"

"My job's not to babysit. I'll wait at the café across the street, inspecting the tourists for our man." He slapped me on the shoulder, chuckled, and walked away.

I hustled past the barrier into the Mozart house. Lightning beat me up the stairs.

Pete and I read some of the information, eyes peeled for the suspect while soaking in the self-guided tour. The first two rooms contained several glass cases with papers. The second room was bigger than the first.

Lightning yanked me along.

"Slow down." I jerked his leash. "Find something?"

Nose an inch from the floor, he sniffed with rapid puffs. A couple of times, dust under the cabinets made him snort. He strained, toenails clicking on the wood floor, to move faster into the next room.

"What's happening?" Pete said. "Must be a strong scent. He's going to choke himself."

I let out more leash. He flew to a corner in the third room, Mozart's birth room, behind a glass bookcase and snapped up a brown piece of cloth, note attached.

I dragged him from under the bookcase, plucking the prizes from his mouth.

"That's the same material as the Phantom's jacket." Pete felt the soft cloth.

"Yeah." I unfolded the note. "He says, 'Can't keep up with an old man? Catch me near the college church this afternoon.'"

"Why are we too slow?" Pete scanned the room to find him.

"Because we're being tourists." I hooked Lightning under my arm and sliced my way through the clumps of sightseers in the fourth room, zipping to the exit.

"Right in front of you." Pete tapped my shoulder.

A man ducked around the corner. I raced to catch him, Pete in close pursuit.

The next room was a mock-up of what Mozart's house might have looked like. I threaded the narrow gaps toward the gift shop at the end. The Phantom hurried down the stairs.

Got him. Four people to clear before the stairs.

An arm whipped around my waist. A hand covered my eyes.

"Guess who?" A boy's voice.

"Jonathan, let go." Pete yanked his hand off. "We're chasing someone."

"In a hurry?" Jonathan didn't let go. "Tell me about it."

I wrestled with his arm and stamped on his foot.

"Ow." He knelt to massage his toes. "Why'd you do that?"

"Later." I dashed for the door, Lightning and my friends in pursuit. I burst into the jammed street. Large groups of tourists wound around each other like currents in a river.

"Do you see him?" I motioned Pete to check out the people.

Jonathan folded his arms and propped himself on the wall next to the exit. He dressed like a tough guy. Black leather jacket, designer jeans, and biker boots.

We almost caught him.

"Lightning." I touched the brown cloth to his nose and set him on the pavement. "Track."

My canine buddy went back to the exit, snooped around the door, the steps, and the ground. He sat on his haunches, staring at me.

"Can't smell him?"

He snorted and lay on his stomach.

"The crowds are too thick." Jonathan shifted. "Who are you looking for?"

"Couldn't find him." Pete appeared and met me at the exit. "We are too slow."

"Jonathan's the reason we didn't catch him." I glared at him. "We're not slow."

"The store was packed." Jonathan scratched Lightning's back. "How can you pin this on me?"

55

"Jonathan Brinker, you're a space cadet." I inched closer. "Just because you're sixteen and bigger than me doesn't mean you know the situation better."

"Okay. Explain." He gestured at a restaurant. "First, let's eat. I'm starved."

"Can't." Pete pointed to the note. "The Phan—the guy will get away. We have to find the college church."

"Oh, that's easy." Brinker pulled a tourist map from his pocket. "Here." He showed us the location. "See, it's on the backside alley from Mozart's Birth House Museum.

"That'll take us ten minutes according to the map," I said. "He'll escape."

"Never fear, *I* am here." Jonathan bowed. "Glad to be of service."

"Right," Pete said.

"I'm not kidding." Jonathan waved for us to follow him. "It's two minutes through the little store alleyways between the streets."

"We have to tell Wilcox first," Pete said.

"Who's that?"

"A Polizei agent assigned to us." Pete wiggled through the sightseers to the café across from the Birth House.

"Tell me more." Jonathan raised his eyebrows at me. "The Polizei?"

Pete saved me, breaking through another clot of people to return.

"Gone." Pete shook his head. "I didn't see him anywhere.

"Willie warned us." I picked up Lightning. "Lead the way, Jonathan."

Chapter Nine

University Plaza

Lightning blasted into a large plaza from a tiny alleyway, no wider than two people side-by-side, with the three of us seconds behind.

"Quick." I pointed in a couple of directions. "Search around. Did we catch up with him?"

The College Church bordered the University Plaza, a large square filled with an outdoor market. Austrian food vendors sold cold meats, cheeses, vegetables, and large pretzels alongside the normal tourist shops with trinkets about Mozart, candy, chocolates and fresh flowers.

Sunshine reflected off the paved street, keeping us warm in spite of the cool sixty degrees Fahrenheit. The aroma of coffee floated in the air. Kids and adults jostled each other to see the merchandise, flowing from one street vendor to another, jamming each nook and cranny.

"Three minutes, Jonathan, not two." I adjusted my jacket. "And the guy's vanished." The coffee smell got to me. "Time for a bretzel."

Bretzels, huge pretzels about a foot long and half-a-foot wide, were a European staple. Most were made from pretzel dough. A few were sweet bread. Several choices of toppings such as chocolate, cinnamon-sugar, cherries, cheesecake, and others were available.

"Count me in," Pete said.

"I need real food." Jonathan motioned at a sausage shop. "I'll get a bratwurst and pommes."

"French fries are worse for you than bretzels." I searched for the best vendor and headed in that direction. "My favorite is the cinnamon-sugar covered donut bretzel."

Pete and me made our choices. The man, dressed in a typical blue-striped shirt and jeans, quoted a price and wrapped them. I fished in my pocket for money and Lightning took off like a shot.

"Come back." I snagged the bretzel and launched. "Pete," I called over my shoulder, "pay the bill."

Jonathan, his mouth stuffed with of a bite of bratwurst, tailed me, leaving Pete by himself.

"Lightning, did you find his scent?"

His tail wagged like a flag in a gentle breeze. He prowled near the flower vendors next to the University Plaza church. He darted around flowers, trotted past the steps of the cathedral, and went around the corner.

I noted the speed of his tail's movement. *Hmmm. Not too excited.* Mozart's piano music filled the air. Was it from the church?

Jonathan tapped my shoulder and pointed toward one side of the building.

"Wait." Breathless, Pete joined us. His cheeks were rosy red.

We jogged to the side of the church. A tape recorder broadcast the Mozart music. Another note was taped to its side. Jonathan read it to us.

"You're late. And running out of time. Look across the plaza."

I dashed back to the street, the flower booth in front of me.

"Next to the meat stand." Pete tapped me. "And the girl's with him."

"Where did she come from?" I stared. "He must have a network of accomplices built up."

The Phantom waved casually at us. His brown coat and hat pulled low over his face helped him blend in. He muscled the girl by her arm into the crowd and disappeared in a connecting passageway toward Getreidegasse.

"What's with the disguise?" Jonathan said. "The trench coat and Fedora hat?"

"Not now." I raced past the brilliant colors of the fresh flowers to cross the plaza. Lightning's speed outstripped mine since he could dart between legs. One man raised a fist and yelled in German when I flashed by him.

Pete and Jonathan joined me while we navigated the congested space.

"That way." Jonathan tagged my right shoulder and forged ahead to a passage that linked to the next street. "He went down this alley."

I angled toward the opening. A group of camera-toting Japanese tourists poured into the plaza, pausing to take pictures. They kept coming and coming. A hundred of them jammed together. We couldn't penetrate the blockade.

"Split up," I yelled. "Pete, you and Jonathan go one more passage to the right, I'll go left." I dashed away, whistling for Lightning to follow, but I didn't see him anywhere.

Feet pounding on the cobblestones, I sped into the nearest passageway entrance and collided with a girl, about my age, dressed in traditional Austrian costume. She bounced away, spilling her basket's contents on the ground. Her wide eyes turned into watery pools at the scattered flowers. She was ready to cry.

59

"Excuse me." I bent, stacking the yellow tulips in her basket as neat as I could. I straightened and smiled. "I'm sorry. I have to go."

Her brown eyes searched my face.

"I've lost my dog." I shrugged.

"Oh." She nodded. Smiling, she waved me on. "Go find him."

In the alley, I dodged people and banged into walls. Halfway to Getreidegasse, I passed a full-sized ceramic bull covered with different colored buttons near a pizza place. I memorized that landmark and exited on Getreidegasse. I whistled for Lightning. He didn't respond. I moved right to trap the Phantom in the closing pincers of our two teams. Jonathan and Pete met me halfway.

"Did you see him?" I said.

"No." Pete sucked in a deep breath. His jacket was off. "Nothing."

"Seems like a wild goose chase to me." Jonathan yawned. "What did this guy do?"

I explained the case while searching for Lightning. "When we split alleyways on either side of the Phantom and the girl, I lost him." We joined the flow of tourists into the alley the Phantom used.

"Where could he be?" I poked my head into stores on the right. Pete and Jonathan scoured the left. After eight stores, I heard a whimper. I quickened my pace. Inside a Christmas shop full of different glittery and glass ornaments, I found Lightning on the floor. A colorful Austrian scarf with winter scenes wrapped around his body restrained his legs. Bright red ribbon wound around his muzzle to keep it shut.

A safety pin pierced the flap of his ear. Another note. "Buddy, that's got to hurt." I unclipped the pin, letting the note flutter to the floor. I knelt. Scooped him into my arms and pressed a tissue against his skin. "The Phantom will wish he had never done that." A surge of adrenalin hit me. I jumped to my feet. "Let's find him."

"Wait." Jonathan captured the piece of paper. "Listen to this first."

> Thirty-six hours will end this game. Then
> I will earn immortal fame.
>
> A re-born Mozart you will hear as the
> Phantom prowls the Fortress near.
>
> Salzburg will suffer more catastrophes
> for failing to see Mozart's spirit in me.
>
> The girl dies at the second sun
> to prove to all that I'm the one.
>
> Death will be your fate, too,
> if stopping me, you pursue.

"What does that mean?" Pete rolled his eyes. "Other than we'll die if we keep this up."

"We only have about thirty-six hours." I ruffled Lightning's hair, the anger subsiding as I analyzed the note and we wandered back to Getreidegasse. "I think his clock must not start until 6:00 P.M. tonight because he says, 'the second sun.' That probably means two sunrises."

"It could mean two days." Jonathan fell in beside me. "That would give us more time."

"Us?" I glanced hard at him. "You're not part of the team."

"Not yet." He rubbed his thighs, groaning. "Try running in biker boots. I'm not sure you could keep up." He slapped his legs. "In any event, I'm your man. I know this town better than the two of you. Who got us through these passageways to get to University Plaza?"

"That doesn't matter." Pete stopped, turning on Jonathan. "Only Gabe and Alex are on this case. They invited Jenna and me to join them." He narrowed his eyes. "You haven't been invited yet."

"Quit." I wedged between the two, separating them from closing in on each other. "That decision is Willie's. He'll be back at four o'clock."

"And where is your brother?"

"At the train station. With Jenna."

"Wilcox is gone." Pete touched my arm. "We should scour the area for more clues on our own."

"Until Willie gives his permission, why don't I hang out with you?" Jonathan raised his eyebrows. "I don't have anything else to do. Dad's on another business trip." His shoulders sagged.

I shrugged. "I'm not sure…"

"Fire," a man yelled. Smoke billowed from the top of the only yellow building on the street—Mozart's Geburtshaus.

"He's started." The color drained from Pete's face. "The Phantom's attacks have begun.

"Run." I set Lightning on the ground and dashed toward the fire.

Chapter Ten

Chase on the Train

"Tickets?" The conductor reached out his hand.

"Alex?" Jenna elbowed me.

"We don't have tickets yet." I straightened my posture and tried to look sophisticated. I felt like I failed. My muscles tensed. "We would like two tickets to Vienna."

The conductor tilted his head. "Ah. An American. Ja?"

"Yes, I mean, ja." I nodded. "American."

"Passport?" He held out his hand. "And where are your parents?"

"They're—" *Did I bring my passport?* My hand slapped my chest. We could be in deep trouble. Thunder, lying by my feet, raised his head at my sudden motion.

Jenna saved me by speaking rapid German while I scrambled to retrieve my passport. She said Mozart several times, pointing toward Vienna. At one point, she put her hand on my shoulder. And with a slight tilt of her head, she spoke in a lower voice, the corners of her mouth lifting in a smile. A shy smile. *Or was it a sly smile?*

My heart calmed as I removed the leather pouch slung around my neck.

"Thank you." The conductor glanced at my passport, closed and returned it. "Alex Zanadu. You are smart, carrying your passport and money in this way. Since you are American, I warn you to keep your dog under strictest control. Understood?"

"Yes, sir."

"Enjoy your trip." He smiled, nodding as he moved behind us.

"What did you say to him?" I turned toward Jenna.

She blushed, not looking me in the eyes.

"Well..." She pushed a blonde strand of hair behind her ear. She glanced at me, then away again. "I said we were on a special trip alone to Vienna to see Mozart's house and return. With our parent's permission."

"Why are you turning pink?" I was suspicious because, like most Germans, Jenna never seemed to become embarrassed.

"I hinted that we were close. That you were totally interested in me." She sank back into the soft, burgundy cushions of the bullet train. "And that you might do something special for me on this trip."

This didn't sound like Jenna at all. She was a sports nut, tough-minded, and pushed my limits with her strong will. We held hands—nothing more.

"Really?" I raised one eyebrow. "What kind of special?"

"You are totally into me, aren't you?" A playful push moved my shoulder, and she smiled.

"I like you, but—"

Thunder shifted, sitting up and putting his muzzle in my lap.

"But what?" Jenna gazed into my eyes for an answer.

"I'm not sure I ever thought about us that way. I'm only fifteen..."

"I should have known better." She twisted away, back straight against her seat. "You American military boys only like American

64

girls for girlfriends." A storm began to build in those blue German eyes.

"Jenna, please. Not now. We're chasing a criminal who kidnapped a girl and plans to hurt her." I reached out and squeezed her hand. "We need to focus."

"Will we talk later?"

"Sure." I brushed the top of her hand. "Later. I promise." I needed to learn what she told that conductor.

"What's the plan?"

"The guy entered the last car. We locate and watch him."

"We have to appear like we're doing something normal." She plucked at some lint on her pants.

"Okay. Let's eat." I stood and offered my hand. "I'm hungry."

"Me too." She stared at my hand for a second before taking it and standing. "Just business, right?"

"Quit picking on me." I faced her, irritated. "If this guy gets away, he'll kill the girl. And then what?"

"Who knows?" Jenna's eyes contained a hint of laughter, but the firm set of her jaw told me she wouldn't let this go. "I'll wait. If we'll have that conversation."

"I promised. And I won't forget." I strolled to the dining car with Thunder and Jenna trailing. My head swiveled back and forth, taking in each passenger's face. I steadied myself as the train took a curve.

We reached our destination without spotting the targets. I held the double doors open. Jenna slid through first, scanning the dining car. Two steps in, she stiffened. She held out her hand for me to join her.

I took the hand, stepped around her, and let the aromas sweep over me. Gravy, meat, hot vegetables, and steaming rice scents filled the air. My stomach rumbled in response. I inspected the area while checking for empty seats. At the table next to the exit door sat a man with his back to me. He faced a girl who appeared to be the right age, about fourteen, with the same height and blonde hair color of the victim's daughter.

The man wore a Fedora hat, perched on his head. He wore the same trench coat, collar pulled up around his neck, that I saw when they entered the train.

"That's them," I whispered to Jenna.

Thunder sniffed and made a low rumble.

I bent down. "Stop it," I said. "Stay quiet."

Jenna tugged me forward to an empty table and sat opposite me. She kept her voice low. "We can't do anything in this car."

I leaned close. "I'll watch them." Without little extra effort, I could spy on the suspects and the exit door. *The Phantom. What a twisted mind.* I admired the artwork and decorations in the dining car, eyes sweeping the car's interior for several minutes.

"Are you there? Earth to Alex." Jenna tapped my fist. "We need to order if we're going to sit here."

"Sorry. Give me a minute." The waiter held his head high, impatient. He ignored me while waiting for my order. The menu choices were expensive. I wanted something cheap that I could leave, if necessary, without feeling bad about it. "I'll have a Cola Light and Pommes." French fries were always good. "Oh, and ketchup as well." I'd almost forgotten that in Europe the customer requested and paid for toppings or sauces separately.

Jenna ordered a Wiener schnitzel and a Perrier.

The waiter was back in minutes with the beverages and our meals.

Jenna sipped, glancing over her glass at me. "What would you like to talk about?"

"Nothing serious. We might have to run at any minute." I swallowed some cola and studied them. "They seem to be fidgeting."

"Okay, Mr. Detective." Jenna bit into her Schnitzel. "What's on your mind?"

"When they leave the…"

The man and girl finished their meal. After a short conversation, they left.

"We'll confront them at their seats." I gulped soda and jammed a handful of fries in my mouth. "I'll zip tie their wrists and have the conductor call the Polizei."

"Is your head on straight?" She latched onto my arm as I rose, drawing me back. "We can't arrest them on the train. Whose authority would you use? I've said this before. You're not a Polizei, Federal or local."

"Okay. You tell me. What's the plan?" I sagged into my seat and ate a few more fries, dipping them in the ketchup first.

"We verify he's the right person and have the conductor call the Polizei to meet us when we arrive." She poured the last of her Perrier water into her glass.

"And I guess we can block their path. They'll have limited exits to leave the train."

"That would help."

"Let's do it." I drained my soda. Rising, I followed the suspect's exit path.

When we passed the location where the man sat, Thunder stopped.

I gripped his collar. "Come on, boy, the man's gone."

He resisted, paws digging into the floor. Ears flat against his skull, his growls scared the diners at the next table.

"He's under control." I forced a smile at the dining car patrons. Jerking his collar, I stage-whispered. "Cut it out. Heel."

At the command, he paced beside me, though his head swiveled back toward the seat before we left the dining area.

"What's going on with him?" Jenna asked. "I haven't seen his ears lay back like that unless there's big trouble."

"I don't know." I forged into the next car. "We can't stop. We've got to keep that guy and girl in our sight at all times."

I halted. Near the end of the car, the man read a paper by the window with the girl sitting beside him in the aisle seat. Opposite them were two empty spots.

I knelt in the aisle to warn Thunder to stay quiet. Then we occupied the seats without any reaction from the man glued to the newspaper. Jenna's polite nod at the girl produced a strange response.

The girl shrank back, tears in her eyes. Her golden locks shook slightly back and forth with almost un-noticeable motions. The man ruffled the paper, and the girl's shoulders twitched.

I whispered to Jenna and left for the men's room. When I returned, I observed the man's face. I motioned for Jenna to join me in the aisle back towards the dining car.

"I haven't seen the right side of his face with the birthmark." I rubbed my jaw. "Otherwise he fits the description. Let's nail him."

"If you're sure." She checked the aisle. "Let's find the conductor."

We left the car, Thunder trailing. He growled in the diner car again. I stopped that with a hard yank. The conductor was near the front of the train. Little time was left—about a half an hour. Jenna talked with the conductor in German for at least five minutes before he agreed to call the Salzburg Police.

I told Jenna to have him ask for Captain Bergmann, Salzburg Polizei, since he knew the whole case.

The conductor left and returned in a few minutes.

"This is under control." He looked around and lowered his voice. "A local Polizei unit will prepare for our arrival. In order not to alarm passengers, we will do nothing special on the train. After the man and girl disembark, the Polizei will take them into custody. The Salzburg Captain has sent their description to Vienna." He patted my arm. "Don't worry."

"What about us?" I shifted my weight. "We're supposed to be part of the Polizei team."

"I suppose you can watch the police take him into custody and when they finish, go with them." The conductor beamed. "You see? All neatly tied up. Afterward, you can have your special announcement at dinner." With that, he winked at Jenna and checked for tickets and the comfort of the passengers.

"I don't like this." Jenna's eyebrows knit together. "It's too easy."

We decelerated into the station, gliding to a halt. Passengers rose to disembark. The noise of the platform filtered in when the doors slid open.

The suspect read his paper until the train came to a complete stop. Keeping the newspaper in front of his face, he rose and turned. With his back to Jenna and me, he dropped the paper. Grasping the girl's arm, he lifted her from the seat and pushed her into the center walkway.

I was in the window seat opposite him. When he entered the aisle, I could see only the left side of his face, not the right side.

Before either of us could step behind them, the passenger on the other side pushed his briefcase between us, blocking our path for a few seconds. Thunder rammed the man's bag, and he glared at me. I held Thunder back. We were losing them.

"Jenna." I alternated tracking the pair while talking with her. "Did you see the man's right side of his face?"

"You mean the birthmark?" She pushed me ahead to follow the man with the briefcase, who made a gentleman's point of letting more and more people between the targets and us.

"Yes. Did you see it?" I watched as the man and girl reached the exit door.

"I'm not sure." She frowned. "I was checking out the girl."

Turning to exit the train, the man's right side of his face became visible. Straight, smooth, and clean. He eyed his watch, shoved the girl off the train and jumped after her.

"He isn't the Phantom." I pounded a fist onto the back of a seat cushion. "We've been tricked."

An explosion flung our car skyward. The lights flickered and died. Passengers crashed into walls. Ragdolls out of control. A man flew over his seat into a woman. She crumpled as they toppled into the mangled exit doors. Shrieks of pain rattled my ears. A guy slumped, face speckled with glistening glass. Carryon luggage slammed into bodies. Something sizzled, releasing a burnt smell. A twisted body with an arm bent at an impossible angle convulsed in sobs by the door. It was chaos.

A crushing blow slammed the back of my head. I blacked out.

Chapter Eleven

Searching St. Peter's Graveyard

"Gabe, hurry up." Pete tugged on my jacket. "We got to get to Mozart's Geburtshaus."

People ran in all directions from the crackling flames reaching into the blue skies. Fire danced from window to window in the brown building to my right, next to Mozart's birthplace. Shrill alarms buzzed. Smoke poured out of the sixth story windows.

A fire engine, with the European siren blaring, "Ner-nee, ner-nee," screeched to a halt. Jumping from the truck, a fireman yelled at the Polizei. The police moved the crowd several buildings from the blaze.

"Hey." Jonathan pointed back the way we came.

Lightning shot past my legs and I yelled. "Stop." He obeyed. I captured him and held him tight.

The Phantom waved and disappeared into a passage going back to the University Plaza.

I pulled Lightning near my lips. "Stay close, buddy. Heel." I set him on the ground and launched down the street.

I led us down the passageway, passing the bull covered with buttons, skirting slow tourists unaware of the fire a block away. We burst into the University Plaza, scanning to see the Phantom.

Lightning barked.

"Okay, boy," I said. "Find him."

Lightning headed for the center of the square, then swept in a wide arc to his left. We stayed on his trail, darting and dodging sightseers through streets, alleys, and walkways. I ducked around an open, horse-drawn carriage as Lightning ran underneath it to keep tracking our suspect.

You won't get away this time.

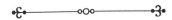

I ran my fingers along a wrought iron fence next to St. Peter's Abbey, which made a light ringing sound. A tour blocked the entrance, but Lightning wouldn't go any other way.

"St. Peter's Abbey houses the oldest library in Austria." The guide pointed at the building. "Adjacent to the main cathedral is a cemetery where you can find the headstone of Mozart's wife and others famous in this town. By the graveyard are the Christian catacombs, used for burial and church services—"

"We need to find another path inside," Jonathan said.

"If we do, we lose the scent." I pointed to the crowd now following the guide. "A little patience, please."

"Gabe, we've got to find the guy soon." Pete followed me through the gate into the cemetery. "Otherwise, we have to go back for the evening."

"Is there another choice?" I kept up with Lightning, who sniffed throughout the graveyard.

The cemetery's neat lawns and colorful flowers made most of the area pleasant. The scent of newly mown lawn combined with other greenery added to the sense of peace and well-being. A few plots, however, were left in disarray with wildflowers and weeds growing in the cracks of the brick pavers. Behind the tombs, against the stone face of the small Mönschberg mountain was an orange-tiled half-roof covering an arched walkway.

"Lightning headed towards the catacombs."

"I'm not going in" Pete stepped aside at the entrance. "I've hate underground places."

"We won't be long." Jonathan slapped him on the back. "Not much to explore."

"Pete." I tugged his shirt. "Wait by the opening. It's the single entry and exit. If the Phantom shows up, tackle him. And yell for help from that bored security guard." I nodded at a blue uniformed man by the iron gate.

Jonathan, Lightning, and I ascended stairs carved into the rock. A dank smell permeated the air. Candles lit the inside. Smoke rose in curls. We left the first room, exploring each of the catacombs. Two chapel areas clogged with tourists slowed our search. Burial places were holes, crevices, and crawlways into larger caves.

Someone tapped my shoulder.

I flinched and whirled, ready for combat.

"Find him yet?" Pete said.

"What are you doing here?" I eased from my crouch.

"You've been gone forever." Pete glanced around, fidgeting. "What have you been doing? Hurry up."

"Searching." I glanced around. "You're supposed to be on guard."

"I couldn't wait." He flinched as someone bumped into him. "Bored."

"Scared, more likely." Jonathan tossed a rock against the wall. "This is a dead end. Let's go."

"Back to the exit." I darted around a group of school kids.

"Lightning's lost the scent." Pete motioned at my buddy, trotting ahead. "I wonder why?"

"Maybe this was a diversion. Hold on." I peered in the dim light behind the altar in the Gertraudenkapelle—Gertrude's Chapel—and shook my head. "Let's go check out the graveyard."

"Wait." Jonathan watched Lightning's tail disappear into a tunnel. "Your dog's found something."

"Hang tight." I hurried to capture him.

He jumped into a man-size hole in the wall. When I caught up, he sniffed the opposite wall of the burial chamber inside.

"Got a lead?" I sucked in air. My lungs burned.

Lightning nosed around the back of a wood coffin on a stone ledge. His tail wagged while he scraped at the wall behind the polished wooden box.

"What's there, boy?" I climbed up on the low stone ledge, glancing behind the coffin. "Well, I'll be…"

In two minutes, I was back out in Gertrude's Chapel, showing the find to Jonathan and Peter.

"Why would he leave a broken toy here?" Pete said. "Doesn't make sense to me. A train engine and a busted passenger car. Weird."

"Seems like a waste of his time." Jonathan fiddled with the train's car. It broke in half, releasing a note that fluttered to the rock floor.

I snatched the paper, reading aloud. "Too bad, so sad."

"That's pretty obvious." Pete motioned with his hand. "Let's go. Outside where we can talk without all these people around."

Tourists surged around us in the catacombs, forcing us to keep moving.

"Okay, up we go." I led the way, wondering about the clue. *What could it mean?*

74

"Mozart was highly involved in the church," Jonathan said. "I mean, Saint Peter's Abbey, not this graveyard or the catacombs."

"So what?" I said.

"Mozart's the key."

"This guy's nuts. Mozart or not." I plowed through the masses to a quieter sidewalk, changing the subject. "And why a broken train? It doesn't make sense."

"Weren't there four leads?" Pete grabbed my arm. "One was at the train station."

"Right." I stiffened. "Alex and Jenna. We've got to warn them." I secured Lightning in my arms and raced toward the graveyard's side entrance.

"Hold on." Puffing, Pete grabbed my jacket at the entrance.

"Come on. Polizei Station. Main street near Mozart's Birth House." I fished out my tourist map. "We can call from—Lightning, stop moving."

Lightning wriggled out of my arms, leaping onto a path near a gravestone. He yipped, almost like a coyote, and sat down.

"Silly dog." Jonathan snickered. "Maybe his nose is stuffed up?"

"I doubt it." Pete read the tombstone. "Mozart's sister, Nannerl, wife of Berchtold zu Sonnenberg. If she lived here, the Phantom might torch her home." Pete sighed. "Maybe this graveyard connects us to places where that menace will strike next."

"Yeah," I said. "But not now. We've got to warn Alex and Jenna. Which way to the Polizei Station?" My gaze speared Jonathan.

"Too long to explain." Jonathan broke into a jog. "Follow me."

We dashed into the street, side-stepping tourists, townspeople, and vehicles, looping past the Dom Plaza, past the Alter Markt, and making a few turns to arrive at the main street by the Salzach River.

"Gentlemen, our destination." Jonathan stepped back. He raised his hand like a model on a game show and bowed.

"Thanks." I slapped him on the back as we went in.

The place was a nightmare. No one paid us any attention. Cops and civilians rushed back and forth. Pete yelled in German, and I pounded on a desk before a policeman called Captain Bergmann for us. He handed me the phone.

"You're too late," the Captain said. "Agent Gardener realized your brother, his girlfriend, and dog hopped a bullet train to Vienna this morning. And we haven't received reports yet for all the survivors."

"Survivors?" I gulped. "You don't mean..."

Chapter Twelve

Next Steps

"Gabe." Pete tugged on my arm, eyes wide. "What's happening?"

"Wait." A tense whisper. "Let me listen." My pulse thundered in my ears.

"The Polizei are fighting a gun battle outside the train at the Vienna Hauptbahnhof." Captain Bergmann paused. Background voices spoke in clipped phrases. "We won't know the outcome until the special SWAT team takes out the shooter."

"There is only one guy?" I jammed the telephone against my ear.

"Yes. There are several people down outside the train, including two policemen. The shooter has a human shield, a girl."

"How will I know when my brother and Pete's sister are safe?" I said.

"Check with me in about an hour, either by phone or in person… I should have more information."

With a click, the receiver went to a dial tone. I placed the phone on its cradle, taking my time, processing. I told the guys.

"We found the clue too late." Pete sat in a chair, head hanging.

"Yeah." I sat next to him. Lightning jumped in my lap. "If we had caught him earlier…" I looked up at Jonathan.

"Are you blaming me?" he said.

"If you hadn't stopped us in the gift shop in Mozart's birth house, we might have him in a jail cell right now."

"If and might. Pretty weak defense." Jonathan lowered himself to a chair facing me. "If this, if that…something else could always have happened, but it didn't. You need to accept life the way it happens."

"Maybe you do," Pete straightened in his chair, "but we don't. We try to plan ahead and outguess the bad guys. We don't just take it."

"Is that right?" Jonathan tilted his head against the wall. "What can we do about the next event? Seems like this Phantom has figured out a slick scheme that's better than your plan."

"Hey," I said. "We need to be figuring out his next steps, not arguing. What was the last clue we got?"

Pete relaxed a minute and rubbed his chin. Jonathan circled his arms around his knees, setting his chin on them.

"What about that grave that Lighting stopped at?" Pete stood. "We need to go back and study that tombstone, to see if there's a clue hidden in the writing."

"Great idea." I bounced to my feet and tapped Jonathan with a toe. "Every moment counts."

Jonathan sighed, unwinding himself. "Okay. I'm coming."

Chapter Thirteen

Train Twister

"Uhh." Jenna moaned. "I smell smoke. What was that?"

"I dunno. A bomb. Maybe." I blinked away the cobwebs and felt the lump on my head. "

Shattered glass lay inches from my face. Gunshots pierced the screams from the people on the train platform. Thunder's barks roared from below.

"Jenna, hide," I said. She was above me.

The train car twisted sideways at either end, tilted to my right. Jammed at a steep angle, the exit toward the dining car seemed twenty feet higher than me or at least half the passenger car away. Smoldering wires from the overhead seat lights sparked and sizzled. Light smoke floated through the cabin. The train's metal walls creaked.

I rolled onto my side, pressing my feet into the headrest of a seat below me. Instead of going up to Jenna, I went sideways, crawling into a seat.

"Mama." A boy, about four years old, cried out. Maybe Italian? He hung near the exit to the Dining Car, bleeding hands clinging to a broken window frame. His legs flailed outside the window over empty space as he fought to drag himself inside. The frame shifted with each of his yells. If it buckled, a fall would be fatal.

Shots punched through metal near him. A cop shouted orders through a loudspeaker.

A limp woman, probably the kid's mom, dangled above him from a left side cabin seat, her seatbelt folding her in half at the waist, her clothes torn.

"Coming," I yelled at the boy. Using seat backs and head rests, I grappled my way back up the slope.

"Jenna." I squeezed her hand when I reached her seat before climbing higher. "I'll help you next."

She gripped my hand and grimaced. Lips firm, she grabbed her leg and tugged to free it.

The kid yelled louder.

"Hang on."

The boy kept calling his mother. His red-rimmed eyes were wet, streaks tracking down his cheeks.

I clambered over the last seat and crouched below, gathering my strength.

Metal groaning, the train slanted more to the right.

"Ready?" Hands beside the window frame. On my knees. One leg hooked a headrest for stability. I shut out the other screams. *Concentrate.*

A red drop splattered on glass near the boy. He screamed. Near hysteria. His mother hadn't moved during my climb.

I stretched for the lift.

A ricochet. I jerked.

The boy slid a couple inches out the window.

Sporadic gunfire continued. Bullets pinged.

I stretched again.

His hands were inches from my fingers.

"Can you reach out to me?" I motioned with my hands.

He loosened his grip to try. Slipped further. He shook his head.

Metal scraped metal above me. The car jolted right. Like a tightrope walker desperate to balance, my arms flew out. *Close.*

Now the kid's stomach hung over the edge. He couldn't hold on long.

"Don't give up." I readjusted my legs for an anchor. "I'll grab your arms. You let go."

The boy's lips trembled.

"Now." I lunged forward at the boy's belt and shirt. Off-balance.

The train lurched again, settling and rotating further right, metal screaming with the strain. The ceiling was a bit lower than the floor.

The boy's weight shifted. Fingers opened. His chest slipped away.

I swiped. Missed. Clamped onto his arms and dragged him close. Wrapped my arms around him. I curled into a ball, tucking his little body inside. And slammed into the ceiling with my shoulder.

The train's shifting made the ceiling a steep-angled chute. We careened back and forth down the slope. I winced when glass dug in. Hit an emergency sprinkler head with a thigh. I felt like a pinball. Jagged edges tore a gash in my forearm. Another sprinkler smacked my back. I landed. Twisted sideways. Shoulder rolled and collided with the door leading to the next car.

Thunder's barking ceased. He poked me with his nose.

"I'm okay." I rubbed his fur.

"Mama." The boy struggled out of my arms and pointed up at the woman swinging from her seatbelt above. The other end of the car.

"Alex, where are you?" Jenna groaned.

"Down here," I said.

A bullet pinged.

Thunder barked.

I covered the kid, melting into another ball. Cries of agony cut the air, I opened up and wobbled to my feet.

"Mama?" I pointed at the woman hanging from her seatbelt. The boy nodded.

I tapped my fingers on my chest and pointed to her. "I get her."

He gripped my hand.

"Wait." I loosened my hand from his and held up a finger.

I drew Thunder close to the boy. "Watch."

Enclosing his hand in mine, we petted Thunder. I left them together.

When I reached Jenna, her foot remained wedged between two seats. Her face was swollen on one side, focused on her dilemma. "I'll come back," I yelled at her. No response.

I kept moving. To get to the woman, I climbed the lower seats like a ladder, using armrests for footholds. Standing under the boy's mother, I slid my utility knife out of my pocket and opened it. Hand on her mid-section, I slashed at one side of the seat belt.

After several tries, the woman fell. A dead weight. I dropped the knife. Her weight collapsed the chair's arm I stood on. We crashed into a glass window below.

Her son screamed.

A grunt of pain escaped my lips. I heard glass crack under the strain. Sharp edges punctured my back and scraped my sides while I fought to stay in the car.

I hooked headrests with my legs, my chest hanging out the window. The lady's legs dangled beside my head. Her upper body was in the train. Weight shifted. Another inch lost. I shoved her at the window. Failed again.

Thunder's bark mingled with the boy's howling, filling the train.

A few seconds later, someone wrapped their arms around my waist. Long hair flowed down my chest. Jenna.

In small stages, in bursts of a few seconds, she lugged a good part of the lady off me and into the train.

My arms burned. Muscles cramped.

"Alex, can you hear me?" Jenna tapped my leg.

"Yes." I clenched my teeth. "Keep pulling her in. Don't stop."

"Alex, can you hear me?" She spoke with a louder voice than normal, kneeling by my side.

"I hear you."

"I'm going to bend her legs." She maneuvered a seat lower. Lay on her stomach and leaned out into space. She snagged one of the woman's legs.

"I'm folding her legs. I may have to push a bit. Don't drop her."

"Gotcha." I tightened my hold.

"Here we go." She brought the lower leg up, bent it to the side and brought the woman's knee inside the train.

I felt pressure for a second. The woman slid, but I clamped on. When the leg was inside, the weight lessened.

"One more." Jenna worked the second leg inside. Jenna unfolded the legs. "I've got her."

I grunted a yes.

The train swayed, metal groaning. A snap caused another six-inch drop.

Without the extra weight on top of me, I wiggled back into the car.

Jenna listened to the woman's heart.

"How's she doing?" I said.

Jenna didn't move. I touched her arm. She flinched, looking my way.

"Is she okay?"

"I can feel her breathe," Jenna shouted at me though I was inches away. "She has a weak heartbeat and pulse."

Why was Jenna yelling? "I'll check how we can lower her down." I straightened, stretching my muscles. *If I turn toward the seats, put the lady over my shoulder, then I could grab the headrests of each seat for a handhold and use the seatbacks below for my feet. Easy.*

"I've got it." I tapped Jenna. "Let me have her."

Jenna cocked her head like she didn't understand.

When I held out my hands, she lifted the woman by the armpits. I draped her over my right shoulder and began my descent. Two steps into the move a loud snap pierced the air. The car collapsed onto the ground.

Chapter Fourteen

Persecuted

"I wonder if any of Mozart's other relatives lived here or were buried here." I paced in front of Nannerl's tombstone. "I don't want to miss any connection, otherwise, the Phantom will hurt more people, and we'll never catch him."

"We can research that tonight." Jonathan looked at his watch. "Hey. I have to meet my dad. Can I meet you guys tomorrow?"

"We don't need one more of us on this case," Pete said. "And you stopped us from catching him in the first place."

"You don't know that for sure. However, we do know that I can navigate the old town, the Altstadt, faster than you two without having to look at a map all the time." Jonathan crossed his arms. "And I know about Mozart. Plus, I'm an expert on the inside of the old fortress on top of the hill. The rooms and different passages can get confusing pretty fast."

"That could be helpful," I said to Pete. "Especially since this guy calls himself the Phantom of the Fortress."

"I don't like him." Pete glared at Jonathan. "And we have too many people involved already."

"Make me the last member of your team." Jonathan shoved his hands in his pockets. "I always get kicked to the curb, anyway. If you did it, that would make you the same as everybody else in my life."

"Jonathan, don't say that." I shook my head. "We're not like that. Tell you what. You meet us at the Salzburg Polizei main police station, and we'll bring you along."

"If the group agrees," Pete said.

"Yeah, if the group agrees." I patted Jonathan' shoulder. "That okay with you? We do have to ask Willie and the Captain if it's all right."

"I guess it's the best you can do." A smile curved his lips back up from his frown.

"See you tomorrow," I said. "Don't be late. Eight o'clock sharp."

"I got it." Jonathan strolled toward the Salzach River, waving over his shoulder as he went.

"Gabe, you're a softie." Pete's hand was on my shoulder. "You're like Italian ice cream, soft and tart."

"Pete, lay off." I brushed his hand away. "The guy's dad doesn't ever do anything for him. He needs a little support now and then."

"Yeah, but what's the cost to us?"

Chapter Fifteen

Smoke

The fall couldn't have been far, but it felt like a hundred feet. The side of the train drove into the ground in a sliding motion as the car in front twisted its path to the ground. I landed with the woman on top of me, squeezing the air out of my chest again. I couldn't breathe for a minute.

Another explosion rocked our car, smaller than the first. Fire burned the seat by the dining car. I rolled the woman off my shoulder and scrambled to my feet.

"Jenna, get up."

She lay on the floor, broken glass glinting in her hair. She faced away from me. I could see her back move with breathing.

"Jenna," I yelled her name again. No response. *Her hearing must be messed up.*

I glanced at the door opposite the fire. Smoke made my eyes water. I saw a blurry clump of metal. Thunder scrabbled over the broken glass and twisted seats, reaching the woman in a moment. He sniffed her body.

"Mama," the young boy ran toward his mother and pushed the dog aside. He lay his head on her shoulder, ignoring her ripped blouse.

"Thunder, over here." I stumbled to Jenna, wincing as she twitched when I touched her from behind. I held out my hand.

She gripped tight and rose, legs shaking. Her blouse was in tatters, slacks torn down the side, Patches of red cloth masked some of the cuts. I supported her waist and walked her to where the woman lay. Our feet crunched through broken glass. Heavier smoke filled the room with a sharp odor of burning fabric and cables.

"Down," I said. I got on my hands and knees. Jenna followed suit. I motioned her to balance the woman on my back. "Thunder, move out," I commanded, coughing from the lungful of smoke. *If we don't escape soon, we'll die of smoke inhalation.* We crawled to the front end of the car, away from the fire. We reached the exit, now five feet off the ground. Twisted metal compacted by the fall jammed the door. It didn't open.

Jenna sat, slumped against the wall, and lay down. "I feel exhausted."

"Stay low." I ignored my worries, covering them with action. I searched for a way out, tense. The train platform blocked any exit through the ceiling skylights. I found a gaping hole on the train's left side, above me. Gulping a breath of air near the floor, I stepped on an armrest in the second row. Holding my breath, I motioned the little boy to come up into my arms.

He hesitated.

I waved rapidly and bent to help him up.

He took my hand.

I wriggled him sideways on my shoulder and pointed at the opening above, a gouged train window.

He bent over my head and rubbed his eyes. Coughed. And nodded.

I balanced him. Stepped on seat armrests and climbed, fueled by the disaster. Smoke thickened higher. Crackling noise came from all around as fire began eating up the flame-retardant seats. We didn't have much time. Maybe a minute. Two at the most.

I slapped the boy's feet. Shoved his rear to get him to stand on my shoulders.

He crouched. Cautious. His hands grasped the opening.

A burst of bullets raked the car.

My thighs trembled. *Ten seconds. Don't quit.*

His hands curled around the opening. He paused.

I gripped his feet and thrust them into the air.

He shot through the opening, falling on his stomach. His feet disappeared, and his head returned.

I waved him on.

He vanished.

A couple of gunshots. One nicked my pants.

I gasped. Inhaled smoke and wheezed. My eyes stung. I lost touch with the train's side and slipped. My chest smashed against the seat back. I bounced off, grabbing for a seat but catching only air. I crashed the last three feet, rolling onto my back.

Thunder investigated, licking my face until I rubbed his neck. "Find an exit." I gave him a pat. He padded away.

Jenna lay next to me, wheezing. Struggling to breathe. The kid's mom lay on her shoulder. Her sides expanded enough for me to know she alive. For now.

Ignoring the pain, I reached out and held Jenna's hand in mine. She smiled and shut her eyes. *I failed her. Us. Terrible.* I couldn't think straight. *So tired.* The last thing I saw was the boy peering down through the haze from the broken window.

Chapter Sixteen

Counting Our Losses

A horrific crash broke the quiet of St. Peter's graveyard.

"Gabe." Pete grabbed my shoulder. "Outside the gate."

We dashed through the gate and looked up the street. A man yelled at a woman on a bicycle.

"Pete, that's the guy who rented the boat to the Phantom this morning." I shot toward the man.

"Gabe. Wait." Pete's voice trailed behind me as I put on the afterburners.

Lightning whipped past me.

The woman yelled, attracting a crowd. The man threw his arms in the air, shouting in German. He faced in our direction and stiffened. Spinning, he ducked out of sight.

Lightning threaded between the legs of people while I kept excusing myself in German. "Entschuldigung." I shouldered my way to the back of the truck.

"Hey." A person dressed in a brown jumpsuit hooked my arm. "You shoved my wife around."

"Sorry." I tugged my arm free. "That guy is a suspect in a—"

"Gabe." Pete struggled to reach me. "Don't reveal anything."

That ticked me off. "Sir." I straightened my clothes. "I believe the Polizei are after that man to question him."

"What has he done?" A large lady in a pink blouse stepped beside the guy in brown. "Someone went to get the Polizei. They'll catch him." She eyed me up and down. "And who are you?"

"We're part of—"

"My friend." Pete sucked in a deep breath. "He's a buddy of mine that likes to investigate accidents." He pulled me back toward him. "I'm teaching him German Polizei reactions to catastrophes. Sorry for any inconvenience." He yanked me away from the crowd.

"What are you doing?" I whirled on him after we were clear of the people.

"Saving your tail. No one needs to know what we're doing." Pete sighed. "You're always—what's that?"

My watch beeped.

"We're late. We missed meeting Willie at four o'clock." I whistled for Lightning. We bolted.

"Do you remember the way back to the main street?" Pete said.

"Maybe." I skirted a horse carriage. "Restrooms are on the right. We go straight through this plaza."

We made the main street in five minutes.

"There's a bus stop." As I ran forward, a bus pulled up. "Pete, hurry up."

"Gabe, it's the wrong line." Pete studied the schedule. "That won't take us to the headquarters. We should ask the Polizei Station over there for help." He pointed at the Polizei symbol about a football field away.

I nodded and sprinted down the street. Rushing into the office, I ran into a police officer on the way out.

"Halt." He grabbed me by the arms and spoke to me in German. I didn't understand it all.

"What?" I said.

"Why you run into me? Speak."

"Well, we're supposed to—"

Pete burst through the door. "Did you ask them?"

"I don't speak German well enough to tell the story."

Pete explained our problem while I gathered Lighting into my arms. The policeman nodded. He led us back to a room and dialed the main Polizei Headquarters for us.

"Where have you been?" Willie's first words weren't angry, but firm.

"We almost caught him a couple of times." I cupped my hand around the mouthpiece to keep the other police officer from hearing. "We need to talk at the Polizei HQ. Can you pick us up?"

"No worries. Be there in ten shakes of a lizard's tail."

"Gabe, what have we left out?" Pete rubbed his temple.

"We've hogged the air time since hopping into Willie's car." I adjusted Lightning in my lap. "I think we covered it all."

"How about my day, mates?" Willie pulled into the station. "A bit of rubbish, it was. Cooked up by my old partner, Wilcox, I suspect."

"He certainly didn't take care of us." I opened the car door and tossed Lightning on the ground. I jumped onto the pavement.

"And disappeared, without a trace." Pete followed me toward the building.

Willie banged through the back door of the Polizei Headquarters, heading for Captain Bergmann's office.

"Well, well. Look what the cat drug in." Wilcox's booming voice greeted us at the office door. "It's high time the junior detective crew showed up."

"Get stuffed. You abandoned my partners." Willie stepped within six inches of Wilcox's face. "Do that again and you'll have to deal with me."

"You Aussies take everything so personal," Wilcox grinned. "While I was in the restroom, your boys ran away."

"Likely story. I reckon we'll have to settle later." Willie side-stepped him and spoke to Bergmann. "Cap'n, how's about a cuppa before we start?"

"Sure." He sat back from a stack of papers on his desk. "Bring me one. Two sugars. No cream."

Pete and I followed Willie outside to the snack room.

"Think he did that on purpose?" I grabbed a diet cola and faced Willie.

"You're darn tootin'. Not to worry. I'll square him away." Willie led the way back, two cups of steaming coffee in his hands.

The Captain rubbed his forehead before he accepted the coffee. Sighed. He glanced at us past three stacks of paper on his desk. Wilcox sat to the side of his desk with Agent Gardener. Our chairs faced the desk's front.

"Captain Bergmann, are my sister and Gabe's brother okay?" Pete rubbed the knees of his jeans.

"They're part of the missing people." The police chief pointed to a blurry fax picture of a mangled train in a station.

"I saw them on the platform of the WESTbahn Zug, a high-speed train, headed to Vienna." Agent Gardener sat forward. "The train boarded. I didn't see anyone suspicious. When the train pulled out, your sister, his brother, and the dog were gone."

"Why didn't you chase them?" I said.

"It wouldn't help unless I was right with them." Gardener's eyes shifted away. "I called the station at Vienna and told the police to have them board the next train to Salzburg when they arrived."

"If you'll allow me." The Captain pointed at the middle car in the picture pinned to the wall. "The explosion ripped through the central dining car of the train. The cars on either side jackknifed into the air, then fell on their sides after a few hours. Emergency vehicles have transported away many victims."

"What about my brother?" The lump in my throat made it hard to speak.

"We can't be sure." Bergmann heaved himself to his feet and touched the car left of the dining car. "Fires erupted in the dining car and this car. There's nothing left of the dining car except metal and ashes. Forensics is checking why the second explosion occurred. That report will come out later. Several cars have been evacuated of the injured and the dead. In the confusion of the emergency, people have to be stabilized at hospitals and identification is secondary. The investigators won't abandon the search until they're found.

"We have to help." Pete's voice rose, his cheeks losing color.

"Calm down, mate." Willie slid an arm around Pete. "The police will do their best. Each hospital and clinic has to report back during a mass casualty to a central police unit. If they're in a hospital, we'll know about it soon."

"I need to brief you on more information," Bergmann continued. "First, the fire department contained the fire next to Mozart's birth house. No one was injured. An arson investigation is in progress."

"We saw the Phantom run away from there." I sipped my soda. "He laughed at the fire after we chased him out of the alleyways."

"That's circumstantial evidence." Wilcox dismissed the idea with a wave of his hand. "No one in court would accept that."

"It's more than you have." Willie let go of Pete and sat forward in his chair.

"We also found two clues in St. Peter's graveyard and catacombs." Pete nudged me.

"Yeah." I tilted my head. "Sort of."

"Spit it out, detective." Wilcox laughed.

"For your information, this is legit." I faced the Captain. "Lightning located a note from the Phantom in the Catacombs." I handed him the train and the note. I reclaimed my seat and guzzled my soda.

"It's not signed," Bergmann said.

I nodded. "But Lightning led us there by a scent trail. It has to be him."

"Can't the department do a handwriting comparison?" Willie said. "Maybe Interpol has the capability?

"That's a headache I don't want." Bergmann sat. "And, yes, our analysis branch analyzed each note from the Phantom and the papers that were in the victim's print shop.

"Wait." I reached into my pocket and produced another note. "This was pinned to Lightning's ear. We have until sunrise on 1 September to solve this case or the girl he kidnapped will die."

The police chief studied the note, scribbling a few things on a pad.

"That's critical, knowing his timeline. We'll have to pursue these other family links from your cemetery visit to protect those establishments. The last bit of my briefing is about another note from the Phantom." He pointed to the three stacks of paper on the desk. "These are notes on the papers you have received from the suspect. The results of our team's analysis are as follows: the paper found in the printer's office is from Mozart's time or very close to it. The writing is not an exact match to Mozart's."

"Cool." I put my empty soda bottle on the floor. "How does that work? How can you tell the paper's from the 1700s?"

"It's complicated." The police chief swiveled to his right, folding his hands in his lap. "Lots of technical details. Experts employ different techniques—microscopes, ink type, and shapes of letters. In this case, they burnt the paper to check its authenticity."

"Since his writing is not exactly like Mozart's, you can tell if he wrote a manuscript, even if it's on the right paper and he uses the right pen." Willie sipped his coffee.

"Correct." Bergmann swiveled his chair directly in front of me. "The manuscript he stole was not a copy. It's real. We have a fragment of that. However, the Phantom left another Mozart man-uscript mixed in with the scattered papers in Herr Gerlach's shop. And that document is a clever forgery done by—."

"I know they're in here. Let me through." Mom appeared seconds later.

The Captain rose. "Gardner and Wilcox, you're dismissed. Everybody else, please wait outside." He extended a hand toward one of the seats. "Mrs. Zanadu, may I talk with you privately for a minute?"

"Why?" Her frantic gaze swept the room. "Where are Alex and Jenna?"

"I'm about to discuss that with you." He nodded and we all filed out.

The restaurant was cheerful, full of people smiling and laughing. Austrian accordion music played in the background. Pol-ka music. The aroma of fried Weiner Schnitzel, a noodle dish with cheese, steaming vegetables, and a buttered steak with mashed pota-toes filled the air at our table. We sat in a booth that was semi-pri-vate towards the back of the restaurant. Unlike the rest of the place, a gloomy cloud hung over the expressions in our tiny world.

"Mrs. Zanadu, the police will find them." Willie drank some water.

"I wish Eli were here. He'd get the Polizei cracking to rescue our kids." She picked at her food with a fork. "All the people that weren't injured have reported in and left." She lifted a piece of as-paragus to her mouth and set it down untouched. "I'm not hungry. I never should have let you talk me into coming here. Everything's falling apart."

"Mrs. Zanadu." Willie patted her hand. "Checking on re-ports might take a while. The kids needed food. We'll go back to HQ soon." He nodded. "This is the right choice."

"Mom, they don't have *all* the reports from the hospitals." I shoveled more cheese noodles in my mouth. "They've got to be somewhere."

"What if they aren't?" Her eyes seemed damp. "What if they were in one of the cars that burned? What will I tell your Father?" She shrank back into the seat.

Lightning jumped onto the bench seat and crawled onto her lap.

"We'll get to the bottom of this tonight." Willie motioned with his fork. "I'm the one to blame because I let the Captain split us up." He speared a piece of steak with Krauterbutter on it and popped it in his mouth. "I'll go back with you to tell the Schultz family and come back to the station."

"Can we go now?" She stroked Lightning's orange hair. "I need to contact Eli, and I want to do it in private."

"No worries." Willie signaled for the waiter. "I'll have them box this up and—"

A policeman walked into the entrance of the restaurant. I spotted him and waved a hand, hoping it was news about Alex. He strode to our table, lips drawn in a tight line.

"Ma'am." He directed his gaze at Mom, his posture straight and rigid. "I have news of your son and friend's daughter."

"Is it bad?" She stopped stroking Lightning. "Are they alive?"

"Ja, they are alive."

Tears flowed down Mom's cheeks. "Oh, thank God."

"But," he swallowed hard, "I must inform you they were in one of the cars that burned."

Chapter Seventeen

Escape from the Krankenhaus

Soaring through the mountain passes like an eagle, I flew the glider with ease

"Alex." Jenna's voice floated in the air.

The radio crackled. *Radio? This glider didn't have a radio.* A gust of wind slammed into the airframe, rocking me from side to side. The man on the radio was urgently telling me something, but I couldn't understand the language. An oversized hawk dove into the right wing, smashing through, tearing the lightly constructed frame, and twisting it at an angle. The shaking worsened.

"Wake up." A familiar voice shouted at me.

Why is Jenna screaming at me? I turned and couldn't see her or the second glider seat.

"Alex, open your eyes," she said.

I stared as my glider tumbled out-of-control to the ground thousands of feet below.

A hand firmly grasped my shoulder. "Can't you hear me?" a man said. "Do something."

"Don't—" I opened my eyes and fought the band restricting my arms.

"Settle down, kid." An Emergency Medical Technician dressed in white patted my chest.

I coughed. My bed jostled, banging into another metal cot—Jenna's. Two men, both in firefighters' uniforms, rushed past me.

Limp, my head rolled right.

"Welcome back." The EMT repositioned my rolling cot. "We sedated you. I've kept you dreaming almost an hour while we sorted out the more serious emergencies."

"What time is it?"

"Almost five o'clock." The med-tech shook his head. "Been busy."

"Keep it moving." A man in blue scrubs directed traffic. "Triage to the right."

Jenna lay on an emergency cot, the kind they use in ambulances. White sheets lay on top of her and the emergency medical techs folded the legs to load her in the vehicle. She shouted and waved her hands, German words spilling out so fast I couldn't translate. I did hear one thing I understood—my name.

One emergency med-tech looked at the other, motioning with his head to re-extend the wheels to the ground.

"Veilen dank." Jenna thanked them with a tight-lipped smile.

"What...how did we..." Hands lifted me up, rolling me onto another ambulance hospital cot. I lost sight of Jenna as a blood pressure cuff inflated and a clear mask covered my nose and mouth. The rush of pure oxygen felt soothing, but I coughed anyway, my throat raw from the smoke.

The Krankenwagen sped to the hospital, carrying Jenna and me side-by-side on the lower of two cot levels. The EMTs worked on us, talking to keep us calm. The siren intruded every few minutes.

Each time Jenna tried to reach out to me, the blonde med-tech repositioned her hand.

"Pretty remarkable escape, I'd say." The blonde said to Jenna. "We weren't sure if you would make it out in time."

"What happened?" Jenna said.

"The gunman made a final stand in front of your train car." She braced Jenna for a turn.

"A Polizei sniper zeroed in and took out the shooter." My EMT, a guy with blue eyes, knelt next to me.

"More important, right before that, firemen spotted a little boy pop out of what was now the top of the train car." The blonde patted Jenna's hand. "With the shooter eliminated, they raced to the car."

"Incredible—they held out their arms but the boy wouldn't jump to them." Blue eyes smiled. "He kept yelling for his Mama and pointed into the smoke pouring from the train."

A call came in from the dispatcher. Blue-eyes went to the front of the ambulance.

"To make a long story short," the blonde said, "several firemen attacked the fire with extinguishers while others threw a ladder against the car. They swarmed onto the top of the car with masks and oxygen tanks. Rigging a harness, a fireman went in and found the mother at the bottom of the car along with both of you."

"Why didn't we die of smoke inhalation?" I said.

"That's easy." Blue-eyes returned. "Smoke rises. Most smoke went out the windows, but not enough to keep you out of danger. The firemen lowered extra oxygen masks and tanks inside. That saved you." He braced himself as the vehicle stopped. "We've arrived."

At the hospital, the EMTs rolled us down the hall, into the elevator, and up to the third floor. After a couple of minutes, zigzagging us through various halls, we arrived in our room, which held beds for four people.

Nurses examined Jenna and me. The EMTs talked to them for about five minutes. They sneaked a few looks at us and left. We remained on the emergency cots.

"What's going on?" Jenna called out to a nurse as they were leaving. "Don't admit us—we have to go back to Salzburg."

The nurse kept walking.

"That didn't work out too well." I sat up on the cot feeling less groggy. I winced at the aching muscles, cuts, and bruises.

Jenna kept staring at the door.

"I said, 'That didn't work out too well.'" I nearly shouted at Jenna.

She turned. "Did you say something? I only heard parts of it. You have to yell at me. The EMT said my hearing would get better soon. He didn't find any ear damage."

"Good. I'd like to—"

Two men walked into the room followed by a police officer.

"This Polizei officer would like to ask for details about the sabotage to the train." The shorter, rotund man waved toward a tall, lean policeman. "Do you know anything that would help?"

"We'll do our best." I shrugged.

"The Polizei in Salzburg called me." The officer stepped forward. "I know about the supposed Phantom of the Fortress and his look-alikes. We nailed the look-alike from the train explosion. He is in serious condition."

"Do you know why we were on the train?" Jenna's loudness startled all three men. "Sorry. It's my hearing. I'll try to read lips. If you speak up, I'll catch a little bit."

"Yes." The officer turned to the short man. "I need to speak with these two privately for a few minutes. I'll call you when we are done."

"Where's my dog?" I said before the policeman could ask any questions. "I've got to have him with me."

"Dogs aren't allowed in the hospital. And though there was a black dog that exited the burned-out train, he ran away before we could catch him. We'll keep looking for him."

"You've got to find him." I swallowed hard. "He's my trained police dog."

"If the dog's trained, he'll know when to return."

"But he's my friend." I slapped the sheets. "I *need* you to find him."

The cop paused, taking a breath before responding.

"What did you want to know?" Jenna drowned out the cop's next words. "We have to get back home."

The man rolled his eyes at the outburst. He glanced at the distance between us and rolled my cot next to Jenna's to ask his questions.

He nodded at me first. "We'll try." He glanced at both of us and raised his volume. "What can you tell me about the look-alike? And the girl?"

Jenna talked first, telling about how nervous the girl had seemed. She provided a detailed description of our efforts to trap the suspects and notify the Vienna police.

"Was there anything unusual about what they did?" The officer flipped a page in his notepad. "Were they in the dining car? Did they act suspicious there?"

"Sort of," I said. "The man acted normal, but the girl was nervous. She seemed scared. Jenna?"

"Let me think."

While she did that, I tried to remember the exact details of our contact with them, but all I could think of was the mother and child.

"Did the little boy and his mother get out all right?" I tapped on my metal cot to get the Polizei's attention.

"Oh." He opened his notebook. "Yes. The little boy told a fireman what was happening. He mentioned his Italian mother and two others. Big helpers, he called them. Since we subdued the suspect, we rushed a firefighting and medical team to your train car. The mother is in stable condition with some internal injuries. The boy's father is on the way to the hospital to pick up the boy."

"Got it!" Jenna slapped her sheets. "Something was strange."

"Tell us." The cop got his pen ready.

"When we followed them after they finished in the dining car, Thunder didn't want to leave the area where they had eaten their meal."

"Oh, man." I fell back onto my bed. "That's an alert sign. I thought he was interested in their scent, but he probably smelled the explosives." I shook my head. "I missed it."

"Is your dog trained for explosives?" The officer's walkie-talkie crackled with a message. "Excuse me. I'll see you later." He rushed out of the room.

"We've got to go home. I mean, back to Salzburg. My Mom will go nuts if I'm not back by the end of the day." I sat up in the cot and threw the sheet off. "Jenna, can you travel?"

Jenna nodded. "My parents, too. They'll think I can't take care of myself." She got out of bed. "We'll have to be sneaky."

"You'll have to be quiet." I grinned. "You sound as loud as a foghorn."

The corners of her mouth twitched up in a grin. She put a finger to her lips.

"Let me check the hallway." I coughed and darted to the door. "All clear."

We retrieved our shoes from the bags under our gurneys, our wallets and other private stuff, and prepared to leave.

I peeked into the corridor. Empty. Our room was next to the exit stairs. We trotted through the exit door, slipping down to the ground floor. We walked out a back service-entrance. After a quick check for unusual activity, we strolled onto the main street. We ducked into the first tourist shop we saw. Jenna bought a floppy hat and sunglasses. I got a baseball cap. We both paid for snacks and faded into the pedestrian traffic unnoticed.

Chapter Eighteen

Implosion

Mom drove Pete and me back to our Gast Haus in Türk, Germany. I kept her focused, helping with traffic and turns.

"Left at the traffic light," I said.

"Gabe, I'm following Willie. I know where we're going." She glanced at me. "I'm glad that you and Pete are all right."

"Mrs. Zanadu," Pete said. "When we get back tonight, my mother will probably want to talk with you."

Mom didn't speak for two more stoplights. Her eyes closed for a second, lips pressed tight, waiting for a BMW to move ahead of her.

"I can imagine your mother has lots of questions." Mom opened her eyes and stepped on the gas. "She has to be scared about your sister being trapped in that train wreck. Until we receive a hospital report on internal injuries, we don't know the severity of their condition. How can I explain this mess to them?" She touched her lips, glancing at Pete in the rearview mirror. "It's all my fault."

"Mrs. Zanadu," Pete said, "Alex and Jenna did this on their own."

We passed the airport on Highway B1. Lines of cars waited to move at most intersections.

"Mom, it's not your—"

"Don't tell me what my responsibilities are, Gabriel Joshua Zanadu." She swerved around a car. "Your father and I will have another conversation before you boys go on any other 'assignments.'" She slammed the brakes for a red light. The seatbelt locked in place as my body flew forward and rebounded into the seat. "Is that understood?"

"Yes, ma'am." The twenty-minute drive seemed to take two hours. I watched the scenery to our Gast Haus without another word.

Willie opened the door for Mom to enter after we parked. A little bell tinkled. Our landlady appeared from her downstairs home behind the small desk area next to the stairs.

"Mrs. Zanadu, I have two messages for you." Her eyes narrowed after glimpsing the papers. "One seemed urgent. Would you like them now?"

"Yes. Immediately." Mom handed me the room key. "Go upstairs, young man, and wait for me."

Willie watched me trudge up to the room and raised his eyebrows. I motioned him to follow me. Lightning led the way. Willie and Pete followed. Pete branched off to his parent's room and Willie stayed with me.

Inside, I shut the outer door of the apartment entryway and stepped through the second door into the living space. Willie reversed a table chair from our dining table and sat. Our combination living/dining/kitchenette room provided several sitting areas.

"Mom's upset." I plopped onto the couch.

"I reckon so. Don't blame her none." Willie shifted his chair to see me better.

"We may be off the case."

"Why do you say that?"

"She told me in the car. No more assignments." I sighed, got up and went to the refrigerator to search for something to drink. Bypassing the soda, lemonade, milk, and iced tea, I chose orange juice. "Iced tea?" I glanced at Willie. He nodded. I carried it to him.

"You'll need to let it set for a while. She'll be all right." Willie took a long drink.

Mom burst into the room.

"They're coming back." She lifted a note into the air. "They'll be in Salzburg on the ten o'clock train this evening from Vienna. They're safe."

"Now that's amazing news." Willie stood.

"Yes. Home by eleven. I wonder what kind of injuries they've had. The note didn't say." Mom's trembling hand touched her cheek. "This is making me a nervous wreck. I'd better sit down." She sat on the end of the couch, placing her trembling hand in the other to steady it. Instead, both hands began to shake.

"Mrs. Z, are you all right?"

"I feel like I'm by myself, taking care of the kids. I'd love to hear—"

Our door buzzer sounded.

"I'll get it." I opened the door in the entryway and Pete was there with his parents. "Come in." I backed up next to the wall and let them pass.

"Rachel." Mrs. Schultz's skirt swished when she rushed to hug my Mom. Pete's dad joined Willie in our combined living room.

I stopped Pete in the apartment's entryway. "What's going on?"

"Mom and Dad heard from the landlady that Alex and Jenna will be back at ten o'clock this evening." I kept my voice low. "Are your parents taking Mom to the Hauptbahnhof to pick them up when their train arrives?"

"I think that's the plan." Pete nodded.

"Got enough room in your van for all of us?"

"No." Pete shifted his feet. "Maybe Willie will help."

We stepped into the main living area. Frieda Schultz was on the couch, arm around Mom, speaking softly to her while she patted her back. Willie moved to one of the table chairs next to Karl Schultz where they engaged in small talk. Pete and I sat on the other side of the table from them.

"I'm going to the station," Willie said. "Since it's only 7:30 P.M., first I'll snoop around Mozart's Geburtshaus and the marketplace area downtown. Afterward, I plan to meet the train at ten."

"Yes." Mr. Schultz scratched his ear. "We do have a small problem." He looked at Mom, speaking in typical German fashion. "Mrs. Zanadu does not seem to be in good enough condition to drive. She's too upset. We will take her."

"Maybe she should take a pill to calm down?" I tilted my head in her direction.

Mrs. Shultz' calming techniques failed. Mom looked even worse. More tears, more uncontrollable sobs, more tissues piling up on the end table.

"She has something to take for this nervousness?" Mr. Schultz gazed right into my eyes.

"Uh, yes, sir. It's a special condition. She keeps them in her bathroom, I think."

"Good." Mr. Schultz got up, took a few steps to the couch and whispered into his wife's ear. She nodded and Mr. Schultz returned to the table.

"All taken care of. As far as transportation tonight..." Herr Schultz scratched his ear again. "Willie, would you be able to take Peter and Gabe with you this evening? Promise to keep things safe?"

"I'll do my best." Willie beamed a smile. "That'll give Mrs. Z a chance to be right as rain when Alex and Jenna arrive."

Mrs. Schultz and Mom went into the bedroom.

"When do you have to go?" I asked Willie.

"Ten minutes, max."

Mrs. Schultz came out, shutting the door to the bedroom after herself.

"Your mother is going to lay down for a few hours before we pick up Jenna and Alex." She arranged her skirt a little, smoothing out a few folds. "She should relax easily. She took two pills for her nerves and another blue pill that looked like a pain reliever."

"Not that," I said. Everyone looked at me.

"What is it, mate?" Willie's eyes widened, demanding an answer.

"She's only supposed to take one of the nerve pills at a time. And the blue pill knocks her into a deep sleep for about eight hours in addition to killing any pain. She won't wake up until tomorrow morning."

"We'll see," Frieda Schultz said. "I'll come back to wake her up at nine-thirty."

"Yeah." I rolled my eyes. "Good luck with that, Mrs. Schultz."

"Excuse us." Willie pushed himself onto his feet before Pete's mom could respond. "The boys and I'll be going. See you at the station, ten o'clock."

The buzzer sounded at the door for the third time that night.

"Now what?" I stomped to the apartment's entry door and flung it open. The landlord towered over me.

"Another note for your mother." He shoved a folded paper into my hands. "It's from your father. Urgent."

"Sure." I backpedaled, note in hand, to give me some space. "I'll make sure she gets it."

The landlord stared at me, waiting.

"Right away." I smiled.

He nodded and left.

I closed the door, reading.

"Mrs. Schultz," I sprinted to her with the note. "My Mom needs to see this as soon as possible." I opened the door to her room. "Mom? Are you awake?"

A murmur came from under the sheets.

I shook my head, closing her room. "When she can think straight, she has to read this note. You can read it. She won't mind."

Frieda Schultz nodded. "Of course." She read it and sat straighter. "I'll do my best in a few hours."

"Thanks." I looked at Willie. "Let's go."

Willie, Pete, and I headed out to the car. Lightning tagged along at my heels.

As we drove away, Willie popped the question. "Well, what was in the note?"

"I couldn't tell, but it's urgent," I said. "Dad wrote to tell Mom, 'Call me right away. Something's come up, and we have to change our plans. Now.'"

Chapter Nineteen

Stashed

The Polizei HQ in Salzburg hummed with precision—even at 8:00 PM. Groups huddled together while other individuals talked on the phone or pounded out words on computer terminals. Captain Hans Bergmann sat at his desk.

"Cap'n, don't you take time off to spend with your family?" Willie snagged a pen off the desk to take notes.

"Normally, I'm at home around six, if the tourists are in a good mood." He rummaged in a drawer for something, couldn't find it, and slammed the drawer shut. "Johansen." He yelled out the door. "Where's that Gerlach file?"

He turned his attention back to us. "These next two evenings may prove to be difficult as they are the last two days of the summer tourist months. The crowds are bigger, more rowdy; a train's exploded; and…" he looked up, "we have a possible killer on the loose."

"I see." Willie relaxed in a chair. "Nothing too unusual." A corner went up on one side of his mouth.

Johansen showed up with file folders. Bergmann snatched them from his hands and slapped the stack on the desk. A curt nod dismissed the officer.

The Captain glared at Willie. With a deliberate deep breath, he forced himself to relax and sit back. "Yes. Everything's under control. How can I assist you tonight?"

Pete and I took two other chairs near Willie and listened. Lightning leaped onto my lap, asking me to scratch his ears by pushing his head into my hand.

"Me and my mates are heading to the Geburtshaus and down around the Marktplatz near University Plaza to check out a few leads." Willie shifted forward. "I need entrance to Mozart's birthplace and no disturbances from your local police. If anything happens, we'll let you know."

"Any news on the other junior detectives?"

"They're arriving at the Hauptbahnhof at ten tonight. We'll meet 'em there." Willie rose. "And return at seven in the morning to bring you up to speed with what we find."

"There is no train scheduled in at ten tonight." Bergmann stood.

"Why wouldn't there be a ten o'clock train?" I jumped to my feet.

"A bomb blew it apart this afternoon." The Captain's jaw tightened. "The next train doesn't arrive until midnight. And it stops at most local towns."

"We have to call my parents," Pete said.

"Give me their number. I'll have one of my men do it." Bergmann looked at Willie. "I'll let my other men know about your activities. Be careful."

I turned to Willie. "I don't care what we're doing, but I have to be at that train station when my brother arrives."

Thanks to Willie's arrangements, we got into Mozart's Geb-urtshaus with no problems. We raced up the stairs two at a time.

"Be quick, mates." Willie walked into the first room. "Was it here that Lightning stopped?"

As if providing an answer, Lightning shot past him into the next room. He ran into the far corner under a display and barked once.

"That's the spot." I bent to look under the document case.

"Let's take a look." On hands and knees, Willie crawled to Lightning. Pete and I followed.

Willie poked around and didn't find any secret panels. "It's a dead end."

"Let me try." I tested the wall myself. No luck. "Lightning's never wrong when he alerts. Maybe it's the opposite side of this wall in the next room?"

We scrambled to our feet and searched the next room's cor-ner. Nothing.

"That's crazy," Pete said. "What's gotten into your dog?"

Lightning danced in place, yipping. When he saw me watch-ing, he ran toward an open doorway.

"What's up, boy?" I said. "That's the internal courtyard."

He kept up the racket and trotted out onto the courtyard's walkway. When I didn't follow, he popped back into the room, barked once, and left again.

"Guess we should follow." I motioned for Pete and Willie to come along. On my way out, I ducked under a rope to run my fin-gers over the dark ebony keys of Amadeus' clavichord, a rectangular piano about the size of a small office desk.

"Get those grungy digits off the ivories, mate."

I jerked my fingers back. "Sorry."

"Come 'ere." He lifted the rope surrounding the piano for me to come out. "This…" He jiggled the rope. "…is for everyone, including coppers like us, yeah?"

"Yeah. But I—"

"No buts." Willie dropped the rope. "This here piano—"

"Clavichord." Pete corrected.

"All right, clavichord." Willie sighed. "You can tell it's special by the keys, right?"

"The keys are opposite the colors of today's pianos." I pointed. "Sharp/flat keys are white and the regular keys dark instead of the other way around like today."

"And Amadeus used this clavichord to compose his favorite opera, *The Magic Flute*." Pete tilted his head at the sign posted on the wall.

"The point is," Willie gave Pete a sharp look with half a grin, "no touching. If you're a detective, you still follow the rules. Don't go wobbly on me. Trackin'?"

"Tracking." I nodded, moving toward the door.

Lightning sat in the center of the path, waiting for us to follow.

Pete scanned the indoor courtyard below, leaning on the black wrought iron railing. "Nothing here."

Lightning barked and trotted away from us, tail swishing in the slight breeze. He made a right at the restroom sign.

"A great time to go to the loo." Willie chuckled.

"I'll get him." I made the corner. Lightning was gone.

"Come here, buddy. Time to leave."

A bark boomed from the men's restroom.

I pushed my way in, flipped the light switch, and found the orange puffball sitting in front of a janitor's closet to my right.

"We've got to go." I reached to pick him up, and he squirmed away, barking.

"What's the difficulty, mate?" The Aussie shoved the door open wide.

I wiggled the doorknob of the closet. "Can you pick a lock?"

"In two shakes of a wallaby's tail." The door opened with ease.

Pete crouched. "Now what's he doing?"

Lightning wiggled past a broom, disappeared under a mop, and sat next to the far right corner.

Willie folded his arms and leaned on the wall. "Let's think about this."

"We walked out of the last room," Pete said, "and turned toward the restrooms."

"Backtracking parallel to the wall of the last room."

"Exactly." Willie snapped his fingers. "We've walked close to the same distance as the room was wide. Your dog wants us to turn right, which takes us back toward the birth room."

"I'm not sure the janitor's closet is deep enough to get back that far." Pete knocked on its rear wall.

"Maybe there's hidden panel here." I squeezed in, past the mops, brooms, buckets, and rags. I prodded the wall and couldn't find a hidden trigger mechanism.

Another bark. Lightning's paws scratched the wall in the corner. He jumped as high as he could."

"I can't find a latch." I rubbed his head. "Let's go."

"Wait," Pete said. "He's pretty sure something's here. Did you push on those L brackets holding the two walls together? That third one up is fancier than the others."

I spotted the bracket and pushed against the sidewall. No movement.

"Try pulling on it," Willie said.

I pulled out my knife, slipped the blade under the edge and lifted. Something gave. I tensed my muscles.

With a stiff release, the L-bracket lifted out. A loud click sounded, and the sidewall swung back to reveal a short passageway. My orange puffball dashed inside.

Chapter Twenty

On the Run

"Alex, duck in here." Jenna dragged me out of the hallway into the family restroom and shut the door. The toilet occupied the end of one car, with passenger seats on one side and the exit to the next car on the other side.

"Jenna—"

She put her finger to my lips. Gradually, when she knew I wouldn't talk, she held her finger up and gave it a slight shake.

Pretty sure that she wanted me to be quiet, I nodded.

She smiled and tilted her head toward the door, hand cupping around her ear.

I followed her directions and put my ear on the door to the corridor. I shrugged when I couldn't hear anything unusual.

She pointed back to the door again.

I sighed, placing my ear a little higher. I heard it.

"Tickets." A man's muffled words penetrated the door. "Please show your tickets. Thank you."

My muscles tightened. I locked the door with a quiet twist of my hand.

Jenna gave me a thumbs up.

Someone pulled on the handle of the door. I stepped back, my pulse picking up.

"Anyone in here?" a woman said in German. "My children need the bathroom."

"Give me a few minutes," Jenna responded in German. "Please come back."

I let out the breath I'd been holding. That was close. I tapped Jenna's arm and mouthed four minutes while holding up the fingers to emphasize the point.

Jenna smiled.

The handle rattled hard.

"One moment please." Jenna's loud response stopped the person outside. She motioned that we had to leave.

I swallowed.

Jenna flushed the toilet, turned on the water basin, wet her hands, and grabbed a handful of paper towels. Unlocking the door, she flung it open and faked stumbling into the waiting redheaded woman and her two toddlers.

I peeked around the edge.

When Jenna tripped over the waiting family, her forward momentum turned the redhead sideways. Paper towels scattered onto several riders and the floor, away from the toilet and past the toddlers.

I glimpsed a few men watching the commotion.

After helping Jenna up, the woman ordered her two children, who were chasing the paper towels, to pick them up. Two other lady passengers helped Jenna.

Satisfied the situation was under control, the men went back to their reading.

I slipped out in the opposite direction, putting the door between me and the passengers. The exit to the next car was behind me. After a moment, I closed the toilet entry.

"Jenna." I rushed forward. "Did you fall?"

"I guess I did." She held onto a seat with the redhead patting her hand. "I'll be fine."

"Let me help pick up those paper towels." I motioned to the redhead that I would help her children.

"Nonsense, young man." The woman waved me off. "My children have forgotten why we are even here. They'll have it all picked up in a minute."

"Thank you." Like a gentleman, I held out an arm for Jenna to take. "Let me help you back to your seat."

"You are such a sweet couple," the redhead said.

"Thanks." Jenna smiled and waved. We left.

In the next car, she tugged her arm from mine.

"That was close," she said. "You need to keep track of that conductor."

"But I feel like I'm stealing," I said. "We're hiding and—"

"It's not stealing," Jenna said. "We're going to pay for these tickets. I don't want Polizei crawling all around us at every stop to put us back in the hospital. That's the reason we told your mom we would arrive at 10:00 PM. She'll tell the police. By the time they figure out we won't arrive until midnight, it'll be too late for them to stick us in a hospital. We'll almost be home."

"We do look a little banged up." I checked over her shoulder. "Rats."

"What?"

"He's coming again." I swiveled to find another place to hide.

"We've hidden in almost all the places we can." Jenna searched the car for another hiding spot.

"I know." I dragged her to the next car and into a seat. "Can we get into the baggage car?"

"I guess… since on this train the porter is also the conductor."

"Good." I glanced back at the train official who talked with a passenger. "Let's go."

We snuck onto the baggage car. Groping in the dim light seeping through the car's entry and exit door windows, we hid behind some big, bulky equipment.

I tapped the glow button on my watch. "Two-and-a-half more hours."

Jenna groaned. "Why couldn't the Phantom have blown up a slow train?"

"Very funny." I rubbed my scalp. "I hope we don't get caught. They might haul us in anyway."

"You're such a pessimist." She slumped back against the wall. "I don't know what makes me want to stay with you."

"Stay with me? What's that mean?"

"Alex, sometimes you are stupid."

"Stupid?"

"Don't leave Germany." She lay her head on my shoulder, blonde hair falling like a cascade. "I haven't found anyone like you. And I've met lots of guys. Didn't you feel something before we almost died?"

"Jenna. We're both fifteen. In the United States, we don't make decisions like this until we're way older."

"I'll be sixteen in December. Four months." She pulled her head away. "In Germany, we decide our lives much sooner than Americans do. We're more responsible."

"You know my Dad has to leave Germany soon. As his son, I can't stay by myself."

"We could work it out." She patted my arm. "You can get your own room with my parents as an exchange student. When you turn sixteen, apply for a work permit. And when you're old enough, we can get serious."

"Jenna." My lips felt dry. I licked them. "You know I like you, right? A lot."

She laid her head on my shoulder in response.

"I…but I'm not going to stay in Germany."

Her fingers clenched my arm. She bolted upright.

"After all we've been through?" Her voice began to rise. "Tell me why you wanted to be my boyfriend. Why do you hold my hand? Why—"

The creak of metal against metal cut her off. Two men, the conductor and someone else, turned on an overhanging light.

"I don't see anyone here," the deeper man's voice said.

"You're right." The conductor's voice agreed. "I'm not moving this equipment, either."

I tried to sink into the floor.

"How many more stops?" deep voice said.

"Several." The conductor shifted several pieces of luggage around. "I found out I have no more luggage stops. Let's play some card games and have a beer."

"Dark or light?"

"What do you care? It's free. Sit down."

We weren't leaving anytime soon.

I searched and touched Jenna's hand. She shoved mine away.

Chapter Twenty-One

Hidden Treasure

"Well done, mate," Willie slapped my back. "Better chase your friend down."

"Gabe, do you need a light?" Pete peered around Willie's shoulder. "Seems a little dark to me."

"Yeah. No light switch." I thrust my head past the opening. "And I see a corner further down."

"Here's a torch." Willie gave me a flashlight.

The light revealed cobwebs and spiders. I heard the scurrying of tiny mice. The flashlight was weak at best. I could barely see. I rounded the corner into pitch-black darkness.

"Keep going," Pete said.

"Letting my eyes adjust." I stood for a minute before moving. The flashlight beam caught something square in the distance. I edged forward, shining the light at my feet. A blur of gray whipped past my toe and headed for Lightning, who pounced. When I reached him, I saw the scared little mouse trapped under his two paws.

"Not now." I snapped my fingers and motioned toward the square.

Lightning lifted a paw and the scared mouse skittered away into the darkness.

I crept forward three steps and reached the wooden box. A bent hasp locking mechanism was on the footlocker. The lock lay smashed on the ground. I opened the box and found three rolled manuscripts covered with a folded note.

"Find anything?" Pete peered around the edge of the corner.

"Jackpot. I found—"

"Don't touch anything," Willie's head appeared over Pete's.

"Too late." I raised the note in my hand.

"Well, stop now. We need to get a fingerprint crew here."

"Where did you find these things?" Captain Bergmann eyed the three scrolls on the desk and the folded note.

"Stashed in a hidden passage," Pete said.

"Behind the room where Mozart was born." I smiled.

"You're sure?" Bergmann said.

"That's where my dog alerted in the house." I patted Lightning.

"Thanks. And have any of you read the note?"

We all shook our heads.

"It's more of the same from the Phantom. Threats and orders. All in German." The Captain took a sip of coffee.

"What about the fingerprints?" Willie asked.

"Negative." The officer sighed. "No positive identification. The suspect is either stupid or losing his marbles. He left two incredibly valuable Mozart manuscripts back from when the boy was four or five."

"I remember three rolled papers." I stroked Lightning's fur.

"Correct. Two originals and a forgery." Another sip of coffee. "However, the Phantom claims the third manuscript is not a forgery, but his work when he was five. That's why I lean toward the unhinged psychological evaluation."

"Is his music any good?" That coffee smell made me hungry. "And can I get some hot chocolate?"

"I don't know about the piano music. I'll turn that over to the experts. As for the chocolate—help yourself." The Captain motioned toward the door.

When I returned, I found Pete, Willie, and the Captain huddled around the desk. I joined in, slurping a little chocolate on the way.

"What's up?" I said.

"The Captain's staff brought in the translation and summary of the Phantom's note." Pete pulled me close. "He plans to trap some Polizei and capture us tomorrow."

Chapter Twenty-Two

The Penetration Plan

"The Phantom's note is a bit confusing because he thinks he is Mozart and owns the town of Salzburg, especially the fortress." Captain Bergmann smoothed out the paper and handed it to me. "You can read the summary of his three demands."

I scanned the typewritten paper.

THE PHANTOM'S DEMANDS

1. Four kids chasing him must meet the Phantom on the Untersberg Mountain; otherwise, he will burn down Mozart's Geburtshaus.

2. Drop off a million Austrian Schillings for the girl's ransom money at Nannerl's restaurant at 6:00 P.M.

3. Should the four children survive the day, they must meet the Phantom at his Fortress in the evening for a historical tour and party.

"Told you he was a tosser. A blooming idiot." Willie winked and glanced at his watch. "Time to scope out the train station and meet the Schultz family."

"Before you go," the Captain tilted forward, "I want to be informed of all your activities and plans. I don't want a mix-up between my folks and yours."

"Understood, Cap'n." Willie hooked his finger at Pete and me. "Off we go, mates."

Lightning trotted after me, jumping into Willie's car as soon as the door was open.

By 11:00 PM the train station felt a bit chilly after the afternoon heat. The temperature hovered in the high sixties. Clouds covered the sky, and a slight drizzle fell. We dodged raindrops moving from Willie's car to the main train station terminal.

"Time for us to make some plans." Willie motioned us to follow. We went down into the mall area of the train station to a coffee shop.

"I'm starving," Pete said.

"Me too." I glanced at Willie. "Do you have money?"

124

"For you mates, anytime."

We all got a sandwich, something to drink, and I got a piece of cake to share with Pete.

"We've got to get into the Fortress when no one else is around to nab that guy." I spoke between bites of sandwich. "And survive to get there tomorrow night."

"Only the four of us." Pete pointed at Willie. "What about you and the other cops? How will they capture him?"

"We may have to wire you." Willie chewed a few times and swallowed. "Whatever you hear, we hear."

"You have equipment that small?" I sliced into the cake. "The portable phones I've seen are about the size of a soda bottle."

"You've not been introduced to any classified projects." Willie's lips curled into a smile. "Tomorrow you'll enter a new world of micro-electronics."

"Time to go." Pete pointed at one of the clocks after a while.

"Yeah. 11:40 P.M." Willie stretched. "Let's get crackin', mates. Or Pete's parents will be waiting for us. We hurried and arrived at the platform first.

Pete's parents rushed from the escalator to join us a few minutes later.

"Gruss Gott." Herr Schmidt nodded at Willie. "I must apologize that we could not wake Mrs. Zanadu." He turned to me. "The note from your father will have to wait until tomorrow."

The five of us stayed close together on the train platform. Lightning curled up on a nearby bench. Scattered people expecting the late arrival loitered near us. Water dripped off the edge of the platform roof above us.

"You did say midnight?" Herr S said.

The minute hand on the clock face clicked onto midnight. A loud, haunting melody floated through the air, first sounding indistinct, as though there wasn't enough air pushing out the notes, ending with a crashing chord that echoed off the rooftops.

"That's from the Fortress." Willie's eyes searched to locate the exact direction.

Willie, Pete, and I faced the sound.

"We'll get him." I patted Pete on the back.

"The bull roars," a grey-haired gentleman spoke from a bench. "What a hideous racket."

The bull? I'd heard that before. It meant something important.

Screeches from the rails interrupted my thoughts and announced the train's arrival. Grinding sounds replaced the music as passenger cars drifted past.

"Where are they?" Mrs. S craned her neck, staring at each window. "Shouldn't they be ready to jump out to greet us?"

"Remain calm," Mr. S said. "They're probably getting their bags."

"They're bags were blown up." Mrs. S raised her voice. "The poor things are probably dazed or have bandages on their heads. Perhaps even worse. Broken arms—"

"Mrs. Schultz, this must be difficult." Willie stepped beside her. "We can hope that both of them felt well enough to travel."

"There they are." I waved at two forms leaving the baggage car.

Alex hopped down to the platform and held out a hand for Jenna. She wrinkled her nose and glided around the outstretched hand. Seeing her parents, she broke into a trot, then a run, clutching her mother and father in a tight hug. She sobbed.

"Mama. Papa." After a while she released them, glaring at Alex.

"You're safe," her mother said. Mrs. Schultz wiped a tissue against her cheeks.

Pete rushed to her side. "Are you hurt?"

"No. But keep Alex away from me." Jenna's shoulders heaved. "I hate him." She wrapped her arms around her mother again.

"Jenna," I got close. "Quit being so dramatic. It can't be that bad."

Pete shook his head.

"What would a *boy* your age know?" She jabbed a finger at me.

Mr. Schultz patted Jenna and her mother as they hugged. He gazed at me, fire lighting his eyes.

I glanced at Willie for support.

"Young man." Herr Schultz strode between his family and me. "Rude. Impertinent. Brash. You are each of these." His veins bulged on his neck. "Another wrong word and..." He waved a finger in my face. "Treat my daughter with respect and courtesy. Do you hear?"

"Sir, I—"

"Yes or no."

I gulped. "Yes."

"I can't believe this young generation." Muttering under his breath, he gathered his family and rushed them down the escalator.

Alex, eyes focused on the ground, still hadn't joined the group.

I ran to him. "You made it." I hugged him even though he hated hugs. "How did you get out of the train wreck? Are you hurt?"

He shook his head.

"Why did you tell us to meet the10:00 P.M. train?" I waited. He didn't answer. "Where's Thunder?"

Alex rubbed his forehead. "I don't know."

Lightning sniffed around Alex's legs and looked at the train.

"He's not here, buddy." I knelt down and ruffled his scalp. "We'll find him."

"It's about time you rocked up." Willie gave Alex a poke on the arm. "We weren't sure you were on the train."

"We didn't want to get pulled off." Alex spoke in a flat tone, pointing at the departing train as it moved to its next stop. "We kept ourselves occupied in the bathrooms or the luggage car. We'll have to pay for the fare later."

"What about Jenna? Shouldn't she pay too?" I faced toward the exit. The platform was empty.

"They didn't take long to clear out," Willie said.

Alex plodded to the exit. "Jenna's having a fit."

"Looks like we'll have lots to catch up on." I matched pace with my brother, Lightning straggling behind. "What happened to Thunder? He—"

"Nothing to tell," Alex said. "The smoke was too much. I blacked out. When I woke up, he was gone."

"Why?" I touched his arm.

He jerked his arm away. "I don't know. Dying dogs often hide when they're hurt enough to die. They want to be alone."

"And the little Sheila?" Willie put an arm on Alex's shoulder. "Having troubles? Her eyes could have frozen you in your tracks when she dismounted the train. Like ice, I'd say." He slapped him on the back. "She'll be right as rain in the morning."

"Not in a million years."

Chapter Twenty-Three

Untersberg

"I say yes." I set the hot chocolate on the police conference room table.

"Gabe." Pete bit off a piece of ham. "I don't agree."

Our 7:00 A.M. continental breakfast at the headquarters had run into a snag.

"We need everyone involved." I threw Lightning another piece of brotchen, which I tore from my breakfast sandwich of cold ham, salami, and cheese. "And Jonathan knows his way around Salzburg." Under the table, the dog nibbled the half-piece of German bread.

"I don't think it's a good idea to expand the team now." Willie sipped from a cup of coffee.

"You won't be with us." I tossed more bread on the floor. "The note mentioned four kids, no adults. You would scare the Phantom away."

"Jonathan's been trouble every time he's around us," Alex said. He straddled a chair in a reverse position, draping himself over the chair back, head laying on his arms like he didn't care about anything.

"Yes, that is true." Pete cut a slice of raisin bread into four pieces and stuffed one in his mouth. "He can be both a help and a problem."

"The Phantom, who happens to be one crazy guy that carries out his threats, wrote he wanted only you four kids on top of the mountain. That means Jenna, Pete, Alex, and Gabe. Not Jonathan." Willie finished his cup and set it down with a clink.

"And why isn't Jenna here?" I spread my hands. "No one's talking. Alex and Jenna won't tell the rest of us what happened."

"Herr Schultz didn't give me any explanation." Willie nodded.

"The man won't care if it's Jenna or Jonathan." I sipped my hot chocolate. "He doesn't know us anyway."

"We don't know that." Pete ate more of his bread.

"We know he threatened to burn down Mozart's Geburtshaus, but the Polizei can protect that place, right?" I checked to see if Lightning needed more food.

"True," Willie said. "What's your plan, mate?"

"Jonathan can take pictures for you like a tourist or something if Jenna ever comes back. He can get around town on public transportation, leaving the four of us alone at crucial times. His knowledge might help us discover clues we need to solve riddles or find certain places in Salzburg." I tossed a piece of ham under the table.

"You have confidence in this kid?" Willie raised his eyebrows.

"Yes—he can do it." I surveyed the room. Pete rubbed the side of his head, and Alex was out of it, staring at the wall. "We've been talking since seven o'clock. It's almost 8:30 A.M. Let him help."

Willie bounced to his feet and stepped in the hallway.

"Call Jonathan Brinker."

"One more thing, before Jonathan arrives." Willie tapped my knee. "You need to be wired for sound." Willie pointed toward the squad room.

"Okay." I smiled. "Should be fun."

The fitting didn't take long and I returned to the group. Jonathan arrived in our meeting room shortly after Pete polished off his raisin bread.

Jonathan beamed a smile at us. "Thanks for taking me on."

"It's more like you'll be tagging along," Willie said. "I'll tell you what you need to know, mate, and no more. You're helping us solve a case, but not everyone here thinks you're the right man for the job or that you'll be any help at all. Today you're a tourist."

Jonathan's smile faded.

"You'll be okay." I stood and called Lightning. "I'm going to make a pit stop before we leave. We can talk in the cable car that takes us to the top of our first stop—Untersberg Mountain."

Pete walked out with me, waiting until we were inside the restroom. "This is a huge mistake."

Lightning yipped his agreement.

I sighed.

The Untersbergbahn's bright red doors welcomed us into the bottom cable car station for the mountain. We were there early, about 9:00 A.M. and the next car left at 9:30 A.M. Willie dropped the four of us off with Lightning and drove to a café to get his third morning coffee. He planned to come back about 10:30 and see what was going on.

"I think it's weird we haven't heard anything about Thunder," Pete said while we waited in a corner.

"My best friend." Alex knelt to pet Lightning. "Gone. Probably dead."

"Don't go there." I touched his shoulder.

He flinched, picked up Lightning, deposited him in my arms, and spoke softly. "You still have your dog." He hunched his shoulders and moved off a few steps, checking out the map of the mountain on the wall.

"Gabe," Pete whispered. "I can see the wire bulging under your shirt. I need to adjust it."

"Good." I scratched my back. "Makes my back itch. Give it a quick rub."

"Stop it." Alex strode over to us. "If the Phantom's watching, he'll know something's different."

"He's not here now," I said. "He said he'd meet us on top of the mountain, not at the bottom."

At least my brother was talking. He didn't talk to Mom at all this morning when Willie and I explained the necessity of our participation to the case. Mom acted normal about it, even after talking with Dad. She wouldn't tell us what changed to the family plans with the exception that we might leave early. She took charge. Warned us not to get hurt. Or take chances. And Alex maintained silence at home. *I guess losing Thunder was a big blow. I'd feel terrible if I lost Lightning.* My throat got suddenly dry.

"Wake up, Gabe." Jonathan thumped me from behind. "Time to get in line for the cable car." Minutes later, we boarded.

Another Alpine day with brilliant sunshine and light blue sky greeted us as the car glided from the bottom station to the top. The temperature was near sixty degrees Fahrenheit at the entry station. At the top, it might be in the low fifties. I adjusted my jacket and backpack during the ride.

"The Untersberg is 1,776 meters tall." Jonathan pointed toward the summit, speaking to a young American couple. "Do you understand German?"

They shook their heads.

"Untersberg means under the mountain." Jonathan's hands showed the relationship. "'Unter' means under and 'Berg' means mountain. And when you entered the Untersbergbahn you entered the town's transportation system, like an electric train, to the mountaintop…"

"Jonathan's got his role down," I whispered to Pete. "So what's bothering Jenna and Alex?"

"I'm not sure. I think Jenna tried to get Alex to make a commitment to her."

"You mean, get married?" My eyes widened. "Alex is only fifteen."

"I'm not sure," Pete said. "She told me she convinced the conductor to let them stay on the train together. Maybe she wanted a ring to go steady or a promise to get engaged later. She's obsessed with Alex lately."

"They already hang out together all the time. Why make it formal?"

"She's got nothing to show for their time together—no ring." Pete made a furtive glance at Alex, several tourists to my left.

"Uh-oh," I said. "A ring's like permanent. Does she know we'll be leaving for good in a few months when my Dad gets reassigned?"

"Look at that view," the young American girl exclaimed, hugging her man. "What a beautiful wedding vacation."

Below us, pasturelands surrounded the town of Salzburg. Tiny grazing cows and goats moved about like dots. I could make out several castles, the airport, other mountains in the distance, and the Autobahn around the city. The red and orange tile roofs on most structures contrasted well with the various wall colors of the houses.

"Here comes a plane to land at the airport." Jonathan pointed out a white Cessna.

Everyone turned to look.

We lurched into the cable car's top station.

"Time to get to work." I picked up Lightning and followed Pete and Alex out of the car.

The exit for the upper station ran through a small hallway connected to a restaurant and gift shop. I zipped up my coat, ready to walk outside.

"Wait." Alex broke his silence again. Our group stopped, letting others jostle past. "Over here." Alex walked to a section of the hallway on the outside of the store. He pointed at one of the backpacks on sale inside. A rolled parchment, similar to the ones we had found with Mozart's composition and the forgery on them, poked out of the side pocket.

"I'm on it." Pete entered the store, greeted the clerk, and browsed, drifting over to the backpack. He unzipped the pocket, checked for anything else, hid the scroll in his coat, and strolled back out. He handed the paper to Alex.

"Hey." I tugged on Pete's coat. "Let me see it first. Who put him in charge?"

"He's the one who found it."

Alex motioned for us to go outside. We followed him past the open-air restaurant where someone sat enjoying a mug of sweet-smelling hot chocolate. We crowded in a circle, except for Jonathan, who strutted about, expanding his chest, exhaling with loud sighs, and commenting to unsuspecting bystanders what a gorgeous view they were seeing.

Alex unrolled the parchment.

"Go on," I said. "Read it. *You* discovered it."

Alex rolled it back up, handed it to me, and walked away.

Chapter Twenty-Four

The Cross

I unrolled the parchment.

"It's just a picture," Pete said from over my shoulder.

Jonathan strolled behind me. "Terrific landscape. Mind if I take a picture over your shoulder?"

"Uh, no." He rested a hand on my shoulder and snapped a shot, probably of the parchment.

The drawing was of a small package on the very top of a cross. The package wasn't noticeable unless you followed the Phantom's arrow to it. Arrows highlighted several pointy objects on the cross above the crossbar that dripped something from their ends.

"We have to get that package," Pete said.

"Alex will be climbing the cross by now." I leaned around Pete to see my brother's location.

"There are two crosses here." Pete showed me a small map of the area. "I think the Phantom's talking about the first one."

"What are the drips from these backward nail things?" I said.

"Might be poison." Pete took a few steps to my right. "And your brother won't wait for us. Five minutes to the cross or less, I bet."

"We need to catch up with him." I tucked the note in my coat. "In his mood, he'll probably puncture his arm on the poison nails."

"Lightning, make him wait." I picked up my dog and tossed him like a bowling ball to give him momentum. I followed at top speed.

The reddish-orange streak sped toward its target. When I ran to catch him, I saw Lightning jump in front of Alex, but he marched on. The ground rose into a steep incline before my brother reached the cross. Lighting flew up the hill, executed a near-perfect fighter-jet style turn, and leaped onto Alex's chest.

Startled, Alex stopped. He lifted the dog until they were face to face. A few quick licks on the chin and the corners of my brother's mouth went up

"Wait." I sprinted the last ten yards, yelling as I went. "Don't do it."

"Do what?" Alex stared back.

"Climb the cross." I panted, putting my hands on my knees.

"I wasn't going to climb it."

"Then why'd you leave without talking to us? You're going to get somebody killed if you don't cut it out."

Pete huffed and puffed as he arrived.

"It's none of your business." Alex put Lightning down.

"Alex," Pete said, "You will get someone hurt." He gulped in air. "We have to work together as a team."

"Says who?"

"Look, I know I'm the girlfriend's brother, but you should forgive people and not hold grudges. Holding grudges makes things worse, not better."

"It's Jenna's fault." He looked away.

"Bro." I tapped him on the shoulder as I climbed the hill past him to the cross. "You keep telling me to act like a Christian when our parents aren't around. Now it's your turn. Don't be hard-hearted. Forgive and forget. That's what Dad and Mom always say."

"Whatever." Alex sat on a rock facing the Salzburg airport.

The cross was anchored to a rock by bolts at the base. Steadying cables held the wooden structure in place against violent windstorms.

"Stand on my shoulders." Pete, still a little out of breath, clapped a hand on my shoulder before I could make my first attempt.

"You should run more," I said. "Or maybe eat less munchies." I studied the cross. "If I'm on your shoulders, I can touch the cross bar, but I'll have to jump to latch on to the top of it."

"Be quick," Pete said. "Even though no one guards these mountain crosses in Germany…" He scanned the area for people. "It's wrong to climb them. They're sacred."

I knelt by the cross, ransacking my backpack. "I'll go as fast as I can. Hopefully, stoneheart will join to help." I located my gloves and tugged them on.

Pete took a quick look around. Some sightseers engaged in conversation at the café, others looked in the opposite direction at the dramatic view, and the rest hiked toward the second cross. Except Jonathan. His camera was out. He raised his right thumb.

"Go." Pete knelt.

I climbed on his back and placed my hands on the cross.

Pete eased upward in increments, ensuring I was steady. Once he was fully extended, I bent my knees.

"Ready?"

"Yes."

I leaped. One hand on each side of the vertical beam, I wrapped my legs around the main post to stop from sliding down. I worked my body higher until my shoulders were above the crossbeam.

"Faster." Pete waved me on.

Avoiding the upper part of the vertical beam, I swung my legs up over the crossbeam and rotated until I was on top. I grabbed the upper vertical post with my left hand, went to my knees on the crossbar, and gently got my feet underneath me. I couldn't see the top of the post.

"Hurry," Pete said. "You're taking too long."

I stood next to the reverse nails and saw a purple tip on each one. Reaching up, I felt the package. It was taped down. I needed both hands for leverage to get it off. I needed to get closer.

I closed my eyes and whispered a prayer, "Don't let me die from poison."

My coat pressed against the nails. I could feel them pushing the coat next to my skin. *A little more.* I stretched. Nails popped through my coat and shirt. *Now.* I yanked with all my might, and the package came free into my hands.

I flailed, trying to keep my balance, and lost the battle. My tail slammed into the cross-brace, followed by my back, knocking my breath out. The package popped out of my hands. Dazed, I fell.

Without air to shout, I could only think the words.

Catch me.

Chapter Twenty-Five

Flying Dragons

I fell to my right, downhill. Like a National Football League wide receiver making a spectacular play, I grabbed the package with both hands. I twisted and tucked my head, bracing for smashing into the rock below and rolling down the hill.

Instead, I slammed into Pete, who fell back. Alex was there to back him up and slowed his crash to the ground. We all sprawled in a heap at the foot of the cross.

Lightning dug into the pile until he found my cheek. His pink tongue made me move.

"Hey, furball," I said, "I'm okay. Check on Pete."

"Stop it," Pete said. "Gabe, call your dog off. He's tickling my ear."

"Lightning, come here." I sat up after Alex and Pete crawled out from our entanglement and struggled to their feet. Pete offered his hand and helped me up.

"What do we have now?" Alex asked.

I paused. He looked interested, holding a hand out to take the package. I handed it to him.

"Looks like a normal package." Pete stepped a little closer to see. "What are those purple holes in your coat?"

"Uh-oh." I unzipped the coat. "Check me out. I may be poisoned."

Pete twisted me sideways until no one else could see. I lifted my shirt.

"You have purple, dotted skin, but I don't see any blood."

"Get it off me."

"In a sec." Pete took a couple of steps, knelt, pulled a handful of grass out of the shadows, and wiped the dewy plants on my chest's purple spots.

Goose bumps prickled my skin. "That's cold."

"Baby." Pete used a tissue from his pocket to wipe off the purple smears.

"That wasn't used, was it?" I cracked a smile.

"Of course." Pete joked. "I only carry used ones in my pocket." He stuffed the tissues into a plastic bag. He went back to the wet grass, rubbed his hands through it, and wiped them on another tissue. "See, no more purple." He held up the tissue for me to see. "And you're clean. No punctures."

"Good," said Alex. "We have work to do." He stepped to the right. "Jonathan, come here."

"You've blown his cover," I said.

"Trust me," my brother said. "The Phantom isn't here and doesn't care. Read for yourself."

The note wasn't a poem or rhyme. The words gave straight-forward instructions. "Go to the second cross and open the back-packs hidden in the rocks nearby. They contain two dragon-fliegt suits, one for each Zanadu boy. Meet me at the Monatschlosschen in Hellbrunn. Fly there if you can. Be there by noon and come alone."

"What's a dragon-fliegt suit?" I said.

"Let me explain." Jonathan beckoned with his finger. "I'll tell you while we hike the trail." He lifted his watch toward me. "Ten o'clock. We'll need a half hour or more to get to the next cross."

"Hurry," Alex's jaw tightened. "That's not much time to find the backpacks."

The path led down a hill on a narrow rocky trail and climbed to a much higher elevation at the second cross. Jonathan started with a brisk walk but reduced the pace for the winding rock trails slippery with moisture.

"Out with it." I tapped Jonathan on the shoulder. "What's the story."

"Dragons were once thought to fly the skies of Germany in older legends." Jonathan negotiated a steep drop. "However, long ago the best flying man could do from these heights was by gliding."

"Yeah," Pete bunched up behind me. "I've seen para-gliders on the mountains lots of times."

"Right." Jonathan smiled. "Hang-gliders and para-gliders. The dragon-fliegt suits allow the flyer to launch a unique hang-glider over the edge and when he's aloft, to tuck his feet back into the sack or special backpack carrier for the suit."

"Hey." Alex bumped into Pete. "Can't you get around those out-of-shape hikers? We're losing time."

"Can't," I said. "The steps fit one person at a time. And there's a huge group coming down."

"They're wobbling a lot." Pete shook his head. "We'll have to let them through."

"Great." Alex picked up a rock and flung it into the steep drop-off to our right.

"Some people," Jonathan said, "say the fliers look like drag-on-flies from a distance." He picked up the pace on the winding stone steps cut into the hill after the tourists passed.

"And what is the "Monatschlosschen?" I said.

"That's easy." Pete, who brought up the rear, wiped sweat from his forehead. "That's the mini-castle or palace that they built in a month at the Hellbrunn Palace complex."

"A month?" I picked up Lightning, who kept checking out the flowers.

"Yes." Pete let a few hikers going down pass him on the narrow path. "Pretty fast. It's not that big."

We reached our destination. I paused at the base of the cross to take in the marvelous view of the valley, Salzburg, and the adjoining mountains.

"Do that later," Alex said. "Let's find those backpacks. It's ten forty-five."

We each went separate ways down the hill. Little paths made by animals led in several directions.

Ten minutes later, I yelled to Pete. "I found them. Go get the others." Another five went by as we gathered together. We pulled out the suits and hang-glider material, which seemed to be partially pre-assembled. The backpack's opening to insert our legs hung from a harness toward the back of the glider. Straps and a harness hung down for the flier. My glider was red and black. Alex's was orange and blue.

"Ever flown one of these before?" Jonathan asked.

"No." Alex and I replied in unison.

Jonathan nodded. "We'll take it—"

"Simple stuff." Pete waved him off.

Alex lifted his eyebrows.

"Sure." Pete lifted the hang bar. "You keep this below you like you're doing a pushup, but keep your arms bent. We adjust the harnesses to make that work for each of you—let the wing do the work. We'll find a place to launch, where the ground drops off dramatically. You run down the hill, jump off, let the updraft raise you higher, stick your feet in the tail for aerodynamics, and fly to the palace."

"Would you like to try?" Alex offered his hang-glider.

"Oh." Pete hesitated, swallowing hard. "Well, by easy, I meant *relatively* easy. And it wouldn't be proper for me to do it." His face brightened with a smile. "The Phantom wants to see you and Gabe."

"Right." Alex slapped Pete's shoulder. "This might be harder than it looks."

"No joke, Sherlock." I lifted the hang-glider with little effort. "Light and maneuverable. I guess we shift our weight to go left or right."

"And ride the thermals to get high enough to make it to the castle," Jonathan said.

"Watch." Pete pointed at several birds with wings extended, floating in the air. Without a single flap of a wing, the birds rose, wheeling away to float to another place. "You can do it. A girl's life is riding on this."

"Let's go." I grabbed my gear and walked to the top of the hill away from the cross.

"Aim for the airport." Jonathan pointed a little to our right.

"That's way too far to fly," Alex said.

"Hellbrunn isn't that far." Jonathan moved his arm further to the right. "Do you see the Salzach River?"

We nodded.

"The A-10 Autobahn goes over it." He indicated the road. "The Hellbrunn Castle and the zoo are on the inside of that intersection, closer to the city. You can't miss it."

I watched the bug-like cars moving on the A-10.

"I can't see the Hellbrunn complex." When I was a kid, people in Germany would tell Mom and Dad 'You can't miss it' and then we would drive hours past the destination.

"The mountain is blocking the view," Pete said. "You'll fly riding the thermals to get high enough to make the distance."

"Aim for the airport first." Jonathan showed us the launching site.

"Look for the zoo after you clear the mountain," Pete said. "That will help."

"Eleven-fifteen." Jonathan glanced up from his watch. "You need to fly."

I was encouraged to see three para-gliders flying on this side of the mountain.

"Check." Pete gave a final tug on my harness. "All systems go."

"Gabe, you go ahead." Alex and Jonathan worked on a twisted strap. "I'll catch up on the descent."

"See you where the eagles fly." I sent a silent prayer into the sky.

"Launch here." Pete led me to a slope that ended in a cliff. "Don't forget. Keep the tip of the glider level, hang on tight to the bar, and let the wing do the work." He adjusted my goggles. "You can do it."

"Thanks for the pep talk." I watched Alex for a second. "I wish your sister and my brother would patch things together. He seems depressed. Not good for something as dangerous as hang-gliding. I'd hate to see him crash."

"What can you expect between a girl and a boy their ages?" Pete checked my straps one final time.

"Yeah. Right." I laughed. "Here goes."

I held the wing above my head, counted down, then followed the path of other fliers. As I got to the edge of the cliff, I leaped, stretching out flat. I felt the bar of the wing slide to the rear, under my waist. I plummeted to the ground hundreds of feet below.

A second passed. I fought the urge to drop my feet and twist in preparation for a fall. I could see the trees rushing up toward me. Huge boulders lay in between the trees. My heart felt like a sledgehammer pounding my chest.

The wing tugged at my back, almost snapping my feet down as I came out of the dive. Unlike a parachutist jolted with a sudden decrease in speed, the wing smoothly leveled out. But I struggled to lift my legs and feet straight back. I needed more altitude. Another cliff. *There.* Another drop-off came into view. I brought the wing around to my right and felt the air lift me higher.

I strained to get my body straight, thrusting a leg back to the pouch. I missed. Too low. My stomach tightened and the tip of one shoe caught on the edge. I worked my foot in and stretched my leg out. The second leg was easier. I zipped up the pouch to my waist.

144

"Gabe."

My name floated out from above me somewhere. Did I imagine it? I focused, noticing my flight path was a collision course with my cliff launch-point. I concentrated, eyes wide. Shift the wing. Roll with it. Steady. I slowed my breathing, tried to control my heart rate. I relaxed my body.

Seconds from impact I felt a surge and soared over the cliff to waves and cheers from my friends. Lighting jumped around in a circle.

I didn't see Alex when I flew over our group. He must have jumped already. I looked below. Nothing. I circled, looking for more thermals or updrafts. I spotted his orange Dragon-fliegt suit about five hundred feet below. He was climbing.

In about five minutes, we were near each other and I motioned to Alex that I was headed to the target, Hellbrunn Castle. He gave me a thumbs-up and I began my descent. The cold air flowed around the wing and my body, making my three-quarters closed jacket flap a little. I surveyed the entire Salzburg area and followed Jonathan's directions. Frozen cheeks made it hard to smile, but I couldn't help it.

At this altitude, it was quiet. Air whistled past the wing and me. Planes taxied at the airport and others made graceful landings. *My landing will be as graceful as a bird.* The blue of the Salzach River contrasted with the green of the fields, forests, and the grey road network. I steered toward a large complex near the intersection of A-10 and the Salzach, descending at a gradual rate. I didn't want to miss the castle.

I hit an air pocket and dropped fifty feet. The lower I went, the choppier the air became. I tensed my stomach muscles. More air pockets reduced my altitude lower than I wanted. I kept my direction on the castle. *Come on, come on. Don't be low.*

Alex swooped over me, his shadow crossing my path. He was dropping faster than I was.

We weren't going to make it. Too late to turn for a pasture. The Hellbrunn Zoo was almost below me. I had to get my feet out of the tailpiece to land with my feet.

I struggled with the zipper first, watching Alex gliding toward a large open area with a few trees and a pond. I wanted to join him, however, my foot was stuck. I let go of the handlebar under my chest with my right hand, finished unzipping my legs, and dragged my left leg out of the tailpiece.

I glanced forward. A cage with a small area large enough to land came into view. Wobbling, I freed my right leg seconds from landing. I tried to flare the front of the wing up like I've seen helicopter pilots do in war movies, except my move was too late for the full effect.

I ran a few steps before the front edge of the wing went down and I tumbled into it, wrecking the entire contraption.

A large crowd of tourists lined the edges of the cage where I landed. A deep ditch separated the cage fence and my landing zone. *Maybe I've landed in a Zebra's run?*

Monkeys chattered to my left, screaming and whooping. A loud clanging sound came from that direction. *Maybe this area houses the larger monkeys—a baboon; a gorilla?*

With frantic motions I released clasps, wiggled out of my harness, untangled my legs, and stepped away from the wrecked Dragon-fliegt. The crowd in front of me yelled and pointed at something behind me.

But before I turned, the roar of the big cat sent a shockwave through my body. *Lion or tiger?* I didn't really want to see.

Chapter Twenty-Six

A Twisted Tale

Okay, God. Need a little help down here. I licked my lips and whirled to face the big cat.

A tiger.

I scanned the hill inside the cage.

No. Make that two tigers.

I dropped to my knees, scanning for a weapon. Stick. Stone. It didn't matter.

The enclosure contained a manmade stream and tiny pool, a rock cave, a rocky hill, and two-foot high grass on either side, with a path created from the large tigers' paws. I was in the grassy area. Loose rocks for throwing would be near the tigers.

I wondered about two cats in one cage. Were they both female? Females were the big hunters in the cat families. Or was that only lions?

Another big roar rang out from the larger tiger. Satisfied for the moment, it sank to the ground, licking a paw.

One down, one to go.

The second tiger decided to investigate the new toy in its cage. Growling, the cat climbed a higher rock formation between us to get a better look. The striped cat was in no hurry. Its toy wasn't going anywhere soon.

I crawled to my downed wing to see if I could make it a weapon. Nothing but busted, twisted struts. Useless. My knife was in my backpack, which was with Pete.

People behind me shouted things in German I couldn't understand. I risked a glance. Outside the fence, a uniformed individual rushed past the crowd. *Zookeeper?*

A man by the fence waved at me. Bent low. Scooped air with his hands and pushed them over his head like he carried a load.

I got it. Moving slow, I reached toward my damaged wing. The tigers watched, both heads tracking my movements. The one in the back looked like it might fall asleep.

Good. Get some rest, little kitty.

I bent and gripped the wing's handlebar.

The smaller tiger changed from a growl to a huge roar. Lips drew back to expose large teeth.

I placed my other hand on the wing and lifted it over my head. The large cat leaped to its feet. The smaller cat roared again.

I faced the tigers, standing as tall as I could, shoulders back, convincing them I was larger than them.

It didn't work.

They decided to investigate. The large tiger went to my left; the smaller one went right.

I pointed the nose of the dragon-fliegt wing at the larger cat, swinging the tail towards the small one.

That slowed their advance. Each cat lowered their body and crept forward through the grass. They paused, near enough to reach me in three or four leaps.

Heart pounding, I filled my lungs to scare them by yelling. Steeled my muscles for a fight.

Metal scraped when the interior door near the back of the tiger's cage opened. A uniformed man appeared and called the cats. They didn't listen. Another uniformed man joined him, carrying two heavy items.

The first man slung the first object like a Frisbee at the big cat. It hit the tiger's hindquarters, and the beast whirled with a growl. The next one hit the second tiger on the shoulder. With a roar, the cat lunged toward the men. They raced into the cage entrance, clanged it shut, and left.

The Frisbees were meat.

The large tiger tore into its feast, laying on the ground, while the second padded back to the other piece. Both cats devoured the food.

I set down the equipment and eased toward the gate between the cats.

The small cat dropped its meat and growled.

I stopped.

The tiger, still on its feet, blocked my path to the exit.

I retreated to the wing, my only defense.

The small cat went back to its lunch. After the meal, both tigers cleaned their paws with great care. The big cat ignored me and retook his position in front of the cave. After the small cat lapped some water from the pond, I became interesting again. It came closer, circling the wing, tail twitching.

I crouched, keeping the wing between us, hoping to throw the ruined glider into the air and lunge out of the way when it attacked.

The big cat rolled on its side and slept. The smaller one swayed, tail sagging. Batting the dragon-suit leg-pouch with a few playful swats, the tiger sank into the grass and closed its eyes.

"Gabe." Alex motioned me to hurry from the cage's inner door. One official gripped his arm. The other swung the steel gate wide. "Quick."

I snuck past the tigers and flew through the gate. Relief flooded my body. Alex slapped me on the back while the zookeepers locked that gate and opened the next one into the zookeeper's prep area.

"Thank you." I extended my hand to the two keepers, but neither one took it.

Instead, the second man locked my arm behind me and pushed me toward the exit of the keeper's area.

In minutes, we were in the head zookeeper's office, a lackluster place. Two windows with mini-blinds let in sunshine. A medium-sized wooden desk with gouges and a worn finish occupied a third of the tiny office. Papers spilled out of the inbox next to a large desktop computer. Four rickety chairs sat against one wall. The keepers that manhandled Alex and me shoved us into two chairs. The zookeeper spoke little English.

"Why you come in this way to the zoo?" He linked his hands together like a bird.

"It's a long story." I crossed my arms. "Could I have a glass of water or something?"

"Nein. No. Answer first. Water later."

"Sir, would you call the Salzburg Polizei?" Alex glared at me. "Please ask for Captain Hans Bergmann. We are working for him at the moment."

"You are children," said one of the tiger's keepers. "Our Polizei do not need children to do their work."

I shifted forward on my seat. "On the contrary—"

The office door slammed open.

The head zookeeper flinched. "No interruptions."

"I do apologize," Willie said, "But these young men are in my custody. If you have questions, call Salzburg Polizei Headquarters."

"And talk with Captain Hans Bergmann?" said the man behind the desk.

"Exactly." Willie motioned for us to stand. "We must leave now."

"Your papers?" The tiger keeper reached out his hand.

Willie pulled out a badge and showed it to him and the head zookeeper.

"Very well." The head zookeeper looked down at a stack of papers on his desk. "You may go."

Chapter Twenty-Seven

Monatschlosschen

Alex told Willie and me about his close call in the rhinoceros' cage as we departed the Zoo on foot.

"I landed near the zookeeper's entrance," Alex said. "The rhino looked for food on the other side of the pond. When I landed, he charged through the water. I shouted for help and wrestled with my straps."

"Didn't the water slow it down?" I said.

Alex shook his head. "Sliced through it like it wasn't there."

"How'd you escape?" Willie picked up the pace.

"The keeper watched me land and raced into the inner cage. He unlocked the inner gate and cracked it open a couple of feet right after I shouted."

"You sure it wasn't a scream?" I smiled.

Alex punched my arm.

I laughed and pushed him.

"Settle down." Willie positioned himself between us. "Go on, Alex."

"I got free of the suit. The rhino exploded from the water at the same time, charging the remaining distance to the gate in seconds. I dove through, and the keeper slammed it shut."

"I'm sure the rhino was ticked." Willie led us onto another path.

"That's an understatement." Alex grinned. "When he couldn't gore me with his horn, he ripped the glider into shreds."

"I don't think the Phantom wants it back," Willie said.

"Anyway, the keeper hustled me out. I saw Gabe in the tiger's cage. Told the keeper in German that my brother needed help and you know the rest of the story."

"We're not done yet." I slowed as we neared Hellbrunn Castle. "We still have to get to the castle built in a month. By the way, Willie, who has Lightning?"

"Pete."

"We have to be alone." Alex handed the note from the cross to Willie. "You guys may need to analyze this as well."

"Yes. We'll do that." He stuffed the note in a pocket. "I may not be able to go to the Monatsschlösschen, but we have it under observation." Willie lifted a palm-sized device from his pocket. "And I can hear any conversation."

We passed onto the castle grounds and stopped.

"Willie, thanks for getting us out of there." I checked the time. "It's almost one o'clock. We were supposed to arrive at noon. If we've missed him, what do we do?"

"Meet me in the castle's parking lot."

"Roger." Alex nodded.

"Race you." I left Alex in my dust.

Partway to the mini-castle I slowed and walked. Alex matched my pace.

"I was thinking," I said.

"That's dangerous." Alex pointed to a path. "Let's go this way."

"What does he want with us now?" I trailed my brother, ignoring the slight.

"What do you mean? Doesn't he want to give us more info about the drop at Nannerl's Restaurant?"

"Maybe." I glanced around, wary of a trap. "This guy is an egomaniac. All he cares about is publicity, right? He might want to scare us, tell us his real reasons for doing this, or he might want to dupe us."

"Dupe us?"

"We're kids, not adults. He might think we won't put two and two together."

"I think the guy's crazy."

"Okay." I heaved a sigh and picked up the pace.

We rounded the corner and caught a full view of the castle. The Monatschlosschen was a golden-yellow three-story building. A stone archway beckoned the visitor to enter into a courtyard, surrounded by two one-story rooms on either side. Contrasting with the gold of the building were green shutters for the windows and a green entry door.

"Come on." I dashed under the arch.

Alex beat me to the doorway. I followed him into the building. We carefully examined each of the eight rooms, then moved up a floor. On the second floor, I rushed toward a corner room, stopping when I glanced into a middle room with a view of Salzburg. I held up my hand.

Alex placed a finger to his lips. He crept near the opposite side of the entry into the middle room. I peeked around the edge.

"Jonathan." My surprise came out more like a hiss than a whisper. "What are you doing here?" The entire floor was empty except for us.

"Sorry," he said. "I thought you two would have been here and left by now. Did you meet," he said, lowering his voice, "the Phantom?"

"No," Alex said.

"I thought as much." He looked out the window again.

"Have you seen him?" I asked.

"No. I've even gone up to the third floor. No Phantom. I haven't seen a person come in the building for ten minutes."

"Why aren't you with the others?" Alex said. "I'm sure Willie wants to know where you are as part of his team."

"I went to the Men's Room." Jonathan shrugged. "I realized that my German background might help if the Phantom spoke to you in German. That's why I'm here."

"Yeah, right." Alex looked away.

"Let me help." Jonathan faced us both. "I notice things you might not see."

"Like what?" Alex folded his arms.

"Like this envelope." Jonathan pulled an envelope out of his pocket. "Even though this is a People's Museum with exhibitions from historical to current times, I was able to spot an unusual envelope in an exhibit."

"Let me see." I reached out to take it.

"Not yet." Jonathan jerked his hand back. "Your brother owes me an apology."

The muscles on Alex's neck stood out as his jaw became hard.

"No apology is required." He crossed his arms on his chest. "I've told everyone that I think we have enough people on the team without you. If you want to show your value, hand it over."

"Don't make a scene." My eyes flicked back and forth between the Alex and Jonathan. "Someone could—"

A small child's footsteps echoed on the stairs, followed by the heavier steps of adults.

"—show up at any time." As the boy raced into the room, I held out my hand to Jonathan, fingers beckoning for the envelope.

"For *you*." Jonathan's surrendered his prize to me, eyes drilling into my brother. "You'll regret your crummy attitude later." Jonathan brushed past Alex and left.

I flipped the envelope over to see the Phantom's scrawl on the seal.

"Open it." Alex stepped closer.

I turned away from the tourists and opened the top. I tugged, noticing the hard, folded note card seemed stuck. I yanked, and metal pieces clunked onto the floor.

The little boy ran over to see what was going on.

Alex stooped, grabbed the objects, and shoved them in his pocket. "Willie's got to see this. Now." He ran for the exit.

I raced to catch him.

Chapter Twenty-Eight

Meeting

"Alex," Willie slapped my knee. "Why don't I take you for a ride?"

"What for?" I slouched in my chair at the Polizei station.

"You'll see." Willie stepped next to me, gripped me under the arm, and nearly lifted me himself until I was on my feet headed to the door.

"I don't feel like doing anything, but if you insist."

We left the others behind, climbed in Willie's Peugeot, and drove away. Willie glanced at me a few times before he spoke.

"You and Jenna seem to be having a tiff."

I sighed.

The sunlight sharpened the contrast between the different colors of green leaves and the trees lining the streets, brightened the manicured gardens with yellow, blue, purple, and red flowers, and highlighted every shade of the pedestrians' clothing.

I should be happy. Even though sunlight reflected off the Salzach River, short-sleeve weather felt good, and the cloudless sky promised exciting things, I wasn't.

"Can we talk about something else?" I kept drowning my thoughts in the scenery, but it felt distant like I was wrapped in glass and couldn't touch the world.

"Mate, this is serious. You're dragging down the team."

"I see. It's about the team. Not about me."

"Not true." Willie hit the turn-signal and changed lanes. "But I can't help if I don't understand." He stopped at a red light. "What's eatin' you? Spill the beans."

"Oh, nothing. I just lost my best friend, Thunder. And a girl I thought I knew seems like a different person."

"When times get rough, you need to think of others, not yourself." Willie accelerated and turned down a small street off the main highway.

"Easy to say." I turned away from Willie to scan the side of the road.

"Mate, I'm not saying it's easy and that you shouldn't care." Willie made another turn. At the end of the street were the bus station and the main train station. "But you should believe things will work out."

"How?" I said. "My dog's as good as dead and a girl I like more than anyone else doesn't want to talk with me."

"That's because you want it all right now. Your way." Willie turned onto a familiar street. "The big man upstairs might have different plans. Have you consulted Him?"

"Sometimes I don't think He listens."

"Really?" Willie slowed the car. "We have a special meeting ahead. I want you to be ready."

"Ready for what?" I sat straighter in my seat.

"I'm gonna let you figure that out, but remember—things aren't always what they seem. Life has lots of lessons. Keep the faith. In here." He tapped his chest. "You may not know it, but others are counting on you."

Willie eased into a parking slot in front of the Hauptbahnhof.

"Be back here in ten." He pointed to the entrance. "Go past the SPAR shop to Gleiss Nine. At the end of the platform on the right side, you'll see a man with a long white beard. His name is Lucilius. He's got some answers for you. Tell him Willie sent you."

"Why aren't you coming?" I opened the door.

"I'm watching the car." Willie's eyes twinkled. "You never know what can happen near a train station. Get moving."

A few people stood around on the platform for Track Nine. I spotted an old man, long white beard, dressed in baggy beggar's clothes on a bench away from the rest of the crowd. People averted their eyes as they passed him. A brown bag lay in his lap. He munched on a sandwich.

"Lucilius?" I stopped a few steps away.

"Who are you?"

"Willie sent me."

"I know Willie, but who are you?" The man set down his sandwich. His grey-green eyes focused on me with intense curiosity. I felt like he was digging deeper than what he saw.

"I'm Alex."

"Short for Alexander, right?"

"Good guess."

"More than a guess. Some say I'm better than Sherlock Holmes." He motioned to the open bench beside him.

I hesitated.

"Time's a' wasting." He pointed to the platform clock.

I sat.

"We can't have a close conversation if you're fifteen feet away. Sit next to me."

I scooted until his lunch bag brushed my leg.

"Good enough." He waited, watching the clock." "Got to catch the next train. It leaves in six minutes."

Chapter Twenty-Nine

Discovery

"Is that the final result?" Captain Bergmann grilled one of his investigators with Jonathan, Pete, and me in the office.

The subordinate's interruption of our discussion made me curious.

He thrust a report onto the Captain's desk, excited about his research.

"Sir, we've pinpointed the perpetrator's identity and validated our musical analysis by our department and in coordination with the Mozart Museum. They are the experts."

"I don't like the conclusion." Bergmann rubbed his jaw after scanning the report. "How could we miss this earlier in the investigation?"

"The Phantom is an expert in forging documents." The man retrieved his papers and rifled through the pages. "Page twelve," he slid the report back on the desk, "summarizes the musical scores and the suspect's superb musical skills. The Museum's analysts are the best in the world regarding Mozart's work."

"Captain," I said, "Who is he? And does this include the manuscripts we just found?"

"Yes and no." He picked up a pen, twirling it in his fingers. He jabbed it at the messenger. "I thought the best Mozart analyst won't arrive in Salzburg from his annual vacation until tomorrow. Correct?"

"But sir," the man spread his hands wide, "you wanted the report today."

"The man we're hunting down is Jürgen Christian Wilhelm Theophilus Meier." Bergmann tapped the papers, ignoring the messenger. "He was born January 17, 1956, exactly 200 years after Mozart."

"He has one of the names of Mozart." Jonathan tilted his head. "Theophilus."

"How do you know that?" Bergmann narrowed his eyes.

"I've studied Mozart a lot."

"Hmm." The Captain jotted a note. "Jürgen Meier's face marred him for life. His birthmark set him apart from others. His sister, who died early, made it worse by scratching that side of his face, mauling him with barbed wire during his younger years."

"Whoa." Pete shook his head. "Bad."

"Very bad." Bergmann sighed. "We've got the doctor's reports. His terrible family and ridicule at school caused him to be a delinquent. However, his piano teacher recognized budding genius."

"So he's as good as Mozart?" I lifted Lightning to my lap.

"Not quite." Bergmann picked up the report. "According to our sources, the boy vanished at age thirteen, angry and deluded. His last written words declared he was the new Mozart and he would have revenge."

"Sir," the forgotten messenger said, "that could be why our Museum can't confirm the second score isn't Mozart's music in his handwriting."

"I want a trustworthy report. We must be certain. Redo the tests. Consult with Vienna's handwriting experts and musicologists. If each confirms the Phantom's composition rivals Mozart's work, the news will rock the music world."

Chapter Thirty

Surprise

I fidgeted. The man didn't say anything but kept eating his lunch.

"You have a question to ask?" Lucilius set down his water bottle.

"Question?" I tilted my head. "Do I have a question? Willie sent me to talk to you."

"Did he say talk?" Lucilius crumpled his empty bag.

"He said you would have some answers."

"I see." He got up, walked to a trashcan, deposited the bag, and returned. "Answers usually come when someone asks a question."

I frowned. Lucilius spoke in riddles. *Was he making fun of me?*

"We have three minutes." The man tipped back his water bottle. "I'm accepting a package upon the train's arrival, so I can't be late." His eyes locked onto mine. He raised his eyebrows.

"Well..." I thought hard. What could I ask? "I'm missing my dog. Do you know where he is?"

"Did you know if you reversed the letters of dog, it spells god?"

"What kind of a person are you?" My eyes stung and nose began to drip. I sniffed loudly. "My dog is gone. He might be dead or hurt bad. We were in a train wreck in Vienna."

A local train pulled into the station at our platform.

The man dug in his baggy pants and pulled out a clean white tissue. He held it out to me. "Your dog is gone, but is God gone?" He stood, ambled to the recycling bin, dropped in his bottle, walked back and knelt beside me. "Be strong and courageous. Time for me to go."

I blew my nose.

Lucilius headed to the last door of the train. A porter appeared next to him and handed him a letter. He accepted the envelope, nodded and climbed a few steps into the train. The whistle blew, and the train picked up speed. Lucilius, half hidden by the door, knelt and reached for something inside. Standing, he released the object, pointed toward me, and smiled. A dark shape leaped to the platform.

"Thunder." I shot out of my seat like I'd been fired from a cannon.

Thunder's barking brought glares from several German bystanders, but I didn't care. We met in the middle of the platform and I flung my arms around his neck.

"Thunder, where have you been?"

His slurpy tongue covered my face as I rubbed his side. Then I buried my head in his furry neck and hugged him hard enough to make him squirm.

Thunder began to pull away, but I tackled him and we wrestled on the platform. Boy and dog, rolling on the tiles. A few minutes later, I patted his side and stood.

"I'm glad you're home, boy." I tickled his ears.

Chapter Thirty-One

Dinner Is Served

A crowd filled the Zipfer Bier Stuben restaurant full to the brim. Chairs scraped as customers settled back to enjoy their food and fellowship at the end of another day.

Our investigative team, brought up-to-date on the latest reports on the Phantom, sat in a corner booth as specified in the suspect's note. The directions stated that three uniformed Polizei must sit near the entrance to the Restaurant, off to one side.

The Zipfer's atmosphere was pleasant. Smiling people in quiet conversation and tables filled with food and drink. But the place looked more like a boisterous beer hall than a family restaurant. Cheap hangings decorated the walls. Several items hung from the ceiling, such as bretzels, brewery signs, paper hangings, and a few lighting fixtures. A quaint Austrian establishment.

"Why are we here?" Jonathan asked.

"The Phantom said he wanted his first ransom installment at the restaurant next to the Mozart widow's house." Willie showed Jonathan the note again. "Haven't you looked at this yet?"

"The red tablecloths, small dining areas, and wooden furniture don't seem to be up to the Phantom's standards," I said. "He likes to go big."

"But my name wasn't on any of the four metal pieces with the Monatschlosschen note." Jonathan fiddled with the note. "It had Gabe, Alex, Pete, and Jenna's names."

"The Phantom won't know the difference." Willie slid the note into a pocket. "He wasn't on the Untersberg or at the Monatschlosschen."

Thunder lay at Alex's feet, but his ears were up. His head swiveled, taking in the entire restaurant as though he was searching for the Phantom. Lightning yawned, curling up on my lap.

"Two minutes left." Pete pointed at the clock. "Shouldn't he be here?"

"This isn't the right place." Jonathan flipped the note back toward Willie. "You detectives don't know what you're doing."

"Nannerl Mozart lived in this building above this restaurant." Willie snatched the note off the table and read it out-loud. "Meet me at 6:00 PM with the million Austrian Schillings for the girl as a good will gesture. Since we are family in Salzburg, as good brothers and sisters come to the Mozart widow's building and place a shopping bag with the ransom in the fancy wooden umbrella stand, next to the carved wooden pillar. You'll find directions inside for our evening adventure if you can read them through your tears."

"More than one widow links to Mozart's family life." Jonathan's teeth showed when he smiled. "Not only was his sister Nannerl a widow, but Mozart's widow moved back to Salzburg, *next* to Tomaselli's Café. Not over the restaurant."

"Then why did he include the phrase 'as good brothers and sisters' if he meant his wife?"

"Tomaselli's is too fancy for that low-life to strike," Pete said.

167

Thunder's back stiffened. A low growl left his throat.

The door at the front of the restaurant swung wide as a man, wearing a hat jammed over his head and a long coat, rushed in. He seemed to be the Phantom's height and build. He headed directly for the umbrella stand next to the wooden column.

The three policemen jumped to their feet, rushed past startled customers, and nabbed him right after he slid something into the stand.

The man whirled, losing his hat. His face had no mutilated birthmark.

One Polizei pinned the man's arms behind him, shoving him against the wall while another barked orders in German. The third policeman darted toward the object the man brought inside.

A stone shattered the main window and crashed into a wine bottle two tables away. Shouts and screams filled the air as guests stampeded for the door.

I threw Lightning toward the action, slid out of my seat and was on my way to the front when an explosion shot flames into the air.

Thunder and Alex raced to the German held by the Polizei. Thunder's menacing growl made the man cower.

Lightning danced around the umbrella stand, now splintered into smoldering pieces of wood.

"That's a distraction, mate." Willie honed in on the man under custody. "And this isn't our man."

"I'm telling you—he's at the other restaurant," Jonathan said. "We should be at Café Tomaselli."

"Where is that?" Pete asked.

"Follow me." Jonathan sprinted to the door.

"Careful," Willie called out to us as we bolted for the door, dogs trailing. "Watch out for a setup."

"He won't fool me twice." I kept moving, nearly knocking over a man with a pipe. "Entschuldigung," I blurted in German, apologizing for brushing against his jacket.

Outside the restaurant, I located Jonathan and raced to make up the distance with the rest of the gang on my tail. The dogs galloped beside me. In a few turns, we neared the café.

Jonathan held out a palm.

We slid to a stop.

"Do we have anything that resembles the package we left in the other restaurant?" Jonathan said.

We stared at him.

"We need something—quick." Jonathan jabbed a finger toward a woman carrying a large shopping bag. "Gabe, snatch that bag and give it to me."

I hesitated.

"Now." He glanced at his watch. "The Polizei will explain it to her."

I dashed across the street.

"Polizei." I jostled the lady, stole the purse, and bounded away, apologizing as I ran. "Entschuldigung" I returned to the group and threw it at Jonathan's like it was a hot coal burning my hand.

Jonathan flew up the steps into the café, elbowing his way past the crowd to the interior.

"Go after him," Alex yelled.

The crowd stepped aside as we jammed our way into the dining area, a few people behind Jonathan. Thunder and Lighting wormed their way to either side of us.

"Classy restaurant," Pete yelled in my ear as we crossed the door's threshold.

"That's it." I pointed past the fancy dining room to the umbrella stand situated next to a carved post of mahogany. Stairs spiraled behind the post.

Jonathan pushed forward to place the package in the stand when a familiar figure appeared.

Several detonations took place, but not near the Phantom. My ears rang. People screamed. Black smoke billowed from several parts of the restaurant.

Alex and I tugged Thunder and Lightning by their collars when they barked, straining to attack.

Waving my finger in a circle, Alex picked up the cue. We both signaled our dogs what to do. They split up, stalking the attacker from both sides.

The Phantom snagged Jonathan and held a pistol to his head.

"One wrong move and the boy dies. Everyone leave." He yelled in English and German. Customers ran, choking on the thick, stinging smoke.

The rest of the team stood in shock.

"Call the dogs off."

Thunder growled.

"Do it." He cocked the pistol held next to Jonathan's head.

"Gabe, Alex." Jonathan's Adam's apple bounced as he swallowed hard. He spoke with terror in his voice. "Help me."

I whistled and called the dogs back. Each one's ears lay flat on their skulls, teeth bared.

"Defeated again?" The Phantom laughed. "It seems the Polizei can't understand my game plan. No Jenna, you lose Jonathan. Don't cross me again or the townspeople will pay a terrible price. Do exactly as I demand. Then we'll have a ball at the palace tonight. Be at the front gate by ten."

The Phantom lowered the pistol to the middle of Jonathan's back, joined the crowd, and left through a side door.

Chapter Thirty-Two

Armoring Up

"Jenna, what are you doing here?" I grabbed the first seat at the Polizei Conference room table, settling Lightning in my lap and my drink on a coaster. "I thought you hated Alex."

"Orders." Jenna tilted her head toward Captain Bergmann.

Pete, sitting beside his sister, shrugged and sighed.

Alex stepped through the door, stiffening when he saw Jenna. He sat opposite her at the table, jaw muscles twitching. Thunder lay at his feet.

Willie entered and surveyed the silent room. "Seems like we're having a real lively time, Cap'n."

Bergmann, sitting at the head of the wooden conference room table, broke his focus on the stack of papers in front of him. "The Phantom specified by name that all four kids be at the fortress tonight." He smiled. "Their morale is your responsibility."

"Guess I'll be taming the tigers tonight." Willie slid into a chair next to Agent Gardener.

The conference table, surrounded by twelve executive chairs, glowed a polished amber color. Behind Captain Hans Bergmann was a map of Salzburg with red X's where the Phantom attacked us or left notes. To his right, angled to allow everyone in the room to see, was a white board with a list of clues.

"Let's review our progress and plans." The Captain stood, moved his chair to his left, and pointed to the clues listed on the board. "At each stage of this operation, when a clue was left, someone or something was hurt…"

The conference room door clicked open, and a man tried to sneak into the room.

"Ah." Bergmann tilted his head and raised an eyebrow. "Agent Wilcox, we're happy you could join us."

"Sorry, boss." Wilcox eyed the floor. "I was—"

"Don't." Bergmann held up a finger. "Wipe the rest of your dinner off of your mouth and sit next to Agent Gardener. By me." The Captain sighed. "As I was saying, at each clue, someone was hurt or in this last case, kidnapped. That would be Jonathan."

"What were the casualties in the two restaurants?" I stroked Lightning's fur as he sat on my lap.

The Captain shook his head. "At the Zipfer Bier Stuben, the explosion sent shards from the umbrella stand into several customers. Five went to the emergency room. The fist-sized rock didn't hit anyone, but the plate glass window pieces wounded nine customers and all three policemen. Nothing serious. At Tomaselli's Café, the story is different. Three people are in serious condition at the hospital, one in the critical care ward, and ten to fifteen suffered from smoke inhalation from the upstairs restaurant."

"Seems like the Polizei stakeout didn't work." Jenna propped her chin on an elbow, glancing with a smirk at Alex.

"More than that." Pete ran a hand through his hair and clenched it into a fist. "I'm tired of the Phantom being one step ahead of us for the entire investigation. We've failed to get anything right or catch him, even though we know him by sight."

"Kid." Agent Gardener's posture straightened from a slouch. "The Polizei knows what it's doing."

"Right," I said. "Captain Bergmann does, but you two agents haven't stopped anything. And you lost about $90,000 in the Bier Stuben."

"Why you snotty little American." Wilcox smacked the tabletop.

"Easy, mate." Willie glared at him. "Don't get stroppy. That little Yank's done better than you."

"Really?" Wilcox sneered. "Did you know he stole a lady's shopping bag?"

"You stole a lady's bag?" Willie looked like he would eat me for dinner.

"Not my fault." I opened my palms face up. "We didn't have a decoy package for the ransom and Jonathan—"

"Enough." Bergmann dropped a pile of documents on the table. "No more bickering."

"Each clue has either led us astray or put us in danger." Bergmann rose and pointed to the whiteboard. "None have been more than a lead to the next meeting or clue until his final note from Tomaselli's Café." He listed four points on the board below a short paragraph. "Wilcox, read these out loud since you want to shoot off your mouth."

"You have failed again." Wilcox read with distaste. "Baloney. What does that guy—"

"Keep reading." Bergmann's voice was flat, threatening.

"No million Austrian Schillings ransom for the girl means someone will die in darkness tonight." Wilcox rolled his eyes. "No ten million Austrian Schillings for Mozart's manuscript and the girl's death will be at fifty-five minutes after midnight in honor of Amadeus Mozart's time of death." Wilcox sighed. "Isn't that lovely?"

"Cut the wisecracks." The Captain drilled him with his eyes.

Wilcox nodded. "You cannot kill me. As Mozart's reincarnation, my time will not come until 5 December. No matter how many you send against me, you will not win. Follow my instructions to the letter or none will survive." He paused.

"This guy's crazy," Pete whispered to me.

I nodded, sipping my hot chocolate, listening to Wilcox.

"Here are the four points:"

"1. 10:00 p.m. – Send Gabe, Alex, Pete, and Jenna with my ransom divided between them.

2. No Polizei, detectives, or other police forces may enter my Festung."

"How can we beat this guy without some help?" Jenna straightened, facing Bergmann.

"Patience." The Captain motioned for Wilcox to continue.

"If my team or I spot any observers or snipers, the children die.

3. Conduct an open-air Mozart concert at midnight in my square, the Mozartplatz. Fill the square to overflowing, lights ablaze, that I might see my glory.

4. At fifty minutes after midnight, play my composition as the finale and look to the Festung's tower for a surprise."

"We don't have much time." Alex rubbed his forehead. "How are we going to catch him?"

"What detective training have you tin lids been getting?" Willie pointed at Alex and me with his chin. "That could make the difference."

"We trained with our dogs at a military K-9 course," Alex said. "And I learned how to pick locks better. Gabe learned how to handcuff people fast."

"We both learned several types of self-defense and taking down of opponents." I shrugged. "I could even take down Wilcox if I wanted to do that."

"You little whippersnapper." Wilcox slammed a fist into his open hand.

The Captain patted Wilcox's shoulder until he leaned back in his seat. "That'll be enough, Agent Wilcox." Bergmann stepped to the door, opened it, and told his secretary to pre-position some sandwiches and drinks in the Polizei's squad room. "Now, let's discuss weapons."

"Now you're talking." Willie took out a pen and a pad. "Here's what I think they need." He scribbled a list and handed it to the Captain.

The Captain took the list, glanced at it, and a smile flitted across his face. He handed the list to Agent Gardener. "Get these items and meet us in thirty minutes in the squad briefing room."

"How about electronic listening devices?" Wilcox leaned back into the executive chair. "We can't expect them to solve this on their own." His lips curved into a half-smile.

"Excellent." Bergmann raised his eyebrows at Wilcox. "What are you waiting for? Go get them. We should have two available."

Wilcox made a noisy exit, bumping roughly into Alex's chair on the way out.

"Get closer." The Captain waved us up to the white board. Willie stood on one side, and he was on the other. "Agent Gretzke has a unique plan."

"Sit over here in your two teams." He wrote Pete and me on one side and Alex and Jenna on the other.

We stood and moved to our new seats. Jenna and Alex dragged their feet.

"Come on. We don't have all day." Willie guided the slowpokes into their places, sitting Alex next to me.

"Does it have to be this way?" Jenna wrinkled her nose, her eyes flicking to Alex.

"Missy," Willie said, "I don't know what's between you two, but we have a maniac who's trying to kill people, and he's almost succeeded several times." He pointed at Alex. "You may not like your partner, but when you split up at the train station you set up a pattern that the Phantom will recognize."

"But what about my brother and me going together?" Jenna's lower lip pushed out in a pout. "We're family, and they're family."

"Are you a whinger now?" Willie's smile lit up his eyes. "Always whining and complaining?"

"No." Jenna shook her head. "But he—"

"It'll be all right," Alex said. "We can work together as a *detective* team, can't we?"

I snickered.

Alex punched me in the arm.

"Stop it." I rubbed the spot he hit. I changed my voice to a higher pitch to imitate Jenna. "You might hurt me." I batted my eyelashes at her.

"Mates." Willie stopped Jenna from jumping out of her seat. "Focus."

Bergmann pulled down another Salzburg map. "Here's a helicopter's view of the Hohensalzburg fortress layout." He tapped a wooden pointer's rubber tip on the map. "Memorize the details to make Willie's plan work."

"We've lost about six hours," Willie said. "The Phantom shortened our evening from his first deadline of dawn tomorrow, to fifty-five minutes after midnight tonight."

"Isn't there something significant about that time?" I scratched my head.

"Yes." Captain Bergmann tapped the table. "That's the time of day Mozart died."

"That guy's a lost cause," Pete said.

"He must have at least one accomplice, if not ten or more." I pointed at the chart. "This castle is humongous."

"The fortress is extensive," the Captain said, "but with expert spotters, the Phantom can keep us out for three hours."

"And we've experienced his bomb-making skills." Black soot still coated Pete's clothes from the Tomaselli Café bombing.

"Here are the main entrance points." The Captain tapped the rubber tip on the paper. "The walking path and road to the primary castle entrance, the supply train approach, the funicular or cable railway, and the walking path that leads to the upper docking station of the funicular."

176

"The lot of you must enter by the walking path." Willie traced the path with his finger. "I don't expect a cakewalk. Be alert for traps. Take in details. This will be hard yakka."

"Hard..." Bergmann's eyebrows lifted in a question.

"Work," I said. "We know that."

"Take torches and use the special tools we'll give you in your backpacks." Willie winked at me.

"Like what?" Pete said. "Do we get special James Bond tools?"

Wilcox strolled in. "Gotcha covered, Captain." He held out two small microphones and wires.

"Thanks." Captain Bergmann set down his pointer. "These tiny microphones will record conversations. But you need to study the chart closely in the squad room to make this all work. That's where we'll outfit you. Let's go."

We stood. Willie made me leave my hot chocolate in the conference room. Wilcox led us further into the maze of offices away from the public areas.

Rows of chairs faced a raised stage area in the squad room. A podium was on the stage to the left, a white projector screen dropped from the ceiling by the wall behind it, and a projector sat on a table. Sandwiches, coffee, sodas, water, tea, and desserts sat on a table near the entryway or back of the room.

"Grab a sandwich, a drink, and a dessert." Captain Bergmann motioned at the table. "It's eight o'clock. Mission prep is as follows: first thirty minutes—memorization of the Festung pictures, second thirty minutes—familiarization with your equipment, and the final thirty minutes is for questions before we drive you to the release point."

Sandwich in hand, I sat next to Pete on one side of the aisle and Jenna sat with Alex on the other side. Jenna purposefully put an empty seat between them. In a half hour, Willie, Agent Gardener, Agent Wilcox, and the Captain discussed over a hundred special features in the fortress, including the towers, the cannons, the military defense architecture, and rooms of special note. These included the organ room, the cistern, the State Rooms, the weapons room, the torture chamber, and the chapel.

Briefing completed, I followed Willie and the others to the equipment room. A female police officer named Greta and her two assistants outfitted us. Wilcox and Gardener spoke with the Captain and left.

"Microphone." Greta handed one to Jenna and me. "You'll be fitted in a moment. And here are walkie-talkies; your communications equipment."

"Keep that commo gear close," Willie rapped me on the head with his knuckles. "Top priority in battle."

"Knives, zip strips for handcuffs, and tiny flashlights." Greta laid the gear on a counter. "The flashlights can be used as a weapon in a fight."

"Backpacks." An assistant waved us over to his area. "Each contains little things like super-strong masking tape, scissors, energy bars, water, rope, gloves, paper, pens, pencils, and one-quarter of the ransom in marked bills."

"Jackets." The other assistant eyed each of us and selected special Polizei protective jackets to wear. "They aren't bulletproof, but can help in rough and tumble situations."

"Jenna." Willie pulled her aside. "Here's the pen camera. They have just one because of their expense." Willie operated the camera while Jenna watched. "Works in all kinds of light. We'll get the photos after the mission. Try it." He gave it to her.

The police techs and armorer packed and fitted our equipment.

"Last chance for a pit stop." Willie pointed toward the restrooms.

"Let's go." I tilted my head toward Alex.

Alex shook his head. "What am I, a girlfriend? I'm good."

When I finished, I got Alex to one side of the group. "Do you still have the key we got from G?"

"Yes." The key hung from a cord around his neck. He pulled it out. "Why?"

178

"You've carried it all this time and didn't use it once." I held out my hand. "Let me carry it for a while."

"Why do you always want my stuff?" He rolled his eyes.

"What's going on?" Willie said. "Clandestine arrangements?"

"My brother won't share." I glared at him. "He's always got to have it all."

"Mates, you're ripping each other apart." Willie leaned against a wall. "We're a team." He looked at Alex. "Aren't we?"

"All right." Alex whipped the key off of his neck and handed it to me. "You'd better have it when I need it."

I smiled and sang the words from "I'll Be There," a number one song sung by Michael Jackson.

"Enough." Willie covered his ears as though in pain. He told me to get the rest of the gang and follow him into a small testing room.

"What's up?" I sat at a desk.

"We've taken care of most of your preparation." Willie sat opposite me and motioned Alex, Jenna, and Pete to sit. "Are we missing something?"

Was this a test? I didn't want to fail on this one.

Everyone was silent for almost half a minute. Willie kept looking at each of us.

"I think we're ready." I gave a thumbs-up. "Let's go."

Willie shook his head. "Try harder. You've prepared physically, mentally, and somewhat emotionally." He glanced at Alex and Jenna. "What's left?"

Alex's eyebrows came together for a second as he thought. His tight fist supported his chin.

Jenna sat ramrod straight in her seat, eyes avoiding Willie's gaze.

Pete licked his lips and stared at the floor.

"I've got it." Alex's hunched shoulders relaxed a little. "We haven't taken time to turn this over to the Man upstairs."

"Bingo." Willie slapped him on the back. "He can take care of anything you've failed to do. What made you realize the answer?"

179

"Tonight's a life or death situation." Alex took a slow breath. "A lot of pressure has been on my shoulders since the train wreck." His face went through a few changes. "But I've realized that I don't have to worry if I talk to God about my problems. He can take care of the issues."

"Most troops going into combat appreciate the commander who provides an opportunity to settle their soul business before taking action." Willie smiled. "Everything works more smoothly. And I know all of you care about one another – you might want to show it better than you have recently."

Willie held out his hands, waiting for Jenna and me to place our hands in his. I took Pete's hand. He reached for Alex. Jenna stiffened as she noticed Alex's outstretched hand toward her.

Chapter Thirty-Three

The Assault

Waiting in the Polizei van for the exact time to walk up the road was like waiting to ride the newest and best roller coaster at an amusement park. My heart pounded.

"Final instructions." Captain Bergmann, standing near the side door, leaned into the dim light of the interior. "Under no circumstances leave your partner. Police teams work in pairs, not solo. Understood?"

"Roger," I said. Everyone else did the same.

"And whatever happens, you have small walkie-talkies to stay in touch." We all nodded. "Believe me, if we could do this any other way, we would. I don't think he'll hurt you; he's after Salzburg's people. He's using you as game pieces."

Agent Gardener, the driver, tapped his watch. "Time."

"We'll monitor everything that happens and bust in through infiltration if we think you're in any danger." Bergmann focused us one more time. "Agent Gretzke will lead that team and ensure you have backup."

"Willie knows how to show up at exactly the right time," I said.

We all glanced at each other, remembering Willie showing up every time we needed him during the Berchtesgaden Salt Mines ordeal a few months ago.

"Fifteen minutes to ten." I jumped out of the van. "We'll need to walk fast to make it to the main entrance by ten."

The dogs leaped out, waggling their tails and sniffing the air. Jenna, Pete, and Alex followed.

I didn't wait but whistled for Lightning to follow and broke into a trot.

"This isn't a race," Jenna said.

"I'm not racing." I tossed the words out as I picked up speed for the first set of stairs. Ten outdoor staircases preceded the first gate, or Sperrbogen, the 1st Guarded Archway. I planned to get a little distance in first, then slow down to a steady climb.

"Wait," Pete said. Being a little chunkier, he couldn't keep up if I went too fast. "You aren't acting like my teammate."

"I know." I slowed my pace until he was beside me. "I didn't want to be walking with the Ice Queen and Mr. Closed Mouth."

"They aren't that bad," Pete said. "But we're all supposed to be one team."

"We're not in the Fortress yet." I patted Pete's shoulder and took the first staircase two steps at a time. "The Ice Queen did seem to thaw after the prayer."

Lightning shot past me to the top of the stairs. He turned and raised an ear.

"Go ahead." I waved at him to let him go further. "But stay in sight."

Lightning flew up the hill. Then a black shadow brushed past me as Thunder raced to catch his playmate. He could take stairs five at a time without slowing down.

"I wasn't sure she was going to take Alex's hand." Pete climbed the staircase one stair at a time.

"Up and down." I faced back up the hill when Pete reached the top of the stairs. "That's their relationship."

We talked about our different viewpoints of our siblings until we arrived at the 1st Guarded Archway, a gateway with walls several feet thick that narrowed the road running through it. A coral colored sign permanently fixed to the gray concrete wall told us the archway was built in 1642.

"What's this?" Pete snagged an envelope half-hidden by the plaque.

"Open it." I got by his shoulder. "Seven minutes left."

"Something more than paper is inside." Pete ripped through the seal, pulled out paper, and several objects fell to the roadway, clinking on the pavement.

"I'll get them." I bent to pick up the metal items. "Read."

"Enclosed is your Get Out of Jail Free card and playing pieces for this game of chance. Each piece has a name on it corresponding to a plaque in the Festung where your next clue lies. One piece per player. Time is short. Split up to meet the deadline or the girl will die. Your time starts at ten o'clock at the next gate."

"Six minutes." Pete glanced at his watch.

Jenna and Alex showed up, walking on the wide edges of either side of the road. The gate's walls cut off the edges, causing them to get closer to each other.

I explained the note.

"Where's my token?" Jenna held out her hand.

"We have to be at the next gate in five minutes." Alex pointed up the hill.

"We'll divide the tokens there," I said. "Run."

We raced up the hill, both dogs running back and forth, excited by the activity.

Rounding a corner, I sprinted toward the arch in a tall white building, the 2nd Guarded Archway. A massive wooden door fitted to the arch blocked the way. The door, split in two at the middle, was shut. A smaller, single lane roadway bordered by two rock walls and tall bushes on either side, one against the castle and the other closer to the town became our approach.

I glanced at my digital watch when I arrived. Thirty seconds to spare. But Jenna and Pete struggled to run after climbing ten sets of stairs.

"Hurry." I cupped my hands around my mouth like a megaphone. "Twenty seconds."

Thunder and Lightning raced back down the hill, barking to encourage our friends to pick up the pace. Ten seconds left.

The bells of the carillon in the Altstadt clanged out a metal melody.

"That's not supposed to be happening." Jenna gulped in some air. "The exhibition times for the carillon to play are—" The left Archway door popped open an inch. We waited for further movement. Nothing.

"Someone has to go through," Pete said.

"I'll go." Jenna pulled the door out and ducked inside.

We followed, searching for the person who unlocked the gate. The ticket area was empty.

I tried the ticket office door. "No dice."

"Keep going." Pete stepped toward the next gate.

"Hold on." Alex grabbed his jacket. "Gabe, show us the tokens. I want to pick which one I get."

I fished the metal pieces out of my pocket and laid them on the ground. A racecar, an iron, a shoe, and a Scottie dog.

"Let's choose which one we want." Jenna scooped up the racecar.

"Hey," I said, "That's my favorite piece."

"Mine too." Pete held out his hand.

Jenna backed away. "I picked it out first." She stuffed the token in her pocket.

"Whatever." Alex took the iron and walked to the next gate.

Pete and I swept up our pieces, a shoe for me and the Scottie for Pete. We jogged to catch up.

"We're going to have to work this together," I said. "Perhaps you two would care to be part of the team with us?"

"We are a part of the team." Jenna didn't slow but picked up her pace.

Thunder and Lightning stopped short of the third gate. Something bothered them. The road narrowed again from a comfortable two-car width to a one car passageway with wrought iron fences on either side. Thunder's half-hearted growl was punctuated by his snuffling about on the ground. Lightning trotted to the edge of the archway, then retreated.

The slam of a wooden door caught us off-guard. We faced the second archway and its closed doors.

"The Phantom knows we're here." Jenna sighed.

"What's bothering the dogs?" Pete got closer to the third archway. Standing at the edge of the entrance, Pete's eyes closed, his face a mask of concentration.

I rushed next to him and heard a faint sound, like a person yelling for help.

"Who is that?" Alex asked. "Do you recognize her?"

"High-pitched like a girl, but I can't make out exact words." I strained to hear.

"All is lost." Jenna nodded. "She's saying that in German."

"She's spooking the dogs. Maybe it's connected to our tokens." I lifted the shoe from my pocket. The beam of my mini-flashlight caught something. "Did you know my iron has an initial on it?" I extended my hand to show the others. "J."

"Interesting." Pete pulled the Scottie dog out of his pocket. "A."

Jenna and Alex checked theirs.

"G," Jenna said.

"P." Alex completed the four letters. "Our first initials."

Jenna handed me the racecar. "Have fun." She took the iron, examining the metal object for a clue.

I flipped the car on its back. Inside, the word *Zeughaus* stood out.

"The shoe has the word *Schüttkasten*." Pete rubbed his forehead. "I think those are close to each other."

"I have *State Rooms* written inside," Alex said.

"And the iron has *Kapelle*." She gave a quick shake of her head. "That's located in the Altes Schloss, or old castle, along with the state rooms."

"To reach our designated spots, each of us has to pass the Zeughaus." I tugged on Pete's shirt. "Together."

"We've wasted fifteen minutes." Alex hit the glow button on his watch. "We can't stop with you if we want to explore all four areas. Jenna and I will search the Altes Schloss. That's why we have two people on each team."

"What about that girl's voice?" Jenna's hands were on her hips. "We have to do something to save her."

Let's solve these riddles quick." I strode toward past the initial arch of the Burgermeister Archway.

The Burgermeister tower straddled the walkway, creating a stone tunnel about twenty paces long and fifteen wide. An entry and exit arch at either end enclosed a high ceiling in between. A few small window-like holes decorated the sides.

Lightning paused a foot short of the entrance arch. He whined.

"Quit acting afraid." I scooped him into my arms, shot a glance at Pete, and strode forward into the tunnel.

"I'm coming." Pete swung his flashlight ahead, broke into a run to catch me, but halfway in settled into a walk.

Jenna and Alex followed at a slower pace. Thunder's growls filled the small stone space when they entered.

I stepped into the open after passing the second archway of this gate, glancing back to see the others.

Pete yelled and leaped forward. Passageway lights sprang to life.

I whirled around. A curtain of burning oil spilled through slit openings in the roof of the exit archway.

Pete sank to his knees, grabbing his left hand. Flames blossomed on his left sleeve and shoulder.

I jumped forward, ripped the coat and his backpack off his body. Pete cried out in agony when I jerked his coat past his left hand.

Inside of the entrance arch, a metal gate slammed into the ground.

"Thunder, get back." The tunnel magnified Alex's yell. He and Jenna, barely visible through the curtain of oil, were three-quarters of the way through the tunnel.

"Don't slip in that oil." Jenna's hand flew to Alex's arm.

"Run," I yelled.

A spear flew from one of the tunnel side windows, catching Jenna's backpack and spinning her around.

Pete moaned and rolled on the ground, grabbing his injured hand.

Alex pushed Thunder toward the first archway and kept Jenna upright by grabbing her backpack.

"Climb." He shoved her toward the gate.

Heated oil gushed out of the overhead slits, flaring into flames while streaming across the concrete toward the trio.

The metal gate looked like a checkerboard with some open squares and some closed. Alex slung Thunder on his left shoulder, stuck his foot into a hole inches off the ground, and searched for a higher handhold. A shoulder-height opening worked for his left hand, but Thunder's weight and the pack made it awkward. His right hand groped for an opening. Nothing.

Jenna wedged her feet into holes a few feet from the ground, near Alex. She found handholds several feet out of Alex's reach and clamped on.

"Put your arm around my waist." Jenna looked down at Alex.

"I'll pull you off."

"Do it."

The flames reached his one foot on the ground.

He jammed his foot near Jenna's, then grabbed her waist with his free arm.

"This won't work long," he said.

"Have a better idea?" Jenna's body, strained by Alex and Thunder's weight, sagged from the safety of the gate toward the flaming oil that covered the floor. "I can't hang on."

"Get rid of your pack," Alex said. "One shoulder at a time."

Jenna let go with her left hand. "My right hand feels like it's tearing." She yelled and wiggled out of the left strap, hand slamming into the gate and bouncing off as the backpack's weight dragged her away.

"I'm falling." She screamed as her right hand lost its grip.

Chapter Thirty-Four

Loose Cannon

Stuck outside the bars by Pete, my breath caught as Jenna's eyes, wide with terror, locked onto Alex and her backpack slammed into the oil.

"Don't quit." My brother, hanging by one arm, stopped her fall. He struggled to lift her closer to the metal grate. "Stop swinging your arms."

Pete groaned in pain on the ground next to me. My gaze darted between him and the final seconds left for Jenna, Alex, and Thunder. *Do something.* I spotted a bulky shape by the exit arch. A box? No. A wheelbarrow. I heard faint words pass between Jenna and Alex.

"Tighten…muscles." He strained to talk. "Lean…forward."

"I'm slipping." Jenna gritted her teeth.

"I know." Alex gritted his teeth. "If I fall…"

I dashed for the wheelbarrow, catching glimpses through the gaps in the sheets of oil pouring down.

"What are you talking about?" Jenna shouted.

"I'll push...you up." Alex's arms shook. "I'll try...save Thunder."

"You can't. I won't let you." Tears choked her words.

"Jenna...I've learned—"

"Alex." I charged at the flaming oil curtain. "Use this." I lifted the bottom of the wheelbarrow. The handles pointed toward the ceiling at an angle, making the wheelbarrow like a motorcycle doing a wheelie using the front tire instead of the back one. I shoved the metal bulk toward the curtain of fire and jumped back.

The oil spilling from the ceiling slowed to drips as the wheelbarrow flew past, but in seconds it fell back on its legs, bouncing and skidding to the right.

I shook my head when it wobbled from one side to the other. *It won't reach them.*

The right support smacked into Jenna's backpack, flipping it upside down. Lurching back to the left, the wheelbarrow skidded into the metal grate.

Alex shoved Jenna's waist hard. He crashed onto the upended metal bucket, the impact tearing Thunder's chest from his iron grip.

Fingers stretching out, Jenna snagged a piece of the grate. Enough to swing the other hand into place. But a foot slid into the flames. She screamed in pain.

Thunder's high-pitched howls filled the tunnel.

"Hang tight." I ran back to where I found the wheelbarrow and commandeered a stiff bristle broom. I sprinted forward, avoiding seepage from the slit above. I cleared a path to Thunder, Jenna, and Alex, pushing the flaming liquid down the tunnel and out the other side. I killed the flames on the pack and near the group. I dropped the broom and surveyed the damage.

On his side, Alex groaned and rubbed his chest. Scrapes from the front wheel covered one cheek, but by curling up during the fall, he stayed out of the oil.

Jenna's left hiking boot was a mess. The partially melted sole would make it hard to walk. Red blotches on her ankle and holes in the calf of her jeans radiated pain. She sobbed.

Thunder squirmed in Alex's arm, his right forepaw lashing out, scraping against the backpack. As Alex tried to calm his buddy, I checked the burned paw. Oil dripped to the pavement. I needed to clean and wrap it.

After a few minutes, Alex stood. I helped Jenna; he carried Thunder. We skated on the oil back up the hill to the exit.

Outside the archway, Alex put Thunder down.

"Pete." Jenna ignored her pain and rushed to his side. "What happened?"

He moaned in response.

I snagged Pete's backpack, set it next to him, selected a few first aid items, and knelt by his side.

"Hey," Jenna said, "Why don't you use your stuff?"

"That's not how it's done." I tugged at her brother's left arm. "We all have med kits in each pack for our use. That's how the military does it."

He winced, then extended his arm. A white area the size of a quarter, surrounded by burned skin, marred the top of his hand. A bulge grew under the skin.

"That's going to cover the entire back of his hand." Jenna took the medical supplies from my hands and gasped when her left pant leg brushed Pete's side.

"You need medical attention yourself." I directed her to the ground. "Let me take care of your brother first." I retrieved the supplies from her and using an alcohol wipe, disinfected Pete's swollen hand, wrapping it with the stretchy white cloth provided.

Alex washed and bandaged Thunder's paw, who lay on his side, a high whine escaping during the application of the medical tape. "Sh-h-h." Alex patted his dog. "You'll be fine."

Jenna was next. Short breaths accompanied the tugging of the ruined pant leg up to her knee. Tough work. The burnt skin and cloth bonding required some extra jerks.

"Hold still." I put cream and bandages on her burns.

"I am." Tears etched her cheeks. "Take it easy." Her lips quivered at any pressure. When I finished, she rolled her pant leg down and scooted next to Pete.

Lightning danced at my feet.

"Yes, little buddy?" I knelt beside him and let him lick my cheek. "Why are you excited? Are you glad we made it?"

As if in response, he backed away and jumped into the air.

"I'm glad too." I patted him on the head, but he yipped at me and trotted toward the Burgermeister tower. "All right."

I stood and followed him to a black door built into the exit archway's side.

Lightning barked once, sat, and put a paw on the door.

I clasped the black bar and tugged to open it. No dice. I set my feet and tried again. I spent a few minutes shoving and yanking on the bar until it came free. The door creaked opened into a pitch-black passage.

I flicked on my flashlight, peering into the hall. Made of cold concrete, the space echoed from the creaking door. Wall sconces missing candles decorated the sides covered by scribbles. I swept the light over the floor and spotted a white envelope.

Lighting dashed inside and retrieved it.

"Very kind of you, old boy." My fake British accent came out from years of practice. "Shall we inform the others?"

We hurried back to the group. Pete was sitting up, blowing his nose and drying his eyes.

"He'll be fine." Jenna stood to her feet.

"I can't use this much." Pete lifted his wrapped left hand. "But after the pain killer gets in my system, I'll be able to make it.

"Let's read the next clue." I held up the envelope, tore it open, and spoke out loud. "You've made it through your first trial by fire. Congratulations. But time is disappearing for your friend and the girl. Find me in the rooms where starry skies can be seen and deliver your packages. But first, use your token to stay alive. I don't want you to miss the midnight concert in my honor."

"That's not much of a clue." Jenna brushed back her hair. "You can see the stars from lots of different points tonight." The clear sky revealed thousands of twinkling stars and a partial moon.

"We have to split up anyway, based on our tokens." I put my backpack back on. "We have an hour and a half until midnight."

"Team one, come in." A crackling came from my walk-ie-talkie.

"Turn that down." Alex tugged on my backpack. "We don't want the Phantom to know we're connected to the Polizei."

I pulled the radio from a side pocket. "Team one here." I turned the volume way down and held it to my ear. After a moment, I turned to the others. "Willie says they're in position on the back-side of the Fortress. If any of us sends a distress signal, they'll storm the castle walls."

"Does he mean the SOS in Morse code?" Pete said. "Three long beeps, three short, and three long?"

"Really." Jenna let out a breath. "I guess I should be happy you listened to the Polizei briefing."

"Don't use those walkie-talkies unless it's an absolute emergency." Alex patted Thunder on the shoulder. "Move out."

Leaving the lit archway behind, Thunder followed the road under the old train railway as we continued our climb. Lightning raced to each new section of wall, sniffing and searching.

"This is the Rosspforte Gate or Horse Gate." Pete pointed at the sign. "After we pass through here, it opens into the main part of the fortress."

The stone ceiling was built in baroque style, with arches meeting in the center above. A light flicked on as we entered the space.

"Here's where we split." I stopped before going too far into the gate. "My race car tells me to visit this place. We'll meet you at the State Rooms when we're done."

"Okay." Alex motioned straight ahead. "Try to meet us in half an hour."

"Got it." I climbed the stairs on the right, Lightning and Pete in tow. We were on the first landing when Jenna shouted.

"Look out."

A loud thump came from their position. We raced back down to the road, halting to watch a cannonball roll past.

"It's a good thing we're not a crowd of marauding invaders," Alex said. He and Jenna stood to one side of the hole in the Rossp-forte Gate's ceiling. "That's the second attack from above."

"Another warning," Pete said. "We'd better be careful around any openings."

"See you at eleven o'clock sharp." Alex led Jenna and Thunder to one side of the passage as he scanned the ceiling, avoiding the overhead hole and stepping out into the courtyard and cool night air.

Chapter Thirty-Five

Sinister Ceiling

I led Jenna and Thunder under the moon and stars, leaving Gabe, Pete, and Lightning at the Horse Gate. More than half the moon reflected light, strong enough to cast slight shadows on the ground. Scattered clouds plunged us into full darkness from time to time.

"Alex, follow the path past the cistern and the Work House into the entrance of the Old Castle." Jenna walked to my right, favoring her left leg.

"I know." I tapped my head. "I've got an excellent memory." My memories of the Fortress map from our Polizei briefings were crystal clear. I knew the exact route I wanted to use to enter the Altstadt.

"I'm still learning my way around," she said. "By the way, were you going to tell me something when we were slipping toward the burning oil?"

"Yes, but not now."

"Why not?" She tossed her hair to one side. "We've got time alone. Or am I not important?"

"Jen-nah." I drew out the last syllable. "You know that's not what I meant. A few minutes ago I was going to…" I couldn't say the next part.

"Sacrifice yourself for me?" She tugged at my sleeve. "It's all right to say you care about me."

"I…I…" I faced her directly.

"Spit it out, Alex." Her eyes started to get misty. "You can say it, can't you?"

I nodded. Swallowed. "Yes. Our time together, the way we care about one another, it's—"

A harsh clang of metal on metal startled us.

Jenna clutched my hand and pointed behind me.

I twisted around.

A man, dressed like a 1700s aristocrat, bowed and motioned us to him. He wore a white wig, a red coat, knickers, white stockings, and black shoes with large gold buckles.

"Are we having a party?" Jenna said. "You're all dressed up."

"Do you recognize me?" He held his chin up, presenting his left side.

"Keep him talking, Jenna," I whispered. I snapped my fingers once.

Thunder slunk into the wall-shadows with an uneven gait.

"I'm not sure I do." Jenna stepped closer. "Are you imitating a person from centuries ago?"

"I am not imitating. I'm the real thing." The man posed again. "One more time. If you fail, I will have no recourse but to punish you."

Thunder stalked his prey.

"Tell him." I faced away from the man and spoke in low tones. "We need two minutes."

"You're like the guy on the candy wrappers." Jenna placed a palm on her forehead, almost like she would faint. "Mozart choco-

196

lates. Yes. You look like Amadeus Mozart."

"I *am* Amadeus." He straightened his posture further. "I have his spirit in me. He lives on in me."

"But what about the other side?" I raised my voice to distract him.

"Come and see my other side." The Phantom vanished around a corner.

Thunder dashed to cut him off but wasn't close enough.

An Old Castle door banged. Suddenly, lights blazed throughout the building.

We raced after the Phantom and found two entrances inside, one wood and one metal.

"I didn't hear a clang this time." I checked both doors. "Thunder?"

He rubbed against my leg on the way to the doors. He sniffed the metal one first, then the wooden one. Finally, he decided. Pawed the wooden door and barked once.

"Let's go." I opened the door and rushed into a broad hallway. A few archways lined the left side, but I heard the telltale creak of steps on the wooden staircase right inside the door.

Thunder surged past me through the door and darted up the stairs.

"Slow down." I bolted after him. At the top of the stairs, I saw another long hallway with more arches.

Thunder skidded and veered left into the second opening.

Our feet pounded the floor as we tried to keep up.

A yelp came from the room.

"No." I dashed inside, pulse pumping.

Thunder lay on his side, a dart sticking out of his flank.

"Spear." Jenna tackled me to the floor.

Chapter Thirty-Six

Victim

"Pete." I knelt to examine a cannon in the Zeughaus. "We need to find the next clue in this armory fast. I bet the others are waiting on us."

Lightning worked his way past several cannons. He sniffed at a pile of cannon balls and moved on.

"I'm doing the best I can, Gabe." Pete lifted both hands in the air, palms up. "I can't invent the guy's notes, can I?"

"No. I'm mad because it's been ten minutes. I bet Alex and Jenna are waiting for us."

"They'll be all right." Pete smiled. "They're probably making up."

"We're supposed to meet them at eleven o'clock. We haven't found anything—"

Lightning barked near a second stack of cannonballs.

I beat Pete to the pile. "Lightning, did you find something?" I bent over the cannonballs and frowned. "Nothing here."

"Exactly," Pete said.

"What?"

"It's not what's here. It's what's missing."

"And that would be…" I looked at the stack of cannonballs. Sixteen rested on the bottom, then nine, then none. "The top one is missing."

"Look again." Pete walked around the square pile on the floor. "How many should be on top of the nine?"

"Four." I felt a chill run down my back.

"And how many cannonballs were dropped on us?"

"One. At the horse gate." I knew what Pete was driving at. "He's going to shoot a cannon at the people in the town square to get his revenge."

"He's going to take four shots," Pete said. "And I bet it will be right after his song is played as the finale."

"It will be his fireworks…"

Lightning barked and tugged the leg of my trousers.

"Yes?" I crouched to pat him on the head. "Did you find something?"

Lightning's tail wagged like it was churning butter. He ran toward a doorway.

"Come on." I shot after him outside and heard a faint voice. A guy.

"Is that who I think it is?" Pete ran to catch up.

"Run." I sprinted toward the muffled sounds, down some stairs, and past restaurant tables. "He's here somewhere."

Lightning darted between my feet. I stumbled but caught myself.

"Got him." I slowed the last two strides to take in the situation. A cable attached to a pole stretched over the wall. A boy, tied up and with a sack on his head, gave another muffled cry for help.

"Pete, help me pull him up."

Four hands made the work easier, as we dragged the squirming bundle toward the top.

"Hold him." I let go of the cable, climbed onto the two-foot thick rock wall, and reached down to grab on. "When I give the signal, jerk back hard." I snagged the cords around his chest and braced my foot against the rock jutting out from the wall. "Ready? Now."

I heaved, struggling with the weight, as Pete pulled hard. We moved the captive inches.

"Again."

About twenty tugs later, the bound and hooded prisoner flopped safe on the paving stones in the restaurant's courtyard. Pete yanked the sack off his head.

"Jonathan." I loosened his flimsy gag. "Found you. You're okay." I cut the zip ties off of his hands.

"Yuck." Jonathan spat on the ground. "That rag in my mouth tasted horrible." He took a deep breath. "I'm glad you saved me. He left me to die."

"The Phantom left you as bait." Pete wrinkled his brow. "He wanted us to find you."

"Why do you say that?" Jonathan freed his feet after rubbing his wrists.

I glanced at my watch. "We don't have much time to meet Jenna and Alex. Ten minutes left and we still haven't found the next clue."

"Where's it at?" Jonathan worked himself to his feet.

"In the Schüttkasten," I said.

"That's the grain storage building." Jonathan pointed to his left. "Quick. This way." He dashed toward the next building.

Chapter Thirty-Seven

Attack

Jenna's body slammed me into the floor. A spear gouged the wall with a loud thunk.

"Thanks." I dragged my aching body off the floor. "I'm glad I'm not the Phantom's pin cushion now."

"Me too." Jenna rolled to her feet.

I peeked over the edge of the exhibit's platform.

"Bring my money upstairs." The Phantom pointed. "A pity to drug your doggy, but I have plans for all of you in the finale." He laughed like a horror movie fiend. "Don't be long." He sprinted upstairs and was gone.

The elevated exhibit hung pieces of ancient armor and weapons from the ceiling by wires to make a battle scene minus the people.

"That's where the Phantom got his spear." I motioned toward two dangling wires on the opposite side of the exhibit.

"He's scary." Jenna rubbed her leg and stood.

I yanked the dart from Thunder and stomped on it.

"Whoa, Alex. Keep it calm."

"He shot my dog."

"He's trying to get you mad."

"He did." I rubbed Thunder's head. "Can you walk, buddy?"

He wobbled to his feet, favoring his right paw. His head swiveled toward Jenna when she patted his back.

"I've got him." She knelt and tickled Thunder's ears.

"I need a weapon." I wrenched a shield from the display and broke free a sword.

"Will you use the sword?" Jenna narrowed her eyes.

"Self-defense. Let's move."

"Give us a minute. I might be a bit slower." She stood, giving commands to Thunder who responded like he was in a fog. "Okay. I'm ready."

"Together." I pressed my lips into a thin line. "We go in as a team; we leave as a team."

Thunder shook his right hind leg a bit, then teetered after Jenna, head hanging low.

At the top of the stairs, I paused, scouting for our attacker. The small room's glass cases, filled with books and military drawings, lined the walls. Some contained examples of old guns. No sign of the Phantom.

I raced through a doorway on the right. A tiled floor and huge columns of marble reminded me of a palace. Dark strips of wood covered the ceiling, arranged in patterns of rectangles cut by diagonal lines. Inside the rectangles, two golden knobs, each shaped like half a golf ball, decorated a blue felt background in the rectangle, one on each side of the diagonal strip.

"The Goldener Saal." The Phantom appeared in the doorway at the end of the hall. He spoke like a tour guide. "You've found one of the starry night scenes created inside my old castle. This great hall with its marble columns is but a beginning to more majesty in the other State Rooms. Archbishops lived below and used these rooms for State events. Would you like to see them?" He held a hand out as if to say "this way" and strolled into the next room.

"He's nuts." I picked up the pace to follow him.

"Sure." Jenna touched my arm. "But go slow for Thunder." We passed thick wooden chairs with leather seats, a long mahogany table, several candelabras, and several marble columns including one with a huge chip gouged out near the top.

"Faster." The Phantom's words floated in the air. Shield in front, I rushed to the threshold and scanned next room. No sign of our host.

"Don't stand around. Come in."

I eased onto the wooden floor, motioning Jenna and Thunder to trail behind. The ceiling matched the last room, but red and blue paint with golden curlicues and patterns covered the wooden walls. The golden knobs décor filled the upper third.

"Drop the money bags in the Chapel." The Phantom appeared in the doorway ahead. "Time is running out. You'll find me near the privy. Hurry." He dashed off.

"The privy?" Jenna shook her head. "How about the toilet?"

"He's stuck in the 1700s." I checked my watch.

"He's a jack-in-the-box." Jenna's volume rose. "Popping in and out like that."

"Quick." I unzipped her backpack's large pocket and removed her part of the money. "I'll take this to the Chapel, come back, and get you." I handed her the shield and sword.

"No." She pushed my hands back. "Too heavy for me. You take them. I have pepper spray. We'll track the Phantom's moves until you get back."

"The toilet's entrance is in the bedroom," I said. "Go through the bedchamber off of the main State Room through this door. Don't follow that nutcase alone."

Jenna nodded.

I squeezed her hand and ran toward the Chapel, passing through the main stateroom that housed a floor to ceiling ceramic stove painted with standout scenes and legs like carved lions. I shot past the door leading to the privy and into the next room. I made a left to enter the Chapel.

A small altar, Biblical story scenes, a large cross, and stained glass windows defined the space's purpose. Plush red cushions on small benches and chairs provided comfortable seating. A few paintings hung on the walls.

I dropped the sword and shield, threw my backpack on a chair, unzipped it, and grabbed the money packages, Jenna's and mine. As I searched for a logical place to leave the cash, I discovered a message sticking out of an offering plate on the altar. I tore it open, speed-reading the contents.

"Put the ransom here. I have a present for you down the stairs next to the privy. Don't delay."

Dumping the packages on top of the golden offering plate, I zipped my bag, swung it onto my shoulders, grabbed my medieval weapons, and dashed to get Jenna and Thunder. When I got to the Goldener Saal, they were gone.

"Jenna," I yelled her name as loud as I could. "Where are you? Say something."

No response.

Chapter Thirty-Eight

Revelation

Jonathan, Pete, Lightning, and I swept through the Granary, examining each area, but hadn't found anything by 10:55 P.M.

"We have to call it quits." I held up my watch. "Five minutes left to find Alex and Jenna.

"I think this place has a cellar," Jonathan said. "Pete could go meet the others while we take a peek."

"We're not supposed to separate." Pete looked at me for support.

"True." I rubbed my chin, rocked back on my heels to think, and snapped my fingers. "I know." I pulled out my walkie-talkie. "Pete, our commo gear has a range of about four hundred feet, right?"

He tugged out his device and turned it over. "Four hundred and twenty feet to be exact."

"Why don't you go to the Old Castle, call Alex and Jenna to get their location, then join them." I turned up the volume and lifted the radio to my mouth. "Team One Alpha to Team One Bravo"

Pete's device crackled and each word came through clear as day.

"Roger." Pete smiled. "I can do it."

"Call when you're safe." I pocketed the commo gear. "If you don't hear from us, don't worry. We'll be in a cellar. The ground might jam the signal. We'll contact you when we're on our way."

"I'll give you five more minutes, then Alex, Jenna, and I will come looking for you."

"Fair enough." I pointed the way.

Pete waved and ran out the door.

Jonathan, Lightning, and I sped in the opposite direction, down a flight of stairs, and out into the outer courtyard toward a massive wooden double door.

"I got it." Jonathan tugged on a handle, opening the right half of the entry.

"The electric bill for this place must be huge." I darted inside and leaped down the stairs two or three at a time.

"Why?" Jonathan kept pace.

"Every part of the castle has been lit up tonight. Is it always like this?"

"For special occasions, I think." Jonathan halted at the first landing. "That's an amazing painting of a joust."

A painting covered the area above a doorway arch that went to a lower level. To the right was a cobblestone landing and on the left, a smooth dirt floor.

"You go left. I'll go right." I examined the space behind a couple of barrels and wooden boxes but found nothing. When I saw Jonathan, he shrugged.

"Come on, Lightning." I hurried down another level and discovered two doors.

"I've heard the rooms behind the doors were used to hold prisoners." Jonathan heaved on one. Creaking, it swung wide. "Maybe they even kept crazy people here."

The space wasn't lit. I brought out my flashlight, clicked it on, and saw an empty room.

"The Phantom's got to be crazy." I moved to the second door and yanked. A piece of paper lay on the floor.

Jonathan swooped in to pick it up before I could reach it. "Got it." He jumped out of the room. "Let's get out of here. This place gives me the creeps."

"Like the guy who captured you." I shut the two doors. "He gives me the creeps too."

"You know," Jonathan paused at the cobblestone landing. "I've got a secret to tell you. You can keep a secret, right?"

"It depends." My muscles tightened in my gut. "If it's illegal or immoral, I might not be able to do that."

"It's nothing like that." Jonathan laughed. "This secret is more about helping capture bad guys than anything. But I have to know you won't break my cover when I tell you. It's something the police asked me to do."

"Oh." I relaxed. "That kind of secret. Will you get in trouble by telling me?"

"No." Jonathan walked over to a keg and sat on it. "But you can't tell the others, or it will compromise our safety."

"Can you tell me as we go?" I lifted my watch towards him. "We have a deadline to meet. We're late."

"Sure." Jonathan eased to his feet. "I've got your word to keep quiet? Our lives could depend upon it."

"Lightning, get going." The orange-red dog flashed up the stairs. "Of course. What are friends for?"

Jonathan patted me on the back. A few steps short of the door he held my arm to stop me. He leaned close, his bad breath like rotten onions.

"I'm a double agent for the Polizei."

Chapter Thirty-Nine

A Tight Squeeze

"Missing someone, Alex?" The Phantom's voice swirled in the air.

"You won't get far." I spun around in the Golden Hall, tracing the sound. *I should never have left her and Thunder alone.*

"Have you forgotten the stairs?" The whisper got stronger.

The note said the Phantom's present waited down the stairs next to the privy. I edged into the hallway toward the toilet.

"Hurry." The voice was louder with each step.

My nerves tingled along my neck. I hurried, dodging from the side room into an elaborate bedchamber. To the right, the privy door hung ajar.

"Run." Laughter followed the clear, cold command.

I flew into the privy. A note lay on the toilet's wooden lid. I dropped the sword. It clattered on the floor while I snatched the paper and flicked it open.

"Unfortunate news. Race required. They won't last long."

The note wasn't signed, but that didn't matter. I crushed it. Hurled it against the wall. I scooped up the sword, clenching its hilt and rushed down the stairs to the left. With my hands full of shield and sword, I could only take three steps at a time. In six jumps I hesitated at a landing. Stairs continued down, but light filtered through a crack of door resting on the doorjamb. Noises seeped into the hall. A chair scraped the floor. *At least I won't need G's key that I gave to Gabe earlier to get in the room.*

My eyes darted from the door on my left to the stairs. *No time to stop.* Heart pumping hard, I sucked in a deep breath. *Which way to go? I need a clue.*

A muffled crash came from behind the door. Jenna cried out.

I kicked the door wide-open and dashed inside.

Chapter Forty

Hot Pursuit

"Did you say double-agent?" I yanked my arm out of his grip and stepped back. "How can I ever trust you?"

"Gabe," Jonathan said in soothing tones, "I couldn't take the secret anymore. Willie thought the best way to keep things smooth was to have an insider crack this guy's moves."

"Willie did this?" I forced myself to take a deep breath. "But you barely joined our team."

Lightning returned. Sensing something wrong, he came by my side and watched the blond-haired boy facing me. His ears stood at full alert.

"The Polizei thought I would make a great double-agent because of ..."

I waited.

"Because of how crazy our last adventure went when we were trapped by the terrorists in the Berchtesgaden Salt Mines." He shook his head. "My broken family life was…an opening for a criminal to exploit." His Adam's apple bobbed with a hard swallow.

"You know I'm concerned about that."

He sniffled, facing away.

"Look, Jonathan." I patted his shoulder. "Your home life is the pits." I glanced at the ceiling, inhaling a deep breath. "I'll trust you, but warn me if you have to do something weird. Wink or raise an eyebrow. Anything to let me know it will work out right in the end."

"You sure?" He pulled out a rag and blew his nose hard. "Because—"

"Team One Alpha, come in."

My walkie-talkie crackled. I fished it out of my jacket.

"You're coming in faint." I turned up the volume. "Is this Team One Bravo?"

"Roger. No contact with Team Two."

"Have you called them on the radio? I mean the walkie-talkie?"

"Yes. No answer. And I've walked all three floors, but got nothing."

"Stay put. We're on our way." I turned the volume down and put the device back in my pocket.

"Don't let that thing go off with the Phantom near you," Jonathan said. "He doesn't want any interference from the outside."

"How do you know that?" My head swiveled for a sharp glance.

"Double-agent, remember?" Jonathan pushed open the door. "He was talking to the girl while he wrote down his requests. I was lying on the floor, tied up like—"

A spear banged against the half-open door and fell to the ground.

"He's here." Jonathan's face went white. "I have to run."

"Go." I shooed him away. "We're going to stop this once and for all."

Lightning was crouched, ready for my command.

211

"Sic 'em."

Lightning flashed out of the open half-door at top speed. I popped the other half-door out, ducking and rolling to my left behind a wooden trashcan container. As I rolled, I glimpsed the Phantom make a break toward the next building, which appeared to be attached to the Granary.

"Get him," I yelled at Lightning. I sprang to my feet, brain churning to project his escape plan.

He headed past the Geierturm, a hexagonal tower, toward the Hasenturm, another oddly shaped tower. He hesitated, saw me charging, and continued around a short tower of the Keep.

I lost him until I cleared the Keep's tower on my right. He flew up a half-flight of stairs, streaking into the Stables and Salt Magazine section of the castle. I cranked up the speed. "Lightning."

Lightning was like a streak of light flowing up the stairs.

My pulse raced, muscles tight. I cornered into the stairs, covered four or five and went sprawling. I banged into the wrought iron handrail and slid down a couple of stairs.

"Missing something?"

I scrambled to my feet, tasting blood. *Must've bit my lip.*

The Phantom thrust his arms and head out a third-floor window, near the outdoor stairway. In his hands, Lightning writhed, fighting the muzzle restraining him.

"I'd hate to see your doggie get hurt from a long fall." The ruthless man laughed. "But he is hard to hold like this. Oops."

Lightning slipped from his hands, flipping to right himself.

Chapter Forty-One

Stranded

Jenna raised her head an inch, looking at me with dazed eyes. Cloth crammed her mouth. A rope bound her to a wooden chair lying sideways on the floor. She couldn't move or speak.

"Are you okay?" I rushed to her side, dropping the sword and shield.

Her eyes closed, head sinking to the ground.

"Hang in there." I threw my backpack down and removed the wad of material from her mouth. In minutes, she lay flat on the floor. "Speak to me, Jenna." I propped her head up and gently shook her shoulders. "Say something."

Eyes fluttering, she mumbled, but the walkie-talkie in my pocket went off.

"Team Two, this is—"

I turned off the knob.

"Say it again." She seemed to be drifting off again. I noticed a dart lying on the floor.

"That scum." I lay Jenna on the floor and moved to Thunder, a few feet away. He struggled to free his legs. Three legs were tied together like a calf in a rodeo. He'd also been muzzled.

"Hey, buddy." I undid the muzzle and removed it. I tickled his ears. "Give me a second." I untangled the rope from his legs.

He jumped to his feet, put his paws on my shoulders and licked my face.

"I'm happy to see you too."

The door to the room slammed shut.

I raced to the door and tried the handle. Locked. I rammed my shoulder into the wood, but it was sturdy.

Jenna stirred.

"You okay, now?" I knelt by her side.

"My head hurts." She rubbed a small bump on her forehead.

"You probably hurt yourself when the chair fell on its side."

"Woozy. Sit me up."

I pushed her to a sitting position, letting her lean back against me for support.

"Whoa." She slid sideways, then caught herself. "What hit me?"

"Apparently, the Phantom darted you like he did Thunder." I nudged her forward to lift her to a standing position.

"Not yet." She fell back on my chest. "You know, you're kind of cute."

"That's the medicine talking." I shifted again, this time going to my knees. "You were ticked off at me. I'm going to help you into the chair."

"But," she slurred the words, "you don't unnerstand."

I carried Jenna, almost like moving a rag doll, arms and legs flopping around. I propped her up, holding her in place while waiting for the medicine to wear off. She shook as though cold. I made her wear my jacket over hers to keep it from sliding off.

214

"I *really* like you and don't wan-chu to leave me. To leave my Germany." She nestled her head under my chin. "You're nic-c-e. Why does shure Dad have to go where the military sends-s-s him? He—"

A noise, halfway between a creak and a crunch, split the air. The wall opposite us trembled.

Thunder barked at the wall, backing up till his tail whacked Jenna on the arm.

"What was-s-s zat?" she said. "Sounds-s-s like someone knocking at my door. You'd better ans-s-swer it."

When I moved away, Jenna drooped to one side, then slid toward the floor. I jumped back, caught her, and lowered her to the floor in a seated position against the wall. I propped her up on one side with the chair.

"Funny," Jenna said. "The wall's-s-s coming closer."

"Right."

The wall crept several inches nearer. It wasn't trembling as much. The noise lessened. I noticed a door on the opposite side and raced to it. When the sunken handle rotated, a wave of relief shot through me. Until I saw it was a tiny utility closet. Built-in shelves covered the inside from thigh level to the top. The bottom area looked big enough for a large sewing machine.

"Tell the wall to shtop...moving." Jenna sat a little straighter. "I don't like it coming that clos-s-se."

"I'm working on it." I ran my fingers over the surface of the other walls, searching for a mechanism to turn the device off, starting with the closet.

We talked while I examined as much as possible, her words getting clearer by the minute. She went silent for a time, closing her eyes.

"Alex." Jenna's fluttered open, eyebrows furrowed. "How long have you been here?" Her hand touched the knot on her head. "Ouch."

"I don't know. Maybe ten minutes." I took a picture off of the wall and saw the square outline of a hidden compartment. "The Phantom shot you with a dart. Don't you remember talking?"

"No. Have you called for help?" Using the chair as a support, Jenna wobbled and rose to her feet, still a bit unsteady.

"I've been busy. But Thunder barked." I pressed hard on the edges of the square to make it pop open. "No response."

"I meant call for help on the radio."

Frustrated, I took a break. "Not yet. I've almost got this panel open. When I get into the secret compartment, I'll shut off this wall. Then we can call for help."

"Have you looked at the wall lately?" Jenna's eyebrows went up, and her head motioned toward the wooden structure.

I faced the wall. About three more feet gone. Four feet left. I didn't have much time. "Give me a minute." I went back to work.

"If you won't call, I will." Jenna pulled out a walkie-talkie. "Team One this is Team Two." She paused and repeated.

"Team Two, this is Team One." Pete's voice came through loud and clear.

"See?" She said to me. Then back on the radio, "Team One, we have an emergency. A wall of our room is pushing towards us and will crush us in about five minutes. Help us stop it." She waited for a response.

I hit the panel with both fists. "Open up."

With a small click, the right side of the panel moved out an inch.

"Team One, do you copy?" Jenna shouted, pitch rising. "Answer me."

Chapter Forty-Two

Lessons in Pain

"So sorry." The Phantom watched me dive to intercept Lightning.

The man's face disappeared while I snatched my buddy out of the air, clutching him to my chest. I curled into a ball. Slammed my shoulder into the cobblestones and rolled past the concrete pad of another door's entryway. I lay stunned for several seconds.

The Phantom leaned out the third story window, his red coat contrasting sharply with the white walls. Stretching, he grabbed the rungs of the fire ladder, then swung from the window to the ladder like a trained gymnast.

I blinked. *Wow. That was strange.*

"Coming?" He laughed and rapidly climbed.

"You'll never get away." I rolled onto my good shoulder. After a silent thank you to the Polizei for the padded coat that absorbed the fall's impact, I removed the muzzle from Lightning, untangled him from the net, and opened my backpack. "In you go."

Lightning jumped inside.

I zipped all but a three-inch section on the top.

Lightning's head popped out. He barked several times as if to say, "What are we waiting for?"

I rolled my right shoulder a couple of times, then sprinted up the stairs. On the third floor, I found the Phantom's escape route. I couldn't grab the rungs outside the room with my right hand without pain, but I could easily get on the wide window ledge and reach it with my left. I scrambled up a staircase's worth of rungs to the top.

The Phantom waved. He straddled the peak of one of a series of slanted roofs, more than a football field away. He laughed hard enough to slip, fall on his back, and slide out of sight.

Gotcha. I covered the six roofs between us with swift rushes up one side and leaping down the other. As I crested the last one, he laughed and darted back the way I'd come. My momentum carried me onto the flat roof of the next building. I reversed my direction.

The man was nimble. He used his hands on the peaks of the roofs to pivot over them like a pommel horse gymnast would do in the Olympics.

"Do you like my stables?" He placed a hand on the ladder leading to the top of the RechtsTurm, the place I left minutes ago. Americans knew it as the Observation Tower. "I love the sights." He clambered up the ladder.

I clenched my jaw tight enough to feel my teeth grind. *He must have been acting when he fell. He baited me.* I copied his vaulting motions as I raced to the base of the Observation Tower, reaching the ladder by the time he swung over the top. I climbed ten rungs when I felt the first pebble. Seconds later a rock bounced off my head. *Ow.* I checked to see what was next and decided to do a fireman's slide back to the roof. When my feet hit the sloped tiles, I threw myself to the left.

A brick whizzed past and crashed onto the roof, sending ceramic chips flying.

"Missed me."

"Obviously on purpose." He grinned. "Now you have learned the old military lesson." The Phantom bowed. "I am pleased to be your teacher. The possessor of the high ground has the advantage." He vanished for a few seconds and returned with a larger rock. "As my father taught me, I will teach you." He dropped the rock onto the roof where it shattered to pieces. "But I must bid you farewell. I don't want to miss the exciting demise of your second team—your brother, his dog, and the girlfriend." With a wave, he left.

I launched at the ladder and climbed with urgency, furious. *You won't get away with this.* I didn't stop at the top of the ladder, but flew down the steps of the observation tower, barely noticing the growing crowd of people in the Mozart Plaza below. I took risks, jumping four or five stairs at a time. When I got to the exit, I didn't see him.

I rolled my right shoulder again to loosen it. A little sore, but not bad. I fished the radio out of my pocket to call Pete. The volume was off. I spun the knob to the right. What I heard next made me dash toward Pete's location.

"—Team One Alpha, please come in." The strain in Pete's voice was clear. "They're gonna die."

Chapter Forty-Three

Fallen Square

"Alex, I lost them." Jenna stared at the walkie-talkie.

I yanked on the wall panel. Though a small gap showed between it and the wall, the mechanism wouldn't budge. "There's got to be another way to get inside."

Thunder barked at me.

"I'm working, buddy. Let me take care of business here; then I'll help you."

He barked a couple of times, then tugged on my pants.

"Team Two, this is the Aussie."

Jenna's eyes went wide.

"Aussie, Team Two." Jenna's words tumbled over each other in her haste to get them out. "We're going to get crushed in this room. The walls are closing in."

"I'm unable to move at this time. Possible spotters in sight. Captain's orders."

"But, we'll be killed."

"No worries. We'll work on a solution." Static created a slight delay. "When all else fails, don't forget to look to the Man upstairs. Aussie, out."

"Talk to me." Jenna's voice began to rise. "Talk to me. Don't leave us hanging." Her shoulders slumped when she flipped the walkie-talkie on the chair. "I guess we're on our own."

The wall was three feet away.

"All right, boy, show me." I heaved a big sigh and followed Thunder to the half-open closet. The wall was forcing the door shut. Inside, near the floor, a small decorative square hung by a corner, revealing a toggle switch. "Great work." I hugged him.

I flipped the toggle switch and heard another click.

"Hey, your box is open now." Jenna moved to the compartment. "And two small panels fell out of the ceiling right next to the back wall."

I looked up through the gaps and saw a big beam, but nothing significant.

"These panels didn't come off on purpose." Jenna held one up. "See the jagged lines?"

Unlike the other trick panels that opened in precise outlines, these pieces of wood appeared rotted, brittle, and broken.

"You're right." I tossed the one in my hand to the side. "At least we can get some fresh air in this room. It's getting a little tight."

I focused on the real trick panel, swung the door wide, and peered inside. Then pounded the wall.

"What?" Jenna said.

"A lock." I rushed past her to my sword and shield. "Quick. We're going to have to jam the wall from closing in on us. Flip the chair on its side."

Jenna grabbed her walkie-talkie off the seat and flipped the chair into position.

The lights went out.

"What made you hit the wall?" She called through the darkness.

"The secret compartment had one thing inside. One." I was glad she couldn't see the anger on my face.

"And it was?"

"A keyhole," I said, "the perfect fit for G's key."

"That's the key you gave…"

"Exactly."

Chapter Forty-Four

Connection

"Gabe, come here." Pete waved me forward.

"What is it?" My lungs burned from the "life or death" sprint to get to Pete. Probably not more than a couple of football fields, but after chasing the Phantom on the rooftops and up and down a tower, I was almost out of gas. I paused a second.

"Alex and Jenna called, then my walkie-talkie went out."

"That's good." I set my backpack down, extracted Lightning, and re-zipped it.

"You don't understand." Pete gripped my shoulder. "The room they're in is closing down on them. They'll get crushed."

"Where are they?"

"I'm not sure." Pete moved up the stairway. "Their tokens sent them to the State Rooms and the Chapel. We should check one or the other."

"Lead the way." I whistled and Lightning took off.

We shot onto the second floor and into the weapons room.

"Someone's been in here." I pointed to the display. A few helmets, swords, and shields seemed to be stuck in the place at odd angles while others seem to be set up like soldiers.

"This soldier's missing his sword and shield." Pete tugged on a frayed wire.

"Someone took a spear too." I picked up one that lay on the floor. "Better take this with me in case we need it."

Lightning barked at me, galloping up another set of stairs.

I circled the exhibit and leaped onto the stairway in time to see my canine spy vanish. "We'd better be quick," I called out to Pete while racing onto the third floor and into the next room, spear at the ready position. When I cleared the doorway, I stopped.

The place was empty. Evenly spaced marble pillars went the length of the hall. Everything seemed in order.

"Where's…that noise…coming from?" Pete huffed and puffed. A grinding and creaking vibrated the floor beneath.

"It's stronger up ahead." I followed my orange fur-ball, who disappeared through the doorway. A short passageway, with arched doorways on the left, led to the Chapel. I put on the afterburner and burst into the Chapel.

"Look." I detoured around the benches and chairs in the room, knocking off one of the red cushions. I picked up the money in the packages. "Alex and Jenna must have left this here."

The shivering of the floor lessened but hadn't stopped.

"Maybe I can reach them now." Pete pulled out his walkie-talkie, pressed the talk button and spoke. "Team Two, this is Team One. Can you hear me?"

"Give me that." I grabbed his radio and keyed the mic. "Team…" I pulled the walkie-talkie away from my ear. "I don't hear any static before I press the talk button." I checked the volume. It was at the max position. "Oh, I see." I showed him the battery indicator on the bottom of his radio. "Red means dead."

"But I didn't use it that much."

"Something in your pocket might have kept the mic open."

"Okay." Pete shrugged and stuffed it in his backpack. "Try yours."

I threw everything in my pocket on the floor and extracted my radio. Turning the volume up, I held it to my mouth.

"Team Two, Team One. Over." I listened for a second and tried again. "Maybe they're batteries are out, too?" I shouldered the pack. "I guess we can look out some windows—"

"Gabe, is that you?" Jenna's voice was shaking.

"Yes."

"Get us out of here. The walls are closing in."

"Can't you block them?"

"Gabe, listen to me." Her pitch rose. "The wall has splintered our chair. We have less than two feet left."

"Where are they?" Pete asked.

I repeated the question into the radio.

"Down the staircase by the privy. It's off the bedchamber."

I looked at Pete and raised my hands palms up. "I didn't memorize the layout Jenna; you'll have to direct me. I'm in the chapel."

"Go to the side doors you passed. The first one you passed is the bedchamber. Go in and the privy is on your right. Hurry. The sword is almost bent in half."

"On our way."

Chapter Forty-Five

Crunch Time

"Alex, help." Jenna stretched out, clutching my left hand. "I can't breathe." She dropped the walkie-talkie and her light.

"Hang tight." I squeezed the hand I couldn't see. Too low. Her arm trembled.

Jenna, Thunder, and I stood lined up in a row, facing the wall with the hidden panel and lock. The lock I didn't have a key to open. To my right, Thunder stared at me, whining as the wall pressed closer toward us from behind. Jenna's flashlight, propped up by shattered pieces of chair, pointed up and to the right, washing our faces in its light.

"Team Two, Team One. Over."

"I can't bend down far enough to get the walkie-talkie." I tried, but the wall prevented any rotation of my shoulders. "You try."

Jenna bent sideways. Her fingers brushed the radio. "Can't." She cried. "I can't believe that idiot brother of yours has the key. That irresponsible loud-mouth—"

"Take it easy." I spoke calming words. "He's coming. We'll make it."

"Team Two, this is Team One. Come in. Over."

"We can't end like this." Jenna shook as sobs wracked her body. "I planned our future. Get married. Have kids Then grandkids. We're going to lose it all."

"Jenna." I tightened my grip on her hand to reassure her. "Dad taught me something that might help."

"What's that?" She shifted and part of the light caught my face.

The wall was inches from the back of my jacket, which she wore on top of her jacket. My own back pressed against the wall to allow breathing room.

"When things are going down, look up." I gazed into her eyes. "That comes from somewhere in the Bible. Think on things above and not about earthly things."

"We're dying." She squirmed against her tightening space. "That's no help."

"When this life's done, we'll graduate upstairs." The wall touched my shoes, pushing them forward. I turned my feet sideways. "Are you ready?"

"Don't go crazy on me. Focus." Jenna's eyes narrowed. "The walls are crushing us. Find a solution."

"We're stuck. Out of options." I shook my head. "But I'm banking on a heavenly intervention."

"No key, no commo, and no stopping this wall." She glared at me. "I'd say your bank is out of cash."

"Life here doesn't last forever." I breathed deep. "That's my point. And spiritual commo is always available." I squeezed her hand again. "Talking with God helps."

"Alex, don't." Blonde hair swished back and forth. Her face, streaked with wet lines, tilted up. Her grip tightened. "Look at that." Her fingernails dug into my skin.

"What?" I stared at the broken planks above and saw nothing for a second.

"Keep watching." Jenna's tone was tight. "See?"

A light swung past the crack.

"Gabe," I yelled. "Down here."

Chapter Forty-Six

A Key Decision

"Gabe," Alex shouted louder than I'd ever heard him before.

"We hear you." I smiled and faced Pete. "How do we get them out?"

We perched on log beams running about four feet above the killer room similar to a maintenance level in a large building where the ductwork for the air conditioning runs. I could see two jagged openings in the ceiling.

"We can't get to the winch and stop it." I pointed to two platforms, one behind and one in front, that run the machinery of the crushing walls.

"You can break through those openings and lift them out." Pete pulled a rope from his backpack. "This should be long enough."

"Gabe, if you don't hurry up I'll break your neck." Alex's voice carried up through the rafters.

"We're going to rig a rope for you to climb out," I called back.

"Too late." Jenna shrieked. "The wall will crush us in minutes. I can't turn."

"Gabe, I need that key," Alex said.

A loud smack echoed from below.

"Hey, you okay?" I whipped the key off my neck, but couldn't see into the room to place it into his hand.

"How are you going to get it to him?" Pete asked.

Lightning shot onto the beam, ran to where the two cracked tiles were, and jumped.

Jenna screamed.

"Got to hurry." I balled the key and cord into my hand to toss it to Alex.

Lightning hit the roof of the room. He scrambled to get his footing, hindquarters slipping into the hole of the right cracked tile. He fell through.

Alex yelled.

"Gabe, don't throw the key," Pete said. "You could miss."

I grabbed the spear, wrapped the key on the tip, and made sure it couldn't fall off.

"That should work." One beam led over the glow below. Like a tightrope walker, I stuck my arms out for balance and slid my feet forward. Slow and steady.

Thunder's low howls, like a wolf baying at the moon, made the hair on the back of my neck stiffen.

"Almost there." I reached a point above the cracked openings. "Pete, light up the target."

His beam danced to where I pointed. Steadied on the hole to my right. Lying on my chest, I extended the spear into the broken panel gap.

"Grab the spear." I held my body in position with my good left arm.

"Too high," Alex said.

I wrapped my legs around the wooden beam and stretched to my limit. Another foot. "How about now?"

"Can't reach it." Alex grunted.

"Drop it," Pete said.

"Into their eyes?" I shifted for a better angle.

"Gabe, drop that spear." Jenna's command made their position clear.

"Duck." I released the spear, flailing as I lost my balance. My legs locked around the beam. I hung upside down.

"My shoulder," Alex yelled.

The shaft of the spear tilted, falling away from sight. But I heard a slight clunk.

"Ow."

"Talk to us," Pete said.

"The spear fell on Jenna's head." Alex gave a short laugh. "That'll be two knots on her head. But I can't reach the key. Can't move anything except my arm. And the tip of the spear is between my elbow and my hand."

I curled up, put my arms around the beam, then crawled back on top. "Lightning can get it for you," I said. "He's small enough to maneuver in that space."

"You tell him." Alex sounded weaker. "Tired."

"Don't give up, Alex and Jenna." Pete got on his belly and crawled from the side of the maintenance level on a different crossbeam to a position above the ceiling holes. "Gabe, this is a better view."

"Lightning." I shifted to the crossbeam Pete straddled. I could see my brother and Jenna better. "Get that key off the spear and into Alex's right hand."

My buddy leaped off the busted chair, onto Jenna's shoulders. He popped onto her head and jumped onto Alex's left shoulder.

"Hurry," Jenna said.

His paws scrabbled on the wall as he extended his head and locked onto the key with his teeth.

I shifted for a clear view. "Pull and twist."

He jerked the key one way and another. Finally, it came free.

"Alex, you still with me?" I watched for a response.

His left hand wiggled a little.

"Lightning, put the key in Alex's hand."

Alex's hand extended toward Lightning who stretched his neck. The key dangled inches from my brother's fingers.

"Keep reaching, Alex," Pete said.

My brother's finger brushed the key.

"Closer, Lightning." I clenched a fist.

Lightning's feet slid a fraction with his efforts.

Alex's fingers closed on the key and Lightning fell into the space between Jenna and my brother.

My buddy's yips of pain made me cringe.

The lock was about a foot above Alex's head.

"Alex." I cupped my hands around my mouth for more volume. "Move your hand up. Insert the key and turn it."

Alex didn't move.

I said it again. When he didn't move, I looked at Pete. "Do something."

"Jenna," Pete said. "Alex has to turn the key in the lock, but he isn't moving. Do something to wake him up. Pinch him or step on his foot."

"Can barely breath." Jenna's words floated up like a whisper.

"Do it now." Pete's face went red as he yelled the instruction.

Alex seemed to jerk.

"The key." I cupped my hands around my mouth and yelled. "Use the key."

His fingers crept up. Inserted the key. Twisted. His hand went limp.

The hum, creaking, and groaning of the floor didn't stop for a long three seconds.

"Alex," I called. "Alex, answer me." I shouted at him. Pete yelled his sister's name at the same time.

Everything fell silent.

232

"Alex, you've got to move. Let me know you're alive." I spotted movement below.

Lightning yipped. Then he let out a low yowl.

I felt my gut clench into a knot.

"Stay with them, buddy." I thrust out my hand like a stop sign. "We'll get you in a minute."

"Gabe, they're gone." A cascade of tears spread down Pete's cheeks. "Crushed to death." His body shook, wracked by grief.

"I'll get you." I shouted at the walls. "Listen to me, Phantom. You're done. Finished." I pounded on the beam. "I won't forget." I swung my arm around, finger pointing into the space above. "I won't forget" Covering my face, I fell forward onto the beam and sobbed.

Chapter Forty-Seven

Dilemma

"Pete." I sat on the cross-brace closest to Lightning, still wiping my face. "We need to make a basket for Lightning and lift him up."

"Okay."

"Then I'm going back to the weapons room for a spear. That killer isn't leaving the castle tonight."

"What about Willie and the Polizei?"

"Who cares what they think? Our brother and sister are…" I couldn't even say the words.

"I care." Willie's head popped in the maintenance door.

"Willie." Pete and I responded at once.

"How's life?" Willie climbed into our space, shining his light on our faces. "Looks bad. Like you both ate rotten kiwis."

"The Phantom…killed…Alex, Jenna, and Thunder." I almost couldn't talk. "I'm gonna take him out."

"Serious?" Willie got a little closer. "He's got you mad as a cut snake."

"What else can he do?" Pete's voice got hoarse. "That murderer is still loose." He wiped his nose.

"He doesn't care about people," I yelled. "He's out to hurt more. Why shouldn't I take him out?"

Willie eased onto my crossbeam.

I sat sideways, facing away.

"You're spewin'." Willie sat next to me.

I felt his clothes brush against mine. "It's not your brother or sister."

"I know." He put his arm on my shoulder. I leaned into him, choking on my tears. "Steady on. Steady on."

When I took a breath, I found Pete underneath his other arm. I hugged them both.

Lightning yipped at us from below.

"I reckon your pal wants some attention." Willie patted my back. "How can he be alive?"

"'Cause he's a furball." I held my hands like I was holding a volleyball. "His hair fluffs out. I bet he's skinnier than Alex's bicep."

"He's guarding the bodies." Pete pointed at the broken panels below. "You can't see them well, but the walls in that room smashed the life out of all three of them."

"They called me." Willie sat on a beam. "I fought until the Captain released me. I'm the single cop he would let in."

"Can you lower me?" I said. "We can set up a rope sling for Lightning."

"I'm the one to go, mate." Willie clambered to his feet.

"No." I let him help me to my feet. "My dog. My brother. I go."

"Are you sure?" Willie's eyes probed mine.

I nodded.

235

"No worries." He shifted to the side. "Pete, be my anchor."

In minutes I glided down, an acid taste in my mouth. On the roof of the sliding wall, I shifted along the edge of the ceiling to the holes where I could lower Lightning's sling between Jenna and Alex. I knelt. A glint of metal caught my attention. A fallen flashlight shone on G's key in the lock a few feet below. I lay down. Grunting, I extended my arm, my fingers wrapping around it while I ignored my dog's barking.

"Gabe," Willie said, "talk to me."

"Found G's key at a weird angle, like it wasn't turned all the way."

"Better not—"

I twisted the key.

A noise, like a thunk, came from below the floor. The wall shook, then crept in reverse.

"Great work." Willie tugged on the rope. "Get your dog."

The rope sling thumped the floor. Following directions, Lightning positioned himself for a lift. I reeled him toward me. When he passed Alex, I thought his arm twitched before it fell like a limp noodle.

"Did you see that?" I called to Willie. "Alex moved."

Lightning bounced out of the sling into my arms. I hugged him tight.

"Up you come." Willie tugged. I returned the signal. The two lifted me in a rapid ascent. The winch controlling the walls movement seemed to pick up the pace, retreating along its earlier path.

Willie and Pete stabilized Lightning and me on the rafters. Back on my stomach, I sent my dog ahead while the three of us crawled to the maintenance door and climbed out into the stairway.

"Did you hear me?" I prodded Willie's side while we rushed down the stairway. "I could swear I saw Alex's arm twitch."

"Sorry, mate." Willie, who reached the landing first, wrestled with the door latch, but it wouldn't open. "I missed it. We'll see soon enough."

236

Lightning stood, nose sniffing the outline of the door until I scooped him into my arms.

The walls fell silent in minutes. None of us could open the room. Willie yanked a hatchet from his backpack. He unsheathed it and hacked the door's latch to splinters.

"Let me." I reached through the splintered door, worked the latch, and the door swung wide. Lightning burst past me.

Alex moaned.

"They're alive." I rushed inside, the rest of the gang on my heels.

Alex's fallen form pinned Jenna's torso face down on the floor.

"Jenna's breathing too." Pete adjusted his sister to lie on her back. "But why does she have on two jackets?"
"Where is Thunder?" Willie glanced around.

Lightning scratched against the sliding door on the far side of the room.

Willie sheathed his hatchet and tugged it open.

Thunder struggled, wiggling his bulk to extract himself from the cramped space. Willie assisted a couple of times. Free, the dog lumbered to Alex's side, lay by his master, and whined.

I shook Alex a little. "Wake up, bro. Time to get up."

Alex stirred a little, hands going to his chest.

Jonathan ran into the room and surveyed the scene. "Why is everyone lying around?"

Chapter Forty-Eight

Tortuous Clue

"Where've you been hanging your hat lately?" Willie stood.

"I...I...the Phantom captured me." Jonathan worked his way closer to me. "Gabe and Pete rescued me."

"A probable trap of some kind that didn't work," Pete said.

Jenna coughed. Pete sank back to his knees. Alex and Thunder were working to get on their feet.

"Slow down," I said to Alex. "Take your time."

"I feel like I was hit by a ten-ton truck." Alex sat. After a few deep breaths, he wrinkled his nose and forehead, teeth on edge. "Ooh. That shoulder's going to hurt."

"You did tell me to drop the spear on you." I shrugged. "Both you and Jenna."

"As a last resort." Jenna pushed to her knees and hands, then thought better of it and sat back down. "My head is throbbing."

"We need to get moving." Jonathan shuffled his feet. "The Phantom sent us another threat."

"And what does that tosser want us to do now?" Willie helped Alex to his feet. "His charade of being Mozart won't last long."

"He said…I mean, his note said to go to the torture chamber by 11:30 PM or learn a hard lesson." Jonathan folded his arms, but his feet and posture kept changing.

"You look a bit nervous, mate." Willie extended an open hand. "Let me see the note."

"You don't believe me?" Jonathan turned away and bent his head, hand covering his face. "No one in this group ever believes me. Why do I even try?" He shook his head.

"Give it up, Jonathan." Willie extended a hand and tapped his arm. "Don't be such a softie. Hand me the note."

"What choice do I have?" He faced the Aussie and extracted a piece of parchment paper, similar to the past ones, and handed it to Willie. "Here."

Willie read the note and shrugged. "Alright, mate. You're clear on this one."

"What's it say?" Jenna climbed to her feet.

"By 11:30 P.M. get the clue at the torture chamber. You'll know what to do. But do it quick, or you'll get hit, with other nasty news. And leave the rest of your money. You've only paid half your admission for the night's concert."

I checked my watch. "We've got ten minutes."

"Can you travel, yet?" Pete looked over Alex, who appeared to have suffered the worst.

"I'll be fine." He stretched and rubbed his ribs. "My rib cage is bigger than Jenna's."

"I wonder if your extra jacket saved me or trapped me." Jenna peeled off the coat and handed it to Alex.

"Good thing you're young." Willie slapped Alex on his uninjured shoulder. "Or your ribs might have been fractured. Off we go."

Pete, Jonathan, and I, along with Lightning, hurried to the building. The torture chamber wasn't a dungeon. The plaque showed it as a room where they kept instruments of torture.

We examined a few cases with no success. The rest of the gang straggled in.

"On time," Pete said. "I have 11:28 P.M."

"Assuming your watch keeps the right time," Jonathan said.

"Did you check inside the exhibits?" Willie pointed at one with several masks in it. "Check that one."

I popped open the display door and looked through the masks. "Bingo."

"Read it." Alex sat on the floor, massaging his chest.

"Not bad. You're on the right track. One clue remains before we experience the glory of my music played in my square, the Mozart Plaza, by Salzburg residents. I've prepared a special feast for the occasion, not from the bakery, but one crammed with meat. To increase your pleasure and mine in preparation for our music and merriment, visit the Keutschach Zisterne, near the fire passage."

"How far is that from here?" Jenna said. "I'm a bit hazy."

"I'll lead you." Jonathan moved toward a doorway. "The fire passage is near the bell tower."

"Do we all have to go?" Alex steadied himself on the wall as he struggled to his feet.

"With that lunatic around, I don't want to leave you like a sitting duck." Willie motioned after Jonathan.

Minutes later, we gathered around the Keutschach Zisterne.

"We're in for a deep discovery here," I said.

"Gabe, quit the puns and wisecracks." Alex sat on the edge of the cistern. "Where's the cover that's supposed to be on here?"

The well was circular, with huge gray blocks at the base and a red marble-like rock that outlined the top and jutted over the blocks outside and inside. The interior hole into the well was as wide as a man is tall. A ladder poked out of the top.

"Normally, yes." Jonathan grabbed a piece of paper sticking out from the orange placard giving the date and name of the well. "Here's the note." He handed it to Willie.

"Twenty-six minutes to midnight." Pete tapped his watch.

"Here we go, mates." Willie unfolded and read the note out loud. "Behind you stands the Glockenturm, where I'll end the life of my captive girl, unless the rest of the money is spilled into the cistern that Keutschach once built. Into the dungeon you must go, but be fast, don't be slow. As the clock strikes midnight, the music will play, the bull will roar, and the people will pay, for mockery, for cruelty, all beyond measure, but I will still obtain my pleasure. In the dungeon you will find, a little girl, sweet and kind. She's unharmed if you do as your told, but make it quick, be brave and be bold."

"Twenty-five minutes." Pete dug through his backpack, took out his money and dropped it into the cistern.

I ripped off my backpack. Threw my package and the two from the Chapel into the well. Done, I re-slung my pack and raced after the others. This building's hallways weren't lit. Flashlights beams bobbed down the curved staircase as I caught up. The stairs followed the exterior of the tower. At the base of the third flight, a door opening spilled light onto the staircase landing.

Alex shuffled in first. And I heard the cackle of the madman's laugh.

"Hurry." The Phantom yelled his instructions. "All of you. In here now."

A scream pierced the building.

"Don't test me."

Our group rushed into the room. Except for me. I snuck to the opposite side of the landing, spying around the door's edge to watch the action.

"See this lovely lady?" I glimpsed the girl, clutching the side of her face, standing like a frightened child about to be slapped. The Phantom held a pistol to her head. "One wrong move and the young lady's life ends now."

A hand clamped over my mouth. I threw an elbow. My attacker tripped me. We fell into darkness on the other side of the door. I wrestled to free my arms with no luck.

"Gabe." A familiar voice.

I thrashed about, even as my mind scrambled to understand.

"It's Jonathan." The whisper was inches from my ear. "Quit struggling."

I stopped bucking.

"I need to talk to you without the rest of the gang." His knee drove into my shoulders. "Can you be quiet?"

I nodded.

He rolled me on my back.

I glared at him.

In the background, the Phantom's voice continued.

"I don't want to do this lady any harm, but the townspeople of Salzburg have insulted me beyond measure. To think that I, the spirit of Amadeus Mozart, have come back to them and they refused to elevate me as their returned hero. Instead, I am mocked because of a terrible birthmark, one that I'm sure they caused by mistreating my mother. However…"

"Listen," Jonathan kept his voice low, "I couldn't warn you with a wink. Things were going down too fast."

I shifted my body to throw him off.

"Cut it out." Jonathan held up a pistol. "This is a sedative gun, like the Phantom used on Thunder and Alex. I stole it, but I'll use it if you don't cooperate."

I relaxed. What else could I do?

"I'm a *double-agent*," he said. "But I can't free everybody until we get that girl away. Understand?"

I tilted my head.

"I can't tell you the whole plan yet. Trust me."

I shook my head.

"Work with me. If you don't, I'll dart you." He sighed. "I *must* have your help. And it has to look convincing."

I shrugged.

"Here's what we do. I let you up. You act like my accomplice and do whatever I tell you. That will fool the Phantom into thinking I've got you brainwashed. When we're finished in the dungeon, we'll grab the girl, and get the cops up here. Can you do that?"

242

I shook my head.

"Okay. Say goodnight." Jonathan raised the pistol.

I felt blood draining from my face. I shook my head again with such force that I wiggled underneath his body.

"See it different now?"

"Do I have a choice?"

"No talking. Do only what I tell you, nothing more. The Phantom will shoot the girl if he suspects something's wrong. And I don't know what kind of pistol he has."

Jonathan yanked me to my feet.

"Brush off." He waived with the pistol over to the door. "Here we go." He winked.

"I see you have them all." Jonathan strutted into the room.

"Who is that behind you?" The Phantom motioned with his head.

"My new accomplice." Jonathan stepped to the side, letting his gun brush against me. "You might say he's my mole in the police operation."

I stiffened.

Jonathan glided behind me and whispered, "Relax, or else."

The room's rock walls enclosed a large space—a circle close to fifty feet wide. A few tiny windows let in starlight near the ceiling, at least ten feet overhead. Willie and the gang, who stood to my left, looked at me, eyes wide. Pete's mouth hung open. Lightning yipped and trotted toward me.

"Guard." I pointed toward the Phantom.

Lightning spun and growled.

"Very funny." The Phantom looked at his pocket watch. "I really must be going to my concert. In eight minutes, the bull will roar."

"Manacles." Jonathan pushed me toward Jenna. "And leg chains. They each have a set in the wall behind them."

"Mate," Willie stepped toward me, "do you know what—"

"Silence." The Phantom thundered. "You will cooperate, or I'll have Jonathan shoot each of you."

Jonathan followed behind me, placing a hood over their heads as I locked each of them up. Jenna first, followed by Alex, Willie, and Pete.

"Leash the dogs to a manacle, then stand by the door, on the inside." Jonathan watched until I was in place, about fifteen feet from my friends.

"Turn around, kneel, and stay that way." Jonathan's finger made a circle in the air.

"Not a sound from the rest of you," said the Phantom. "Or I'll shoot the girl."

I waited a minute.

Two gunshots rang out.

"No," I shouted. I bent forward, head in my hands. *What have I done?*

Jonathan grabbed my coat and half-lifted, shoved me to my feet.

"Out the door." Once through, he slammed the metal door shut and threw the bolt. "Look inside and make sure the boss is with the girl."

I slid open a panel in the door. Eyes wet with tears, I wiped them several times before I saw more than blurry shapes.

"They're going out the side exit." The Phantom used his pistol, prodding the young girl to move. They passed the desk and chairs, leaving through a doorway with a grate that lowered with a clang.

"What else do you see?"

"My friends manacled to the walls."

"And?" Jonathan continued.

"Thunder and Lightning, lying on the floor in a pool of blood." I took a ragged breath. "Dead."

A roar came from the side exit passage closed off by the metal grate like a cage.

"Is that—" I said.

"The lion's here." Jonathan nodded. "We can leave now."

244

Chapter Forty-Nine

Hidden Truth

We climbed the three flights of stairs to the ground level.

"Alright, Gabe. That's far enough." Jonathan sat on an old wooden bench made out of logs. "It won't be long now."

"Long for what?"

A huge noise cut through the air. Starting low, but gaining volume and intensity, the orchestral music flowed from the front of the fortress.

"The Phantom programmed 'The Bull' to go off at midnight with his music instead of Haydn's *Kaiserhymne*. It's like a player-piano that uses organ pipes." Jonathan kicked a few pebbles away from his foot. "The guy is a genius."

"He's a crazy man." I slid a little to the right.

"Going somewhere?" Jonathan played with his pistol and glanced at me. "We still have lots of work to do before his grand finale."

"We're going to let him finish that?" I shook my head. "If we do that, the man has won. He's tricked the Polizei, the town, and us. But he isn't only going to play music; he's going to launch cannon balls at the crowd. He'll kill someone, as though all the pain and misery he's created these past few days wasn't painful enough."

"The man is kind-of like I have been, only worse." Jonathan motioned for me to sit closer. "His whole life was full of joking, kidding, pranks, and practical jokes because of his face. One side like Mozart, the other a horrible mess. How would you feel if people picked on you day and night?"

"I'd feel bad. But that doesn't give him the right to hurt other people like this."

"No, but you understand his pain." Jonathan tapped his lips in time to the music. "Listen. I mean, really listen to his music. This is one of his pieces and is probably as good as any Mozart wrote. But he'll never get the acclaim, the fame, the fortune that belongs to that work because he's disfigured."

"That's not true," I said. "If that was his goal, he could have gone through a publisher, a music dealer, an agent—someone who knew the value of his music."

"Look, I know it's a long shot, but why not let him get away with the money?" Jonathan stood, went to a point where he could see through an opening in the wall to the town below. "What would that hurt the people? If we could get him to take the money and run, he might have a chance at producing more music like this." He closed his eyes; corners upraised in a smile. "It's incredible."

"You're nuts." I stood. "You shot Lightning and Thunder. And you want me to follow you?"

"I didn't shoot them." Jonathan whirled. "Is that what you think? I didn't do it. The girl shot them."

"What?" I faced him, feeling the heat rise to my face. "She's a captive. The Phantom would never give her a gun. She couldn't have shot them."

"You were turned around, remember?" Jonathan got within an inch of my face. "The Phantom made me watch the whole thing in silence. The girl," he paused and gulped, "he kept his gun stuck in the middle of her back and gave her a choice. She could shoot the dogs or she could shoot Willie." Jonathan's hand holding the gun started to shake. "I couldn't stop it. She chose the dogs."

"I don't believe you." I backed away.

"You don't have to." Jonathan brushed at his face with his left hand. "I saw it. He'd beat me later if I didn't."

I studied Jonathan. He sniffed another time, then glanced at his watch.

"If we're going to capture the guy, we've got to go now."

Jonathan led the way, talking to me as we climbed the stairs for several stories. We entered a circular room with brick floor and a wooden ceiling. Arched windows let in light. Bricks filled a wooden archway built into one side of the wall.

"That arch used to be a bathroom." Jonathan tilted his head at the walled-up area. "Opposite side is an exit to reach the bell tower." He pointed to wooden steps leading into another room.

A noise below signaled we had company. I stepped away from the stairs and watched the Phantom, gun in one hand, push the girl toward us.

"Good work, Jonathan." The kidnapper sat the girl on the brick floor by the old bathroom. "Now we must finish our plans."

Our plans? I fixed Jonathan with a stony stare.

Jonathan rotated to hide the right side of his face from his boss and flicked a quick wink.

"Yes. All is going according to plan." He strode over to the Phantom, motioning me to sit by the girl. "Shall we prepare the cannonballs for firing at the conclusion of your newest composition? At one o'clock?"

"Only if you've converted that young detective." The kidnapper wrinkled his brow as he checked me out, then harrumphed, in a regal way. "He seems a little below our station in life."

"I picked him because his father is military." Jonathan nodded. "He has the right training."

"We'll see." The Phantom walked over and stood in front of me. "Do you understand why the townspeople must pay?"

Jonathan smiled behind the man's back at me and nodded. He waved for me to stand.

The girl turned away.

"Yes, sir." I couldn't believe I was saying the words. "Jonathan explained the whole thing to me. I think you were treated unfairly by Salzburg." I clenched my teeth.

"Will you help Jonathan?" The man got next to my face.

I jerked back. The stench from his foul breath nauseated me.

"Willingly?" He smirked.

"Yes." *I will help him get the Polizei and capture you.* "Willingly."

"Then I'll give you a weapon. Another anesthetizing gun like this."

Jonathan's thumb went up, then disappeared before the Phantom strode to a crate by the concrete wall. He picked up a pistol, loaded a dart, and handed it to me.

"No funny stuff," the Phantom said. "Unlike our guns, your dart contains saline solution, but the gun appears deadly. I find it amazing how the mind can confuse what it sees and hears with reality." He chuckled.

"We need to finalize the last details with our new partner on board." The madman spoke in Jonathan's direction. "But the first part is private." He faced me. "You guard the prisoner." He waved me away and led Jonathan down a level.

I tiptoed to the stairway, caught sight of them taking chairs at a table, sitting, and pulling out a diagram. I snuck back to the girl, head resting on her knees with arms around her legs, and touched her arm.

She jerked away, startled.

Finger to my mouth, I knelt next to her and whispered. "Heidi, right?"

Her eyes tracked me. She arched an eyebrow.

"You speak English?"

She nodded.

"I'm going to rescue you with my friend, Jonathan."

She shook her head, hair flying near my face.

"Yes. I mean it." I kept my voice low but stronger. "We will rescue you, but we can't do it now."

Chairs scraped below. I leaped to my feet and pulled the pistol up, but the music outside and conversation below continued.

I bent close to her ear.

"Jonathan—" When I said his name her hair flew into my face again.

"You don't trust Jonathan?"

She widened her eyes and gave a vigorous nod.

"Oh." I tried to reassure her. "He's pretending because he's a double agent."

Another flurry of blonde strands raked my face.

She motioned for me to go to the stairway.

I started, looked back to see her nod, and went onto my knees next to the opening to hear the conversation. The music outside flowed around their words.

"Trickery always brings the best results," the Phantom said. "You've done a marvelous job."

"You should have seen Gabe when I told him I was a double agent." Jonathan's exaggerated motions communicated his excitement. "He fell like a star falling from the sky." Jonathan drew an arc in the air. "When I told him the girl shot the dogs, he resisted. But I convinced him it was the truth." Jonathan put his hand on his chest and did a micro-bow from his seated position.

I was thunderstruck. *What other lies has he told me?* I felt the blood rushing to my face again. I was *such* a fool. I lay on my stomach to hear the faint discussion better.

"You must make him a complete believer in you if our final plan is to work." The boss leaned forward. "We'll take the girl and the money."

"I can do that." Jonathan nodded.

"After the lion's finished his brother and friends, he'll have to join us."

"Gabe will make a great ally."

"And always delegate the dirty work to a person...or an animal." A devilish smile crossed the Phantom's lips.

"Because he helped us set the trap, he's become one us." Jonathan grinned. "Too good to be true."

"And if you can sow seeds of doubt about his faith background, then he will be ours for life." The Phantom stood. "But now that you have him and the girl, I have time to make the Polizei intruder pay for breaking my rules. One last visit to the dungeon should do it. Time to get moving."

I rolled away from the opening, rose, and paced in front of Heidi.

She gazed at me, eyebrows raised as though asking if I believed her.

I lifted my right thumb and gave her a curt nod. I'd have to be a better actor than Jonathan to win this battle.

"Communicating with the prisoner?" Jonathan's hand clasped my shoulder while he looked down into my eyes. "I saw your signal."

"Yes." Another thumbs-up. "I'm making sure she understands she has no chance of escape or rescue."

Chapter Fifty

Polizei Palaver

We crunched across rooftop gravel. Jonathan stopped a few feet from the edge of a wall next to a cannon.

"We've set up four cannons with direction and range to hit the Mozartplatz."

"Where the crowd will be?"

"Yes." He pointed to the fuses next to each cannon. "Fifteen-minutes. We light them early."

"And?" I said.

"Run to the Phantom."

The orchestra's music floated up from the town.

"The explosion happens at the end of his musical composition?" I drifted toward one of the cannons' fuses.

"Don't touch." Jonathan motioned for me to come back. "I've aligned each one perfectly."

"I thought you were a double-agent." I motioned for the girl to sit down by a door where she could still hear us.

Jonathan went behind the girl, yanked her arms behind her around a cast iron pipe with metal fittings, and zip tied her wrists together. He tugged me after him toward a dilapidated structure. He kept his voice low.

"Yes, but now isn't the time for revealing it to the girl."

"When will it be time?" I began to raise my voice.

"Keep it down." Jonathan whacked my coat and drew me closer. "We have to get the police involved now. Then we tell the girl."

"How are we going to call the Polizei?" His double-talk amazed me.

"I hope you understand. I have to keep up an act for the Phantom, the girl, and our team to keep this going."

"Oh. I understand."

"We'll use your walkie-talkie." Jonathan held out his hand, waiting for the radio.

"This only has a range of 420 feet." I slipped the radio out of my backpack and handed it to him.

"True," Jonathan said. "But I have a repeater, or should I say, an amplifier in the corner." We arrived at the rundown shed. He opened the door and stepped inside.

The shed's exterior appeared to be a worn-down centuries-old tower. But modern electronics equipment glowed in the dark.

Jonathan connected the walkie-talkie with a cord to an electronic panel halfway up the rack of equipment. "Polizei HQ, this is Team One, over."

"Team One, this is Polizei HQ. We read you loud and clear."

Jonathan provided directions in German as fast as machine-gun fire, rattling off places and times for the Polizei to gather and storm the fortress. "Make sure all your teams are in place and move exactly at zero-zero-three-zero minutes. Acknowledge."

"Team One, this is Polizei HQ. We acknowledge that you're disabling security cameras on the main entrance to the castle, coming through the Burgermeisterturm at 0030 hours. Also, we will send a team of twelve to the embankment by the Zeughaus, also called the Magazine, and have them scale the wall at the same time. Where will the Phantom be at that time? Also, what is the location of the Aussie?"

"The Aussie is occupied at this time." Jonathan winked at me. "The Phantom is in the Keep in his State Room."

"Team One, acknowledged. What is the best avenue of approach?"

"Execute on time. Must break contact. Team One, out." Jonathan disconnected the walkie-talkie.

"Why'd you tell them those lies? No one's at the Magazine. And the Phantom's in the Bell Tower." I blocked Jonathan from exiting the shack.

"Back up, Gabe." Jonathan waved me away. "I thought you were brighter than that."

"But if they go to the wrong place, the Phantom will get away." I didn't budge.

"We have about ten minutes; then we'll take him down." Jonathan pointed outside. "I'll explain, but I have to lock up. Don't make me use this." He fingered the butt of the pistol sticking out of his belt.

I backed up.

Jonathan locked the door, looked at his watch, and darted to his right. "Come on. I'll tell you on the way."

Leaving the girl, I dashed after Jonathan who ran full tilt into the buildings. Legs pumping as fast as possible, I glimpsed him dashing out of the buildings, across the courtyard, and into the Magazine building.

I shot up the stairs and tracked his pounding steps to a room on the third floor. When I raced in, he was setting a timer next to what looked like a release ratchet on a set of gears.

"Zero-zero-thirty-five. Done. Let's go" Jonathan flew past me back out the door.

I trailed him, calling out. "You said you'd explain."

"I will," he said over his shoulder as he leaped down the stairs. "It's all in the master's plan."

Down we went, back out into the courtyard and toward the Burgermeisterturm. As we neared that location, he ducked into another building, went up some stairs, through a long passageway and stopped in a bedroom-sized room near a long slit in the floor.

I knelt to check it out. I recognized the opening where hot oil flowed onto the street below, almost burning Alex and Jenna.

By the opening was a long metal container, like a long trough for feeding cattle, on hinges. Coals and firewood flamed underneath, heating a steaming liquid. The only furniture in the room was a wooden stool in a corner against the back wall.

"Liquid fire," Jonathan said. "Triggered by the police squad's entry into the third gate near the Burgermeisterturm, the oil will splatter on the police."

"That didn't work on us."

"You were fortunate." Jonathan worked with a few knobs in a control box. "That was the medieval way. But I'm spicing it up with some modern touches. When the men enter this third gate section, the iron gates, front and back, drop when the first man reaches the photoelectric beam under this slit. The oil container rolls to dump the boiling oil onto his head. Even better are the fans set to blow the scorching liquid onto the rest of the team."

"They'll be blinded. Scalded. Scarred for life." I drifted closer to Jonathan and the controls. I needed to stop this craziness.

"Gabe, you're already too far into this to quit now." Jonathan clicked a switch, closed the box, and spun the combination dial on its cover. "I can testify in court that you willingly manacled your brother, Willie, and friends to the wall. When the lion gets in that room, it'll rip them to shreds." Jonathan backed up towards the wall. "Now that I have the two traps set for the police here, the humiliation of Salzburg will be complete, like the Phantom predicted." He stopped next to a wooden door.

I tensed to lunge at him.

"I thought you would understand how the plight of the Phantom is a replica of my life." His hand caressed the butt of the pistol. "But I guess you don't have enough charity to see how much pain we've been put through."

"I can help, Jonathan." I inched closer. "I believe in you. I can probably get the judge to give you psychiatric help."

"For what?" His eyes shot daggers in my direction. "To go back with my father who doesn't care for me at all?" His face twisted into a sneer. "Or should I let a *friend* like you take care of me?" He drew the pistol.

"Don't shoot." I calculated how much closer I could get. "Why did you lie to me about being a double-agent?"

"It's no lie." He opened the door behind him, leaning against its edge to relax. "I am a double-agent. Against the Polizei." He slipped behind the door, firing his weapon.

I leaped sideways to avoid the dart, smashing my body into the gray stone wall. The dart sunk into the shoulder of my jacket. I dropped.

The door slammed, a key turned, and a slit opened in the door at eye level.

"You fell for it all." Jonathan grinned. "You are such a loser. In five minutes, the Polizei will be burned with oil here. Five minutes later, a sling full of logs will crush the other team halfway up their climb" He laughed. "And at the end, the noble younger brother will be helpless to stop the destruction unleashed by the lion or the cannons." With one last hysterical laugh, the metal plate slid shut, and I was left alone.

Chapter Fifty-One

The Chase

I tugged the needle out of the padded shoulder of my jacket and tossed it in a corner. Eyeing the boiling liquid, I searched for something to stop the flow of oil onto the Polizei.

Perpendicular windows, too tiny for me to slide through sideways were on three sides of the room. A gap between the wooden roof and the gray walls left a possible way out, but the overhang stuck out too far for me to see the end of it.

Three minutes left.

I stepped on a concrete buttress near the gap in the room's ceiling. Maybe if I could get one of the two-by-six ceiling boards loose, I could brace it against the wall near the slit in the floor and keep the boiling oil holder from tipping over when it released. Or I could bash in the lockbox.

I found a loose board and tugged. Bending an inch, it sprang back into place when I released it. I locked both hands around it and jumped off the buttress, hanging in the air above the floor. I bounced up and down with my weight. With a crack, it broke and I fell to the floor.

The piece in my hand was about a foot long. Too short.

I surveyed the room. A tall stool sat in one corner. If I could break it apart, I could use the four legs to prop up the metal trough of oil.

One minute.

I flipped the stool, with the seat on the floor and legs sticking into the air. I slid my body between the four legs, then pushed. Splintering the braces, then the seat, the legs came off.

I wedged a leg between the wall and the upper edge of the trough. The legs were a little long, but the mortar for the stones provided more space to make a tight connection on one end and the trough metal was soft enough to give a fraction of an inch. I wrestled a leg in at each end and two in the middle, spaced equally apart. While placing the last leg in the middle, the gates below me crashed into the ground, and the trough trembled.

Oil lapped the edge of the trough as a stool leg slipped to a tighter position and spilled a few drops on my hands. The machine tried to overcome the resistance.

"Jiminy Christmas," I shouted, shaking the burning liquid dots off the back of my hand.

The machine shuddered. I sidestepped to get over the last leg propped against the vat.

"It's a trap," I yelled through the slit in the floor. "The Phantom has set a trap."

"What?" A loud Polizei's voice came from below.

I gazed at the oil vat, shivering with the pressure from the gears to turn it over and the legs digging into the mortar. It might not hold. Hands shaking, I knelt, placing my body and head right over the slit, praying the legs would continue working.

"Tell the other squad scaling the wall it's a trap. Four cannons on the Kuenburg Bastion are aimed at the Mozartplatz. You capture the Phantom; I'll catch the accomplice."

Another drop of burning oil hit my neck. I yelled, jerked away, and rubbed the injury.

The trough vibrated as though it would flip at any minute.

"Guard all the exits from the Fortress. The Phantom plans to escape with the girl."

One of the gears snapped.

I dove and rolled away.

The pin holding the gears together broke enough to allow the rotator arm to spin freely.

I lay quiet for a few heartbeats and closed my eyes, thankful to be alive.

"We'll warn them and set up a perimeter," the policeman said.

I slid from under a stool leg, bounced to my feet and ran to the buttress. Climbing to the roof gap, I leaped at a wooden post holding up the outer edge of the roof. Sliding down the weathered wood, I landed on a small terrace.

I checked my watch—0033 hours. I got to the courtyard and hesitated. Left to stop the logs, right to rescue the girl and the others. I turned right. The Polizei knew about Jonathan's trap for the other team.

I raced up the stairs and out onto the Kuenburg Bastion. Heidi shook her head at me. *Good. Jonathan must be checking the logs.*

I darted toward the nearest cannon's fuse which sputtered as it burned toward the cannon.

"Not so fast, hotshot." Jonathan stepped out of the shadows.

"I'm not stopping for you." I grabbed some gravel and threw it in his direction, ducking by a cannon.

A clink of a dart sounded on the other side of the cannon.

"I like you even though you're confused," Jonathan said. "I'll give you a fighting chance. You can have this. Only two shots left in the clip."

I got my breathing under control. My heart pounded. A pistol skidded in the gravel a few feet from my position.

"Go on. Pick it up." Jonathan's voice seemed to shift location.

I lunged low, picked up the pistol, and dodged left.

A shot cracked in the darkness. Gravel flew and a spurt of dust rose from the impact area. Bullets.

"You have time to save the girl or your friends and family, but not both." He laughed. "Tamper with the fuses or cannons, all which are booby-trapped, and you won't be saving anyone. Enjoy the show."

A door slammed.

"You don't scare me." I peeked around the cannon.

No movement.

I cautiously stood.

Heidi struggled with her wrists.

I sped to her side.

"Get this off me."

I spotted a jagged edge on one of the pipe's metal bands, a few feet off the ground, "Stand up." I sawed off the plastic zip tie in seconds.

"Quick." She sprinted to the door. "Before you got back, Jonathan bragged that he's setting up another trap for the Polizei. And preparing his getaway on the old supply train that slides away from the town." She paused.

"Go on. I have to rescue my brother and friends from a hungry lion."

"What about your dogs?"

"The Phantom killed them."

Her hand went to her mouth as a look of horror crept into her eyes. "I'm sorry. I thought—"

"Thirteen minutes left. We'll talk later."

She nodded and slipped through the doorway.

I turned back to the cannons, determined to stop the bloodshed somehow.

Chapter Fifty-Two

Dungeon

"Alex. Wake up, mate."

Willie? I felt like trash that someone compacted and jumped on to make sure it was squashed. *Why couldn't I see?*

"Rise and shine." Chains rattled. "You acting a bit muzzy."

"Muzzy?" I croaked.

"Yeah. My new Aussie word. Muddled and fuzzy. Muzzy."

Metal rustled when I placed one manacled hand on the ground to get up off my knees. I grimaced. Pain spiked from the left side of my face. My entire body ached.

"Did you sleep long?" I got one hand to my head and tugged off the hood. Light hurt. Eyes closed, I pushed on my left temple, trying to kill the headache.

"Nah," Willie said. "Just taking a kip. Seems I was a bit knackered."

"You don't look like you were napping to me." Willie came into focus as my eyes swept the room. "Your left eye's bulging."

"I think all us guys enjoyed the typical castle beatings from the Phantom's final visit. With extra hits to the head for good measure." Willie pointed at Pete, who moaned and rubbed his right cheek. Jenna hung limp. "I suspect he was serious about no Polizei intervention."

"Let's get out of these manacles." I tugged to rip them out of the wall.

"No good mate." Willie jangled his chains. "These are at least a half-inch thick and the bolts in the walls could hold back a bull."

"They mus-s-s-t have hit us-s-s with a s-s-sedative." Pete's slurred speech was little more than a whisper.

"My stomach." Jenna bent forward with the dry heaves.

"They did something to all of us." Pete sounded better. "Including the dogs."

Thunder and Lightning lay next to each other, each on their side. Between the two of them lay a pool of red.

"I'm going to teach that Jonathan—" I shook a fist toward the door.

A metal bolt rasped, and the door trembled slightly.

"I didn't know you possessed such mighty powers," Willie said.

Jonathan flung the wooden door to the side and threw the blonde girl into the middle of the room. She fell near Thunder and Lightning.

"That will teach you to follow me." He strode in and kicked her.

"Jonathan, can you only hit those who are tied up first?" I rattled my chains. "Take these off of me and see how fast I'll put you on the ground."

"Easy, mate." Willie held up a hand as though to stop me. "Don't waste your time on him. He's just an assistant."

"Think you're smart?" Jonathan left the girl doubled up on the floor, straightened, and sauntered over to Willie. "Six minutes. The Phantom's music won't drown out your screams."

The lion behind the cage paced, growling.

"But this can make it more painful." He drew a switchblade and opened it. "A scar—"

"Put that toy away." The Phantom appeared in the door, wrestling with something in the hallway. "We are running out of time."

Chapter Fifty-Three

The Reckoning

The Phantom dragged me through the door.

"Gabe," Pete strained against his restraints.

Though I fought like a cornered badger, the man hurled me next to Heidi.

"Enough of this nonsense." The Phantom brushed his hands together like he was removing dirt from his palms. "In five minutes I'll sound my victory." Head held high, he thrust a fist skyward. "And punish the unbelieving." His hand chopped the air.

"Not while I'm around." I rolled to my feet. "I stopped your flaming oil."

"Mere distractions, my boy." The Phantom's lips curled up in a smile. "They kept you and Jonathan busy. The cannons fire at one o'clock, after my new composition timed to start at the time of Mozart's death, five minutes before one. The townspeople reap their proper reward, and I slide to freedom. But I'm afraid you'll miss the action. Remember the special feast I promised you? Our lion's famished for a live meal."

The golden beast roared.

"Restless." The Phantom chuckled.

A huge orchestral noise wafted through a tiny window.

"Ah. That A-major chord with all instruments playing at full volume is my cue. As they say in Austria, 'Auf Wiedersehen.'"

"My performance is finished." Jonathan bowed. "I played the double-agent role rather well, don't you think?" He stepped out, slammed the door shut, and threw the bolt.

"Mate, get us out of these manacles." Willie waved me next to the door. "He put the keys in a box near the door."

I raced to the wooden key box mounted on the wall. "Locked."

"Smash it." Alex pointed at a piece of broken stone about the size of my hand on the floor.

I snatched it up.

The side passage grating in front of the lion began to rise.

"Now, Gabe." Alex got my attention back on the box.

I smashed the key box with the rock. I barely made a dent. After two more strikes, I threw the stone across the room.

"Help Heidi," Jenna said.

"Block the grate." Pete pointed to the desk.

"Focus on the lock." Willie yelled above the others.

They all talked at once.

I sprinted back to Heidi to help her stand.

The grate reached about six inches off the floor.

"Our backpacks," Pete yelled. "We've got tools."

"Shoot the lion first." Heidi grabbed my arm. "Remember your pistol? It might work on the lion." She sank back to her knees, groaning and clutching her stomach.

"Listen to the Sheila, mate." Willie nodded. "Same stuff they hit us with, right? Knocked me out."

"He's four or five times as big," Pete said. "You'll need more than one."

"Two shots left if Jonathan told the truth." I whipped out the gun. Hurried toward the lion.

The gap widened between grate and floor to more than a foot. The lion roared, deafening me. His paw swiped at my feet.

"Take a shoulder shot," Jenna said. "Or hindquarters. Either should get it into his system fast the way he's walking around."

I aimed. Fired into his shoulder. His swung a paw at the cage's grate.

"Thunder." Alex's voice distracted me. "You're alive."

I glanced to my left. The black-furred body stirred. He tried to sit up and fell back down.

"Lightning?" I called out louder. "Lightning? Hey, old pal, do something."

He sneezed a couple times, then his head sank into the red pool under his head.

"Gabe, shoot the lion." Jenna yelled at me with all her strength. "If you don't stop him, it won't matter if your dog is alive or dead."

I gulped and reoriented the gun on the lion and shot as it leaped into the gate, making it bulge inward toward me. I couldn't tell exactly where the second shot hit.

"It's not long until the cannons go off." Pete kicked at his bag and missed it. "Gabe, get over here and use this stuff."

I stuffed the gun into my belt, skirted the desk, and darted to Pete's pack, wondering where I had left mine.

Heidi struggled to her feet, limped to a wall, and went back to her knees. Dry heaves wracked her body.

"What am I looking for?" My heart thumped loud in my chest. I scattered the contents on the floor.

"Anything to stop the lion." Pete's voice got louder.

I sifted through the pile—a dead walkie-talkie, rope, pepper spray, compass, Swiss Army knife, useless pens and more. I swept away the worthless junk in frustration. "Give me a hint." A couple water bottles rolled.

"Dump the water on Thunder and Lightning," Alex said. "Quick. That should wake them up more. Then they can help."

"Take the rope," Jenna said. "Make a lariat and capture the lion's mouth with a noose. Yank it tight."

"And when," I pocketed the knife, yelling at her, "do I have time for that?" I rushed with the bottles to Thunder and Lightning, emptying them on their heads and rubbing their soaked fur. Both struggled to their feet.

The cage was close to two feet off the ground. The metal ground against the stone walls. The lion almost squeezed under, but couldn't get past the steel spikes projecting from the base of the grate.

"Good on ya, mate." Willie shook a chain to get my attention. "Take that knife and open the lockbox."

"I'll do it." Heidi stood, legs less shaky. "I've picked locks for my father when he's lost his keys. You tie a lasso."

"Two minutes." Pete kept looking at his watch. "We'll never stop those cannons."

"I fixed that." I knelt, working to get a noose ready for the lion. "He won't be firing any cannons."

"How'd you do that?" Pete said. "Didn't we count four cannonballs missing?"

"Five." I kept working. "He dropped one on us, remember?"

"How could we forget?" Jenna's voice dripped with ice. "And you're going to have a lot of explaining to do when we get out of here."

The lion shoved its head under the gate.

"Why isn't he sleeping, yet?" Jenna waved an arm at the beast. "You darted him twice."

The lion's shoulders heaved, but the gate's projections dug in, preventing him from sliding through.

"Almost have it." Heidi's fingers gentle, deliberate movements got a little rotation on the knife blade. "These old locks are pretty simple if you can get one section to rotate."

"You're doing a fabulous job," Alex said.

266

Jenna's eyes darted between the blonde working the lock and Alex's gaze. "Don't get too happy. She hasn't unlocked us, yet."

Thunder took a step, steadied himself, and barked at the lion.

"No, you black bundle of fur." Alex's chains scraped the floor as he stretched them to their limit. "That lion will eat you for a snack."

Thunder didn't back up, but his barks got louder as he regained his strength.

Lightning wobbled, righted himself, and trotted to me, each step surer than the last. He put his paws on my shoulders as I bent over my work, facing the lion. He brushed his tongue against my cheek, which felt like sandpaper cleaning my skin. His reddish whiskers brushed my nose and mouth.

"Lightning, I'm glad to see you too." I held him in one hand and the completed noose in another. "Where is this blood coming from?"

I wiped off my face.

Lightning continued to lick the places I missed.

"Do you like this?" I held up my hand, and he lapped at it.

"That's not blood," Jenna said.

I sniffed my hand. "Fake blood. But no odor."

"Jonathan's a deceitful young man, isn't he?" Willie said. "I'd recommend…"

With a roar, the lion wiggled free of the gate into our circular prison. He shook his mane as though to clear his thoughts. To his far left, Heidi stood near the lockbox by the bolted door. In the middle section of wall, about forty feet away hung the rest of the gang. I was to the lion's right, close to the wall, but in front of me were Thunder and Lightning, two chairs and a small desk.

Thunder responded with a series of barks and my buddy joined him. We couldn't hear the music anymore.

"I have the keys." Heidi held up a key ring in victory.

The lion surveyed his options.

Chapter Fifty-Four

Lion's Share

"Don't move." I raised a palm toward Heidi, yelling and dodging left to attract the lion.

The big cat didn't take the bait. He faced Heidi and gathered his feet underneath himself to strike.

Heidi turned pale, hand over mouth.

"Hey." I rushed forward, snatched the fist-sized stone I threw earlier, and hurled it like a baseball pitcher at the lion. The stone caught him behind the ear. He roared and spun toward me.

Thunder and Lightning split up, backing up on either side of the desk, barking at the furious feline.

"Heidi." Alex rattled his chains. "Toss the keys. Quick."

I dashed to the two chairs by the desk, grabbed one and turned it upside down like a lion tamer does in a circus.

Heidi shook so bad that her throw fell far short of Alex.

"She's all right, little lady." Willie talked in loud, but steady tones. "Pick up the key ring and run to Alex.

"Th-th-the lion." She pointed my way.

"Gabe's got the lion's attention."

The big cat roared, crouching again to leap. The dogs lunged toward him.

"Get back here." I felt the cords of muscles stand out on my neck. I acted without thinking, chasing the dogs.

Heidi hesitated. Dashed to the keys. They jangled as she sped to Alex.

"I c-can't get the key in the lock."

"You're shaking," Alex said. "Deep breath. You can do it."

I risked a glimpse as Heidi steadied her hands. I passed the desk and stopped.

Lightning darted in to nip the lion's flank.

The lion, slowed by the effect of the earlier darts, swatted at Lightning and missed.

Thunder was next, his massive frame and jaws a better match. He snapped at the lion's other side, tearing away golden fur in his mouth.

The lion swung his right paw, and Thunder sailed several feet, smashing into the wall. He went limp, stunned. The lion stepped in his direction.

"Not while I'm in charge." I swung my lion-taming chair from my side and threw it in the big cat's face. It nicked his right eye and ear.

The golden beast's thunder drove me back into the desk.

Lightning made another run but failed to avoid a claw. I heard him screech as it penetrated his flesh. He rolled to the side.

I glanced toward Heidi and Alex. One manacle fell to the floor. Heidi worked on the second. Willie was next. Thunder lay silent on the floor. Lightning whimpered feet away from Heidi.

The lion didn't crouch, but swayed toward Lightning, blinking its right eye. Low, guttural growls filled the room.

The cat's intent clear, I grabbed the other chair back with two hands. The light wood didn't give me much advantage against a lion.

"Hey," I yelled.

The cat didn't change course.

"King of the jungle." I headed straight for the head and swung the chair.

The lion dodged sideways. A leg caught its jaw, but the cat reacted with lightning speed, knocking the furniture out of my hands. He changed direction. I could almost see my reflection in his eyes.

I scrambled behind the desk, searching for something to throw.

Alex, Willie, Pete, and Jenna screamed, trying to distract the cat. The snarling lion didn't care. Slow but sure, he crouched for a final spring.

I settled on my two tranquilizer guns. I could throw them at his eyes for serious injury, which might just delay the inevitable. The first gun hadn't been fired, leaving one dart. *Was it really a salt-water solution and not sedative?* That didn't make sense. But I didn't have time to find out.

The lion pounced.

I shot the gun in my left hand, threw the one in my right.

A roar shook my guts as I dove away.

Chapter Fifty-Five

Fireworks at One

I hit the concrete floor and rolled back into a corner.

The lion landed, wobbled a bit, and collapsed on the floor.

"That's a cracker of a lion taming act, mate." Willie rubbed his freed wrists. "Remind me to hire you on if I ever own a circus."

Alex steadied Thunder on his feet. He seemed dizzy.

Heidi used the keys to release Jenna and Pete.

"Twenty-five seconds." Pete stuffed the pile of items on the floor into his backpack and threw it on his shoulders. "We have to stop them."

"Heidi, is there a key to this door back here?" I motioned behind me. "I know where the Phantom and his assistant will be."

"Found it." Heidi rushed over with the key and opened the door.

"I've got Lightning." Pete took my buddy, opened his backpack and laid him inside. "I heard a little whimper. "We'll have to take him to the vet when we're done."

"Let's gag this lion, first." Alex whipped my amateurish noose around the sleeping lion's mouth and tied it around the neck like a horse's halter to keep it secure on the muzzle.

"Fifteen seconds." Pete stood near the door. "We'll never make it."

"We don't have to," I said. "I told you I fixed the cannons. Now we have to go trap the Phantom and Jonathan at the old supply funicular."

We dashed out of the dungeon and up one flight of stairs when the bell rang on top of the tower. The cannons fired in rapid succession. I stopped.

"I thought you fixed those cannons," Jenna said. "I counted all four going off."

"But, I...I..."

"Shake it off, mate." Willie patted me on the shoulder. "Show us the way."

We made the courtyard, lit by the blazing fireworks above. The bell in the tower continued to ring, joined by the Bull playing another Phantom masterpiece.

"This is the long way around." Jenna kept pace with me.

"Yes." I took a deep breath. "But they are going through the Schlangengang and then coming down."

"The guard passageway?" Jenna was losing ground.

"Jonathan thought they should stay hidden," I explained over my shoulder as I slipped through the supply storeroom door into the launching level for the supply train, an early funicular.

The old cart was gone. Straw covering the floor seemed shoved aside near the tracks and strewn in several directions by the door.

"They've beaten us here," Heidi said

"Looks like a rush job to me." Alex poked around with his feet.

"If we don't catch them before they reach the town below," Pete said, "they'll vanish."

"Oh, we haven't left quite yet." The Phantom, revolver leveled, stepped out of a doorway about fifteen feet away.

"And I'd like to build a fire first." Jonathan emerged from a matching doorway opposite his boss. "By the way, Gabe, you have a knack for leading your friends into traps."

"You're not getting away with this." I stared at the Phantom's gun.

Thunder growled.

"Oh, I think we will." The Phantom, still garbed as the boy genius, Mozart, clutched a dark cloak, hat, and gloves in his other hand. "I rigged the dynamite store to blow when our cart glides a quarter of the length to the bottom. In town, I'll be a tourist out for a ride with his son."

Thunder eased forward to the left.

"And call your dog off. Though Jonathan didn't want to kill your precious pets, I have no such limitations."

Alex commanded, "Thunder, heel." He obeyed.

"What's that?" Willie pointed at a thin, plastic pipe resting on a table. "A pipe bomb?"

"Not quite." Jonathan chuckled. "A special trigger I designed for the explosion." He picked up the short, foot-long pipe. "Ingenious, I'd say."

"How could a dummy like you rig an explosion?" Pete snorted.

"Figures you'd be the critic." Jonathan showed us the pipe. A gap ran its entire length. "I've wrapped the train's ascending cable with duct tape. The thicker wire doesn't bother the pulley system, but it's too large for this pipe."

"Enough. Turn around." The Phantom made a circle with his gun.

We faced to the rear. Several support poles and a few feet separated us from the back wall.

"Tie them to the poles." The boss gave instructions. "Bags near the wall. Cage the dog's first."

"Bet your trigger won't work." I peeked at Jonathan.

A shot rang out, shattering a lantern that hung on the wall.

"Keep your eyes forward." The Phantom's cold tone made my neck hairs rise. "Or the girl's next."

"I wouldn't test him." Jonathan motioned to Alex. "Lock your dog in this cage."

Alex stepped toward one of two plastic kennel cages by the wall. "Thunder." Alex opened the door. "Inside."

His dog barked at Jonathan.

"Settle." Alex waved him to the opening, pushed him through, and locked the door.

Jonathan shoved Alex, who stumbled, toward the support beam. "Move."

Thunder barked with fury, baring his teeth and rocking the kennel.

"To answer your earlier question…" Jonathan secured our arms behind us around the poles, starting with Alex and progressing down the line to me. "My invention works. I'll flex open the pipe's gap to mount it on the cable up here and wrap it with tape. A wood pressure plate will hold it in place. The wire slides through harmlessly while we descend to safety. About two minutes after we leave, the explosions begin."

"Homemade gadgets never work." I shook my head.

He smiled. "When the pipe's pressure reaches the right intensity, the wooden plate gives way. The pipe and pressure plate slam against the packet containing phosphorus, breaking it open. The phosphorus burns when exposed to air, setting hay bales and kerosene trails ablaze. The kerosene-doused straw lights a few twenty-second fuses for blasting caps, which explode the dynamite and det cord." He tugged, yanking the rope on my wrists until it dug into my skin.

"Impressive." I winced.

"That and a few other strategically placed gas cans light more fuses for the rest of the explosives. The pipe disintegrates and the wooden pressure plate burns, making the fire seem to be an unfortunate accident of poorly stored blasting caps and dynamite."

"A tidy solution," Willie said. "Except for the prisoners attached to the poles."

"This building will be torn apart." Jonathan smiled. "And we all love huge explosions, fires, and fireworks, right?"

"One last reminder to this wretched town as to what I think of their hospitality." The Phantom laughed. "Jonathan, let them watch your trigger work. Hurry."

He swung a few of us to face the cable pulleys but stiffened in front of me.

"Where's your dog?" Jonathan got in my face. "Is he in your bag?" Jonathan kicked my backpack hard against the wall. The pack thudded without any other sound.

My jaw tightened, eyes forming tears in the corners. "Not all of us made it."

"Leave him," the Phantom said. "It doesn't matter. What could he do? We're off."

A new rail car, which Jonathan slid from a battered shed at the top of the tracks, rolled into view.

"Gabe, you are naive." Jonathan laughed. "That old rail car was a tourist exhibit and would never have worked on this track. I'll miss your gullibility." He prepped the pipe on the cable.

The Phantom and Jonathan jumped in the car, lying flat to disguise their exit.

The car slid out of view.

"How much time do we have?" I asked.

"About one minute and fifty seconds." Pete shook his head. "You'll never make it."

"Lightning." I worked my hands down the pole, lay flat on the ground, hooked Pete's backpack with my feet, and drug it next to my side. "Can you hear me?"

A muffled yip came through the bag.

I scrambled to my knees, bit into a metal zipper, and tugged it open a few inches.

My buddy's nose poked out.

"Give me a sec." I switched zipper pulls and opened the other side a smidge.

Lightning's head popped up. He yipped.

"Out."

He wiggled while I yanked on the zipper, then he sprawled onto the floor. He couldn't move much.

"Time's evaporating. Hurry." Jenna jerked at her ropes.

"Knife." I thrust my back pocket toward Lightning. "Pull it out."

He gnawed at my back pocket without success.

"Turn this way." Heidi, on my left, tapped me with her foot. "I can push the knife enough to make it stick out of your pocket. Then he can snag it."

"Great." I faced away from her.

"I've been counting," Pete said. "We have about a minute left."

"Gabe," Heidi said, "Stand tall to loosen the tension on your pants. When I push the knife up, squat slow to keep it in position."

As I did this, Jenna spoke up. "How are you going to get free? You need an open blade in your hands to use it, right?

"Ye of little faith," I said. "Watch and learn."

"Make it quick." Willie scuffed a foot across the floor. "The stone block floor won't catch fire, but the clumps of straw and wood interior will. If we don't get blown to bits, we'll burn to death."

"Pretty optimistic, aren't we?" Jenna said.

"Got it." I felt the knife sticking out of my pocket. I lowered myself with Heidi's foot on my pocket until my pants tightened.

"You have to kneel," Alex said.

"I know, I know." I sank to my knees, ensuring the knife stayed in place. "One of you needs to figure out how to stop the dynamite from going off. I'm not going to be able to free anyone else in time."

"Speaking of time, you have forty-five seconds," Pete said.

Lightning followed my directions, grasping the knife, lifting it out, and placing it in my hands.

I flipped open the best blade and dropped it.

"We're gonna die." Jenna looked away.

"No rush, mate." Willie sighed. "No worries."

We lost five seconds. I fumbled for the handle, snagged it, and sawed the rope.

"Thirty seconds."

"Thanks, Pete." I nodded. "The cord snapped. "How do I disarm the firing mechanism?" I darted toward the trigger.

Alex, Willie, Heidi, and Jenna each had a solution but drowned out one another's words.

"Ten seconds," Pete yelled. "Give or take."

"Pull the actuator off the narrow cable." Alex tilted his head at the pipe.

"What?" I said.

The wrapped cable appeared, pressing the plastic pipe into the pressure plate. Soon we'd explode into dust.

I rushed forward and sprawled on my stomach to grab the pressure plate, willing it to stop.

Chapter Fifty-Six

Finale

"Gabe, rip the pipe off the cable," Jenna shouted.

"Can't." I dropped the knife, wrestling with the pressure plate and home-made trigger, but neither budged.

"Do something." Pete strained against his ropes.

Lightning barked in my ear. Ran toward the control room.

In a flash, I was on my feet, racing inside. I jammed the tram's emergency stop button, jolting the getaway car.

At the same time, the pressure plate slammed into the phosphorus packet, lighting hay bales which sparked the kerosene trails through the straw. Three fiery lines spread like a spider's web through the building.

"Cut us loose," Heidi said.

"Fifteen second left on the fuses until the dynamite blows." Pete jerked against his restraints.

Rifle shots cracked from below me. A control room window shattered. Needle-like pain erupted in my left shoulder. A glass shard tipped in red clattered to the floor.

"Get that knife over here, mate." Willie's voice cut through the noise.

"Lightning, quick." I waved him toward the exploded phosphorus. "Get the knife to Willie."

Smoke curled up into the ceiling from the trails of flame. The flickering light highlighted the gang frantically wrestling with their tied hands.

A hole appeared in the remaining glass by my right ear, the bullet seeming to whine inside my head. I dropped, bouncing back to a crouch. I searched for the ascent button and punched it. The cable reversed direction. The Phantom and Jonathan's car crept back to its launching point.

Explosions rocked the building. I heard screams from Jenna and Heidi. The rest of the glass in the booth shattered and fell to the floor. Det cord demolished two roof-supporting poles. I raised my head and gazed at the flaming inferno. Lightning, thrown by the blasts, lay fifteen feet from the control cabin. He whimpered. The knife was in his mouth, but his head rested on the ground.

I dashed for my dog and the knife. The main fires were at the ends of the building. Smoke filled the air. I got low. Rushed to Heidi. I slashed her free of the rope and lay Lightning at her feet.

"Thanks." She gasped for air.

"Free the others. Get out." I motioned at the other poles, some leaning at odd angles.

"I'll kill you." The Phantom's voice rose above the crackle of the flames.

A bullet nicked the pole near Heidi's head. Another whizzed by and she yelled.

"Down." I jerked her to the floor. Warm, sticky fluid covered my hand. A bullet had grazed Heidi's upper arm.

"You're hit, but not bad." I reached for the knife.

"Don't." She snatched her hand away from mine. "I'll free them. You stop the Phantom." Her eyes held a glint of steel I hadn't seen before. She clenched her teeth. "Go on."

Two more shots prodded me away. I dashed toward a bale of hay. Looked back and saw Heidi creeping over to free Pete.

"Come and get me." I flew toward the flames by a wooden beam on the outer wall, leading the Phantom and Jonathan away from the others. The heat ratcheted up. I felt like I was inches away from a bonfire.

"Gotcha." Jonathan, outlined in flaming wood, rose and lined me up in his sights. "You should've joined us when you had the chance."

"Never." I pointed at the ceiling." "Look out."

"Nice trick." Jonathan smiled. "Won't work."

The burning roof collapsed on him with a thunderous roar. Dust and ashes floated in the air.

The crashing noise disguised the crack of a shot. White-hot pain climbed my right leg.

"Can't escape every bullet." The Phantom grinned. Coughed. Smoke was getting thick.

"Your apprentice is trapped under that burning log." I motioned behind him.

Out of his sight, Pete, Alex, and Thunder flitted behind barriers, headed my way.

"He is one of many pawns." The Phantom was about twenty steps away. "I'll gather more. And I won't have to put up with the likes of you." His gun zeroed in on my heart.

Another explosion. A section of the roof between me and the rest of the gang caved in, orange flames creating a wall of fire. Intense heat ruined any chance of rescue.

The distraction gave me an out. I rolled left. The Phantom's bullet punched through the hay bale inches from my previous spot. I hobbled to something like a horse's stall, complete with wooden bucket, rags, and a stool. But no exit.

An older man coughed near the stall. The Phantom.

With my left leg, I stepped on the stool and peeked over the edge, smoke burning my eyes. I sensed a movement. A blur went left to right. I hustled back to the corner. Snatched a rag. Stood on the stool, found a square rafter still not burning, and dragged myself on top, bucket in one hand. Like a wounded tightrope walker, I inched forward, swaying back and forth. The rag covering my face kept most of the smoke out and my groans in. In minutes the fire or smoke would kill us.

Below me, a gun poked out of the haze.

I wiped at my blurry, stinging eyes.

A hand and arm appeared.

I jumped. Swung the bucket hard. It connected with a crunch. We fell like discarded toy soldiers into a pile on the ground. Jonathan's screams seemed weaker.

I had to get air.

I crawled into the horse stall. One outside wall was solid stone. The other, wooden. A sliver of lamplight glowed on the floor. *Cracked wood.* I spun my body, legs to the wall. Kicked hard. Twice. A small section splintered out. I shoved my face in the hole. Breathed deeply four or five times. Above Jonathan's agonized shouts, I heard other voices.

"Willie," I yelled. "Alex. Help."

No answer.

After a few more breaths, I crouched, rag tight to my face, and tried sprinting along the stone wall. More like falling forward. Pain seared my leg. *Need a door out—quick. Five steps. Ten. Twenty—found it!*

Locked, of course.

I grabbed a fallen two-by-four and pounded on the handle. I coughed. Felt light-headed. I went to my knees. Shadows opened the door. Rumbling voices flowed past while angels carried me away.

"Get him back from the door." Willie's voice was clear after a few clean gulps of air.

"Pete," Alex said, "set him against this wall."

My eyes cleared. A wall of flame backlit the rock face of the building.

"Okay, buddy?" Pete jostled my shoulder.

"How long since the explosion?" I said.

"Couple of minutes, I think." Pete patted my shoulder.

"Lightning?"

"Haven't seen him."

"Inside." I wobbled to my feet. Sheer agony.

"You're not going anywhere." Jenna held me against the wall. "You can barely stand."

I rocked from bad to good leg. "The Phantom. Jonathan. We have to rescue them."

"He's right." Heidi nodded. "We can't let them burn."

"Alex." I flinched as my right foot took my weight. "Send Thunder to find Lightning. He can do it."

"Willie?" I scanned for him. He raced into view with several cloths soaked in water. I called out. "We're going to rescue—"

"Cracker of an idea." He tossed a rag to each of us. "Split into teams." He tapped Jenna and pointed the way he had come. "Get some water. Blankets. First Aid kits."

"Thunder and Alex find Lighting." I grabbed a rag. "Follow me to the Phantom and Jonathan." I overrode the jolts of pain while we sped to the door I exited from earlier.

"Stay low," Willie said.

I made a beeline for the Phantom.

"He's too big for me." I grimaced. Clutched my leg, hacking on a gritty breath.

Willie nodded. "Pete. You and me." Snagging the Phantom's arms, they dragged him out.

"Jonathan?" Heidi raised her eyebrows.

Waving gray air away from my face, I led the way. A thick rafter, stuck in a larger log-pile, pinned Jonathan's left leg. The scene looked like a game of pick-up-sticks.

I knelt. "If we move one beam the wrong way, the rest will slide on top of him."

"Gabe?" Jonathan whispered.

"We've got you." I placed a hand on his back.

"Why...rescue..."

"Later." I glanced for something to pry him out.

"There." Heidi rushed to a few two-by-fours, each charred on one end. She paused, shoulders heaving with labored breaths. Waving smoke from her face, she retraced her path.

We positioned ourselves, two-by-fours braced on broken wood for leverage.

"Now," I said. We tugged together. The logs shifted dangerously.

Jonathan shrieked like a tortured man. "Stop."

We released the pressure and inspected the log jam.

"Heidi." A raw throat made my words hoarse. "I'll pull the lever. You haul him out from the logs."

She nodded and scrambled into position.

"Again." I struggled, shoving the wooden beam below my waist, straining with all my weight.

The log jam rustled. Debris slid down.

"Hurry," I yelled.

Heidi yanked Jonathan's bulk back a few feet, clearing the avalanche of logs.

I threw the two-by-four into the pile. Heidi jumped to her feet. I stepped toward her to help evacuate Jonathan, but collapsed, resting partly in her arms.

"My gunshot wound." I choked on the bad air. "Can't walk."

With gentle hands, she laid me flat and raced away.

Jonathan's hand dug into my shoulder, his croak barely discernable. "Why?"

"Leaving you to die would kill me. The inner Gabe. God's in charge and cares about everyone. Even though you used and betrayed me, you still matter."

For the second time that day, Willie and Heidi lugged me out of the burning building. Smoke billowed from the windows. They propped me against a wall to let me watch the action.

"'Bout time." Jenna knelt, laying a slow-moving Lightning by my side and throwing a blanket over me.

I coughed. "Women." I shifted the blanket and noticed Heidi. Her lips pressed together in a firm line, eyebrows raised in a question.

My cheeks heated up. "I didn't mean *all* women. I...I meant her." I tilted my chin at Jenna.

"Well, well." Jenna smiled. "You do like girls."

"I didn't say that." I gritted my teeth while she inspected the bullet wound. My words came out in spurts. "I didn't want...Heidi to get the impression...ah...that my comment was about every girl I know." I sucked in some air, grinning. "I reserved that remark for you."

"Is it Heidi now?" Jenna chuckled. "You've changed into a real teenager."

"Cut it out, sis," Pete said. "Or we'll be here all night."

A small firetruck, siren blaring, appeared on the road next to the building. Firemen poured out of the vehicle. A few Polizei cars followed. A Krankenwagen, brakes screeching, halted by me and ambulance techs jumped out to triage the patients.

"Good police work." Willie clapped a hand on my shoulder. "We eliminated obvious exit points and covered the rest."

"Excellent," Heidi said. "I'm glad to be rescued." She glanced at each of us. I thought her eyes lingered on me.

"So what happens to Jonathan and the Phantom?" Pete shouldered his pack.

"A fair question." Willie scratched his head. "But we have a lot of those after all this hard yakka. Let's head to the Polizei HQ for a cuppa and a wrap-up of this operation. Well, except for Gabe and Lightning. They need some medical attention first."

"Yakka?" Heidi said.

"Work." I smiled at her. "He's an Aussie."

"Don't forget your best friend." Jenna winked as she walked past. "He is your best friend, right?"

"Cut it out," Pete said.

Lightning lay on the gray stone floor.

"Hey, bud, let's go." I bent over to tickle his ears.

Lightning struggled to his feet, took a few halting steps, then lay down.

"Sorry, bud." Concern tinged my words. "I forgot." I slid my hands underneath him and lifted him close to my chest. "That lion must have knocked you for a loop."

Chapter Fifty-Seven

Assessment

"Any idea?" I asked, scratching Lightning's ear.

"Possible internal injuries," said the emergency room doc, "but I fix people, not dogs." The sterile treatment bay curtain around us shut out prying eyes.

"Can you do anything?" Willie asked.

"I'll try."

Willie insisted we all see the hospital emergency room staff before we went to the Polizei HQ. Earlier, we bypassed a few seated patients waiting to be seen when he waved his detective badge at the admitting nurse.

"The results of the x-rays are promising." The doctor looked at me. "Lucky boy. No arteries or bones hit, no bullet fragments, clean entry and exit holes, and minimal bleeding."

"A flesh wound, I'd say." Willie grinned.

"Then get me out of here." I sat up.

"Not so fast, cowboy." Willie pressed me back down. "They've cleaned you out, but you're getting a special ride home."

"Two-thirty in the morning, Willie." Alex yawned as he and Jenna joined Lightning and me in the treatment bay. "Do we have to debrief tonight?"

"Details fade in the morning after a night's sleep." Willie checked on the treatment of Pete and Heidi's injuries.

"Lightning's got to see a vet." I ruffled my buddy's hair, avoiding the white bandages covering his abdomen. "The doc let me wrap him for tonight."

"Thunder's not in the best shape." Alex's dog lay near his feet.

"Pete has a concussion." Jenna massaged her stomach. "The Phantom or Jonathan must have beat us when we were knocked out."

"No guessing," Willie said. "We need to report facts. That's why the microphones on Pete and Gabe will be invaluable."

"Did you guys hear what happened to Pete and me with Jonathan?" I leaned closer to Alex.

"No cross-talk." Willie stepped out to talk to a nurse, came back with Heidi, whose arm was wrapped, and Pete. An attendant brought in a wheelchair. I settled in, and our gang went to a small classroom near the emergency room.

"Here's a witness statement." Willie handed each of us a piece of paper. "If you need more sheets, take them from this stack. The Chief says he wants a summary from each of you. Write down any facts you saw or heard. Don't write anything someone else told you. Just your stories. Got it?"

"Roger." I rubbed Lightning's head.

"When you get these finished, I'll take them and see you in the afternoon at the Polizei HQ for a full report and backbrief."

"One question before I go," I handed in my report, handling Lighting with light moves. "That emergency room was empty. Where were the other casualties from the Mozart Plaza?"

"And what casualties would those be?" Willie grinned.

"The ones from the four cannons the Phantom fired."

"There weren't any."

"But—"

"See you tomorrow afternoon." Willie patted me on the shoulder, hooked a finger at an ambulance attendant, and waved as the ambulance van took the four of us back to our parents at the apartments across the border.

Heidi and her mother appeared by Willie's side, watching until we were out of sight.

Chapter Fifty-Eight

Debriefing

I woke to blinding sunshine.

Alex walked into the room and yawned. "Out of bed, sleepy-head." He threw a pillow at me.

"You're up early." I stared at the clock. Ten-thirty A.M.

"I'd say you're a little late."

Yawning, the past couple of days flashed through my mind. I felt exhausted because we arrived at our room in Türk at three-thirty in the morning. "Must be the drugs. Or the short night's sleep." My right leg throbbed. "See you at noon."

"Oh, no, you don't," Mom said. "Get up, get dressed, and pack. This is our last day here. We have to be out by noon and get your dogs to the vet. Alex, help your brother."

We both groaned.

Salzburg gleamed in the afternoon sun as our two-car cara-van entered the city. The Schultz family followed behind us.

I glanced at the fortress surrounded by yellow tape and po-lice vehicles while Mom navigated the streets to the Polizei HQ.

"The townspeople probably have no idea what happened last night." Alex patted Thunder.

"I won't be able to forget." I felt my pulse quicken.

"The police called me several times today to thank you for your actions." Mom made a left turn. "I'm still not happy about your involvement."

I didn't argue. If Mom did things her way, we'd never have any excitement or help others. *Some of these townspeople could have died last night.* I stroked Lightning's hair, a lump in my throat. *We almost didn't make it.*

Mom parked the car. The Schultz's joined us, and Pete posi-tioned my wheelchair, settled me onto the cushion, and. pushed me through the front doors of the Salzburg Polizei HQ.

"Welcome." The Captain waited for us at the head of the conference table. The team, or what was left of the team, assembled with coffee cups, sodas, and water. "This part is short. You will scat-ter to various debriefing rooms, then return here and we will piece everything together for you. Mrs. Zanadu, Mr. and Mrs. Schultz, please accompany me to my office." He gave a curt nod, rose, and walked past, slapping each of us on our backs. His teeth shone in a huge smile.

"Mates, we're almost done." Willie's twinkling eyes and bouncy steps showed his good mood.

I wasn't sure I would like my debriefing. A sense of dread filled my gut. What if they discovered all the terrible decisions I had made? I'd never be allowed to do this again. Pete wheeled me to my debriefing room.

The room was dark and barely large enough for the furniture. A gray metal desk set near one wall with a padded executive chair. Opposite the desk was another gray, padded chair with thick metal legs pushed up against the wall. No windows. I felt like I was already in prison. How would I feel behind prison bars for my treachery?

I shifted on the cushions in the wheelchair, locking the wheels, resting my feet on the supports, feeling small. I slumped against the back, wedging Lightning's basket on the left side of my lap.

The light burst on, startling me.

"Gabe, you look upset about something." Willie stepped in front of me, putting a hand on my shoulder. "What's spoiled your party?"

"Nothing." I should have felt better. Willie was probably the sole individual I could trust to tell the entire sordid story, but I felt ashamed. My cheeks burned.

Lightning tried to assure me with a lick, but I pushed him down.

"Oh, I see." Willie shut the door and leaned against it, arms folded. "We're ashamed?"

He read me like a book.

"No one's perfect." He circled the desk and sat. "Tell me now, or you'll feel guilty the rest of your life."

"I didn't mean for it to happen that way." Once the water burst through the damn, it gushed out of me. "I didn't want to betray anyone. Jonathan lied to me."

"What did he say?"

"He told me he was a double-agent for you."

"Is Jonathan trustworthy?"

Caught. Like me, Willie knew that Jonathan acted strangely during our last mishap in the Salt Mines. He lied even back then.

"But he told me…" Rats. I knew I was lying to myself. A tear formed. "I almost let you and the rest of the gang get torn apart by a lion."

"Gabe, that was a result of your actions, but we might have been trapped even without your cooperation. The Phantom and Jonathan planned the operation down to the last details. We suspect he was working with the wrong side before you met him."

"But his background...his dad's absence..."

"Even bad circumstances cannot excuse poor behavior. He made wrong choices."

I closed my eyes, a hand going to my forehead. "I wanted to solve the case by myself, to be in charge of part of the operation." I sighed. "I was a loner. Jonathan seemed to have the answers. I listened to him, trusted him. I even tried to beat him at his own game when I realized I'd been a sucker. But none of that is an excuse."

An hour passed before we finished discussing the entire ordeal.

"Time to see the Captain." Willie slid his legs off the desk.

"You didn't take any notes."

"Not necessary." Willie shifted in his chair. "This was a private session to help you adjust to what happened. Feel better?"

"Well..." I thought about it for an instant. "Yeah." I felt a little lighter. Willie didn't blame me for all the bad things that happened. I scratched Lightning's ears. "But what about the other members of our team. They'll think I'm a traitor."

"Their debriefers have shared certain parts of your recorded conversations with Jonathan. They know he dragged you where you didn't want to go."

"That helps."

"Yeah."

"You know about G, right?"

Willie nodded. "He's pretty special."

"How can he know the details he shares with us *before* they happen? And give us a key that saves our lives?"

"How people know things in advance is difficult to explain. But the Phantom was not a secret to every person in Salzburg, correct?"

"Yes. That's right."

"And wouldn't you say G's poem included a partial focus on a bigger plan? How many keys did he give you?" Willie's eyes sparkled.

"I guess he hinted about staying true to the original plan. Seven keys, seven adventures."

"Maybe he'll reveal his hidden purpose at the end of the seventh adventure."

"When I see him," I nodded, "I've got a lot of questions for him."

"Time for the major conference room meeting." Willie stood and circled the desk. He unlocked the wheels of my chair, swiveling me out the door to the big debrief.

I cradled Lightning in my arms.

Chapter Fifty-Nine

Unanswered Questions

Lightning squirmed in my lap.

The conference room, filled to capacity, felt a little claustrophobic. People jammed into standing positions behind the chairs where all the detectives, policemen, Willie and the rest of our team sat. Thunder was under the table at our feet.

The Captain squeezed past the opposite side of the table and the wall. A policeman drew the blue velvet curtains over the windows.

Thunder yelped, bumping into Alex's leg.

"Someone get your tail?" Alex reached under the table.

"Ah, bring the dogs to the front." Captain Bergmann waved them up. "Will they sit quietly?"

I nodded. Alex picked up Lighting in his basket and walked Thunder to his place. They lay under the projection screen. My brother returned to his seat.

"Before our slide show, I want to congratulate our two canine heroes. They've helped us retrieve the stolen documents and rescue Heidi Gerlach."

The Captain clapped his hands. We all applauded. I eased to my feet, standing on the good leg. The rest of the group joined me in short order.

After we sat again, the Captain dimmed the lights and went over the entire operation. While he discussed our preparations, I tugged on Willie's sleeve and whispered, "Where's Wilcox?"

Willie whispered in my ear. "The Chief's got something special for him."

A short while later, Bergmann finished, and the lights brightened. I raised a hand.

"What happened to the cannons?" I said. "I cut the fuses, but I heard them fire anyway."

"Excellent question." Bergmann took the slideshow back to the picture of the Kuenburg Bastion with the four cannons facing the Mozartplatz. He went to the hidden slides in his presentation, selected the unhide option on the menu, and clicked on one slide.

On the screen, I saw four shapes in black next to each cannon.

"After you saved the Polizei Squad from being burned alive with oil, we received a call on our radio. Our squad scaling the fortress wall aborted their mission in the nick of time, except for two policemen who received minor injuries. But more importantly, we sent an undercover, black ops team to the bastion. They analyzed the booby traps set for anyone redirecting the cannons' aim from the plaza."

"I don't get it," Jenna said.

The Captain motioned to Willie.

"We couldn't move the cannons left or right. The only option not booby-trapped by the Phantom was to tilt them at a higher angle." Willie winked. "The cannon balls didn't land anywhere near the square."

"But I cut the fuses."

"They were decoys." Bergmann flipped to another hidden slide—a close-up of each cannon. Attached to each cannon were two separate fuses with timers and lighting devices. "Jonathan armed each cannon with a tamper-proof timer which couldn't be halted. When the cannons fired, the cannonballs flew with a higher arc than planned, causing damage to a few buildings, but no injuries."

"What's going to happen to the Phantom?" Pete said.

"The Phantom, Jonathan, the Phantom's mother, Agent Wilcox, the look-alikes we've captured, and a few other accomplices will go behind bars." The Captain pointed at Willie. "Agent Gretzke."

"Wilcox?" I straightened in my chair.

"Yes." Willie stood and went up to the front. "I found traces of evidence that Agent Wilcox accepted bribes from the Phantom."

No wonder Wilcox wasn't in the room. That's probably why he abandoned Pete and me at the Mozart Geburtshaus. It made perfect sense.

"Mates." Willie squared his shoulders, tilting his head toward Bergmann. "I alerted the Captain that I've been tracking him since an incident where he left me stranded on an Australian operation. Further evidence relating to his accepting bribes came to light after we finished the operation."

Murmurs flowed around the room.

"That'll be enough," Bergmann said. "We must be vigilant, even with our own operators."

"The final part of this briefing is important." Willie's normal smile widened.

The door to the room flew open. Light flooded the room as man in a chef's hat wheeled in a huge sheet cake.

"Salzburg remains an exceptional tourist destination for those celebrating Mozart and his accomplishments. Today will be the City Celebration—thanks to our Junior Detectives: Alex, Gabe, Pete, Jenna, and their canine partners, Thunder and Lightning."

A punchbowl filled with pink sherbet floating on a bubbly, pink liquid came next, followed by Mom, Dad, and the Schultz parents.

"Let's celebrate." Willie grabbed pieces of cake and passed them out while Mom and Mrs. Schultz served the punch.

About the Author

 Aaron—author, coach, speaker, ghostwriter, and entrepreneur—thrives on a challenging life filled with ministering and mentoring others.

Here are a few fun facts:

- Aaron loves playing guitar, singing, running, hiking, and many other outdoor activities. "Activity sparks creativity," he says. "I enjoy God's creation and glorifying Him."

- Aaron stays busy with organizations and positions. He is Fort Hood Coordinator and Bible Study Leader for Officers' Christian Fellowship. Aaron also serves as President, Military Officers' Association of America (MOAA), Central Texas Chapter, and is a member of the American Christian Fiction Writers and Texas Authors, Inc.

- Aaron is a retired U.S. Army Colonel. He loves God and being a husband, father, and grandpa. He and his wife live in Belton, Texas. They have two married sons and three grandchildren.

Check out this free e-article, Passion for God. Interested? Go to Aaron's website, ZookBooks.org, for your free download.

Made in the USA
Lexington, KY
08 September 2017